# Dead Man Deep

Glasgow-born Lynne McEwan is a former newspaper photographer turned crime author. She's covered stories including the Fall of the Berlin Wall and the first Gulf War in addition to many high profile murder cases. She currently lives in Lincoln and is in the final year of an MA in Crime Fiction at the University of East Anglia.

# Also by Lynne McEwan

## Detective Shona Oliver

# Dead Man Deep

## LYNNE McEWAN

First published in the United Kingdom in 2022 by

Canelo
Unit 9, 5th Floor
Cargo Works, 1–2 Hatfields
London, SE1 9PG
United Kingdom

A CIP catalogue record for this book is available from the British Library.

Print ISBN 978 1 80032 434 3
Ebook ISBN 978 1 80032 433 6

Look for more great books at www.canelo.co

Printed and bound in Great Britain by Clays Ltd, Elcograf S.p.A.

1

*For the fish and the fishermen and those working to save marine ecosystems everywhere.*

# Chapter 1

The lifeboat pager hauled Shona Oliver from her sleep. She threw back the covers and turned on the light. Next to her, husband Rob groaned, dragging the duvet back over his head.

'Shout.' Her phone showed four a.m. 'Rob, don't forget about the guests. Make sure Becca gets some breakfast.' She pulled on leggings and a long-sleeved T-shirt.

Coat, shoes, keys.

Downstairs in the kitchen, she grabbed a fleece, hopping towards the back door as she tugged at her trainers. The security light came on, a solid yellow beam in the pitch dark. Outside, the freshness of the air hit her. It was early May, the end of a long winter that still cast its shadow in the wind's chill. The birds were just stirring. She turned the key in her four-year-old Audi A3 and set off on the short drive down the hill to Kirkness Lifeboat Station.

Skipper Tommy McCall had the boat hall doors open and the tractor idling. As she got out of the car, Shona glimpsed headlights on the winding road down into the village. Callum Stewart, the village's twenty-two-year-old postman, was racing along the seafront from his girlfriend Paula's flat at the rear of the Royal Hotel.

'What's the shout?' Shona called to Tommy as she stepped into her immersion suit. She pulled the seal over her head, catching it in the loose curls of her dark brown bob.

'Immediate launch. Mayday call from Kilcatrin Island,' Tommy replied. 'It's within the Ministry of Defence base. Coastguard has tasked us due to the state of the tide. It'll be a couple of hours before they can get a vehicle from the firing ranges over the causeway to the island.'

Six minutes after she'd jumped out of bed, Shona was aboard the *Margaret Wilson* as they swept out into the Solway Firth with Tommy on the helm. Callum Stewart knelt opposite her, and they both gripped tightly to the anchor points as they left the scattered lights of Kirkness behind and headed south-east across a short, choppy sea.

Tommy pointed to the D-class lifeboat's navigation console showing a chart of the coastline. 'Kilcatrin Island is small and tidal. All this belongs to the MoD firing range.' He indicated an area on the screen overlaid with red hatching. It covered a river estuary and a large block of land and coastline. 'But the island isn't used for exercises. It's a bird sanctuary.'

'Any information on our caller?' Shona asked, above the roar of the outboard.

'Not much.'

Shona couldn't see Tommy's weathered face in the faint light from the consul, but she heard the tension in his voice.

'Someone pressed the red button on a handheld VHF radio. No vessel ID but coastguard got a GPS position off it. It's on the shoreline.'

She knew if the mayday came from a ship, they were already aground and every second was vital.

Shona shivered and thought of Rob asleep in bed. He'd be up soon to fetch a couple of B&B guests from the Caledonian Sleeper train in Carlisle. The fact he was willing to drive the two-hour-plus round trip across the border into Cumbria and back showed how desperate he was to keep clients happy. Despite the plushness of their boutique B&B, the financial problems that had surfaced the previous autumn meant they needed every booking.

Twenty minutes later, the lifeboat approached the low mound of the tidal island which sat a few hundred yards off the rocky promontory of Kilcatrin Airds. Shona radioed for an update but the coastguard had heard nothing more from the stricken vessel.

As they came closer, a square outline loomed on the mainland cliff, black against the dark blue of the sky.

'Tommy, what's that?' Shona said. 'Is that an MoD installation?'

The skipper shook his head. 'That's St Catrin's chapel. It's how the area gets its local name.'

Since her arrival in Kirkness, she'd quickly become accustomed to the duality of place names in the area, one on the maps, the other used by local people. Some communities hedged their bets and mentioned both on the village signs.

'It's a superstition 'round here,' Tommy continued, 'that shipwreck bodies must be buried close to where they wash ashore, or their spirits won't rest. The chapel grew up next to a graveyard.'

'So what's the local name?' Shona had a feeling she wouldn't like the answer.

'Deadman's Point.'

The chart showed a small inlet on the edge of the river estuary. They circled the island with no sign of the damaged yacht or working vessel.

'How close are we to the last known position?' Shona said, as she and Callum took torches from the waterproof kit bag.

'Coming up on it now,' Tommy replied.

Shona scanned the shoreline. Rocks like serrated teeth ran out at a sharp angle to the beach, cruel ridges emerging from the waves in the falling tide.

Her torchlight danced in response to the rocking lifeboat. She glimpsed a white object resembling a football net lying on the beach. Looking closer, Shona saw the goalposts were, in fact, a sealed rectangle surrounding the net. It lay next to a jumble of items which could have come from a wrecked boat.

'Target sighted.' She shot out an arm and kept it there, pointing like a weathervane towards the objects on the beach as Tommy turned the lifeboat through ninety degrees and edged them forward between the rocks.

'First assessment, Shona,' Tommy said. 'Watch yourself on those rocks. Keep your gloves on.'

Shona went over the bow, her immersion suit slipping against the Hypalon material of the hull. The black water came up to her chest. A wave slapped her face. She shook the salt water from her eyes and felt forward with her steel toe-capped boots, knocking against rocks as she half-swam towards the shore. Soon her knee struck soft sand, and she waded the rest of the way. She turned to check the position of the lifeboat. The *Margaret Wilson* rode the dark sea, white edges of foam around her bows.

'You okay?' Callum called out.

'Fine, Cal,' Shona replied. 'Stand by with the first aid bag.'

Loose shingle and cockle shells crunched under foot. Shona's eyes stung from the salt water. She blinked away tears as she swept her narrow torch beam across a scattering of clothes, a cool box and the strange white object. Then she saw him.

He lay face down, dressed in fisherman's chest waders, a piece of sacking material tied across his shoulders. His oilskin jacket looked as if it had been shredded by the rocks as he'd come ashore. No sign of a boat beyond the flotsam of a toolbox, bait buckets and plastic diesel cans.

She carefully turned him over, her breath catching in her throat. It wasn't his jacket that hung from his arms in strips but his skin, red and blistered. His face, like an over-ripened fruit, was beyond recognition and beyond the lifeboat's help. For a second she thought he'd been in the water for weeks, but then she remembered the mayday call.

She searched around for any sign of the handheld VHF radio that had made the distress call. The inky sky was lightening but the small, west-facing beach still lay in deep shadow. Over the salt-smell of the shore there was another, sharper scent: a mixture of onions and burnt rubber. Had there been a fire? Shona climbed further up the shallow shingle bank, holding the torch high.

'Hello,' she called. 'Lifeboat. Is there anyone here?'

To her right, there came a low, animal moan barely louder than the retreating waves. In the shelter of a large boulder, a shape moved, resolving slowly into human form. A boy, no more than ten years old, younger than her own daughter, Becca. He lay on his side and wore jeans and a blue hoodie. There was blistering to his face and hands, white flecks around his mouth. All signs of chemical burns.

'You're okay now,' Shona said, as she kneeled beside him. 'We'll get you sorted.'

It took only a moment for her to realise the seriousness of his injuries. At the sound of her voice, he rolled onto his back.

'Stay still, try not to move.' She leaned out from behind the boulder. She could just see the lifeboat and Callum alert in the bow.

'One confirmed delta,' she shouted. 'One casualty. First aid bag.'

She turned her attention back to the boy.

His eyes were swollen shut but his burnt hand reached up, grasping at the air in front of him. 'Mum. Mum.' His breath came shallow and fast, barely a murmur.

Shona took his blistered hand. 'What's your name, darlin'? Try to stay awake for me.' He needed oxygen and was already in shock.

'Mum…'

She felt his grip weaken. He was slipping under.

Behind her, the sun touched the far headland with gold. Shona looked out towards the *Margaret Wilson*. Where was Callum with the first aid bag? On Kilcatrin Island, daylight reached around the low hill, the shadows thinning. Tiny glimmers sprang up on the beach, a giant shoal of jellyfish washed ashore.

Shona rubbed away the tears with the back of her gloved hand and looked again. The realisation struck her like a blow.

'Stop!' she yelled to Callum as he waded ashore. 'Don't come any further.'

It wasn't jellyfish. Kilcatrin was MoD land, a firing range. All around her were not jellyfish, but the blinking glass eyes of hundreds upon hundreds of phosphorous shells.

# Chapter 2

Shona rolled the boy onto his side and cleared the froth from his mouth with her gloved fingers. Satisfied he was still breathing, she stepped carefully across the shingle to where Callum stood frozen in the surf. Around him she saw the floating grenades, like small, frosted milk bottles, as the retreating waves dumped more of their deadly cargo every minute.

Callum held the first aid bag clear of the sea. At six foot three inches, he was almost a foot taller than Shona but in every other way he looked up to her. Shona's years at Tower RNLI, the busiest lifeboat station in the UK, earned her respect from all the Kirkness crew but Callum in particular was willing to learn from her experience.

Preservation of life was the priority. She wasn't going to leave the boy and she couldn't recover him on her own. 'Okay, Callum, watch your step and follow my route up.'

She'd dealt with phosphorous once before, while stationed on the Thames. A woman mud-larking had picked up what she thought was a piece of amber from the beach by the Tate Modern. As phosphorous dries, it hardens. When it comes into contact with air, it ignites, burning at over a thousand degrees, and cannot be extinguished with water. The lucky tourist had laid down her jacket on the beach just before her pocket burst into flames. These bombs on Kilcatrin Island contained liquid.

Contact with the skin or breathing in the fumes if the glass broke would be bad enough, but as the tide receded, the danger would only increase.

The boy groaned in protest as Shona put the oxygen mask over his face.

'We need to get him out of here quick,' Shona said. 'Did Tommy call for a helicopter?'

Callum shook his head. 'Coastguard's tasked it on another job out in the Irish Sea. It'll be at least an hour 'fore it can get to us.'

Shona looked from the boy to the falling tide. The closest paramedics were across the causeway on the other side of the island, but it would still be covered. She took the orange plastic sheeting from the first aid bag.

'We'll have to carry him.'

Together, they rolled the boy as gently as they could onto the sheet, folding it round him until he was completely protected. Callum picked him up and held him clear of the water as Shona led the way. Carefully, they waded out to the *Margaret Wilson* as Tommy fought to keep her steady in the rolling waves as the glass grenades chimed against her hull and each other like some lethal percussion.

In the lifeboat, when the boy tried to claw the mask from his face, Shona gently pushed it back and cradled him against her, his hand gripping hers.

'Mum, Mum,' the boy moaned.

On the mainland, the blackness of the cliffs was fading, punctuated by the flashing blue light of the paramedics on standby to cross the causeway.

'The MoD should have warned us,' Shona said between gritted teeth.

'This stuff didnae come from the firing range. It's older. World War Two.' Tommy's face was grim. 'I'd say it's from Beaufort's Dyke.'

She racked her brains for the briefing information she'd been given when she started her detective inspector's post two years ago. Beaufort's Dyke, a deep trench in the seabed between Scotland and Northern Ireland used as an arms dump since World War One.

'But that's out in the North Channel. Got to be thirty miles west of here.'

'Aye, but remember how this place got its name? The currents bring all sorts into the Solway.'

Shona took a deep breath. If what Tommy said was true, this wasn't about one death and a seriously injured child. She had a major environmental incident on her hands. Perfect timing for the early May bank holiday.

She looked down at the unconscious boy wrapped like a chrysalis in waterproof orange sheeting, which in the dawn light seemed to accentuate the bluish tone of his skin. She prayed the death toll wouldn't rise any further.

'Who is he? What were they doing there?' Callum said. Shona had recovered the VHF radio lying next to the boy and quickly checked the dead man for a wallet or mobile phone but found nothing.

Tommy shook his head. 'No sign of a boat, they must have come across the causeway.'

'It's was a bird sanctuary, right?' Callum said over the noise of the outboard engine. 'May is the start of the nesting season. Maybe they were after eggs?'

Shona hoped not. Egg thieves would travel almost any distance. If they were local, there was a better chance of identifying them quickly and tracing the family.

'That was a haaf-net on the beach,' Tommy said. 'It could have washed up, but it might have belonged to the victim.'

Shona had heard of haaf-netting, a traditional fishing practice on both sides of the Solway, introduced by the Vikings a thousand years ago. Men waded out into the tide, a rectangular structure of poles strung with a net on their shoulders, to catch salmon.

'Don't you need a licence for that?' Shona asked.

'Aye,' Tommy replied.

'So the council should have a list?'

'It doesnae mean the victim applied for one,' Tommy began, but the coastguard on the radio, relaying instructions for their final approach, interrupted him.

The ambulance crew Shona saw waiting on the slipway wore full hazmat suits and respirators. The nearby MoD Land Rovers also had personnel standing by in similar attire but these men were armed. Behind them were army fire trucks and a tanker wagon.

'They want us to deposit the casualty on the slipway so we don't contaminate the paramedics by direct contact,' Tommy relayed from the coastguard as they neared the shore.

It felt like an act of abandonment to leave the child lying alone on the stone quayside for even a second, but as Shona stepped back from the approaching paramedics, she felt a rush of relief that he would now get the medical care he desperately needed. She turned to climb back aboard the *Margaret Wilson*, when one of the paramedics called out to her, pointing towards his goggles. It was only then that she remembered her streaming eyes.

The soldiers came forward, beckoning Tommy and Callum up the slipway to where others stood ready with power washers linked to the tankers.

'We'll hold your vessel until we're satisfied it's decontaminated,' a man in a respirator who didn't introduce himself said.

'I'm Detective Inspector Shona Oliver of Dumfries and Galloway Police. Who's in charge here?' Shona demanded.

'All in good time… ma'am,' he added at Shona's glare.

'The body on the island? That's a crime scene. I want it cordoned off.' Shona saw the ambulance containing the boy disappear into the half-leaved trees that reached almost to the shore.

'In hand, ma'am. We need to deconn you. Get your eyes looked at. Then I'll get you up to command.'

Shona had no choice but to submit, her slight frame almost bowled over by the power washers. She watched the *Margaret Wilson*, named for the Solway Martyr, a young woman drowned for her beliefs, receive similar treatment. An MoD team manoeuvred the lifeboat onto a cradle, hauled up the beach to be hosed down.

'Watch what you're doing with my boat,' Tommy muttered as he stood between Shona and Callum, frowning. The three lifeboat volunteers were told to take off their dripping immersion suits. A soldier handed Shona a pair of battered flip-flops and a green army fleece at least three sizes too big. She pulled it on over her damp T-shirt, shivering.

A paramedic washed out Shona's eyes and advised her to go straight to Dumfries Royal Infirmary if she felt at all unwell in the next forty-eight hours. Tommy's reminder to wear her gloves had avoided skin contact and potentially serious injury.

'I need access to a phone. Now,' Shona told the soldier nearest her, and this time she wasn't taking no for an answer.

–

It was a few minutes past six a.m. but DS Murdo O'Halloran answered after the first ring.

'Boss?'

Shona pictured him, table set for breakfast in the neat cottage he shared with wife Joan, sensible suit jacket over the back of the chair and his ex-rugby player's face frowning. He'd know a call this early didn't bode well. When she updated him, he let out a long breath.

'Jeezo. That's not good,' he said with typical understatement. 'Sure you're okay, boss?'

'I'm fine. Can you send a car out to me at Kilcatrin? And give the control room a heads-up. There'll be a joint MoD and Police press statement going out in a minute. The media strategy will be to inform and reassure but expect the phones to light up. We'll need to close the beaches till we know the extent of this. I've already spoken to Division. Since it's the bank holiday, we want to alert people and ask them not to travel into the area.'

'Not gonna be popular, are we?'

'Everyone from the volunteer coastguards to the RSPB bird wardens will check their bit of the shoreline, but we've three hundred miles of coast to cover. With one fatality and a critically injured child, I'm prepared to be as unpopular as it takes.'

'Any idea on the victim?'

'No ID. Male, average height, dark hair, but his facial injuries make things tricky. We might get fingerprints, but this will probably be a DNA job. The MoD say they've taped off the crime scene. Soon as it's safe, we'll need forensics down here. Tommy thinks the man might be a haaf-netter. There was gear on the beach. Can you get onto whoever runs the fishing licences? I'll call you when I get back to Kirkness.'

A squad car picked Shona, Callum and Tommy up from Kilcatrin Ranges guard post. Tommy was reluctant to leave his boat behind but was persuaded he could collect her the next day after final checks.

Back at the RNLI station, the echo of their voices in the boat hall was a physical reminder of *Margaret Wilson*'s absence as they updated the shore crew, whose pagers had sounded at the same time as Shona's and had been busy preparing for the crew's return. Upstairs, in the mezzanine kitchen area, one volunteer had set up breakfast: foil parcels containing morning rolls filled with bacon, scrambled egg and square sausage heaped on plates. Despite not having eaten, Shona couldn't face anything, but the others tucked in.

Shona went straight to her locker and grabbed her phone. Tommy set to work on the paperwork and debrief but Shona was only half listening as she scrolled through her missed calls from Rob, and from her boss, acting DCI Jim Robinson. There were also several from her friend Laura Carlin.

Laura's husband, Tony, was a fisherman and a lifeboat volunteer. Shona and Laura had bonded on girls' nights out over the shared experiences of post-natal depression and difficult marriages. Laura had made a fruitless attempt to lure Shona into her latest fundraising project for the lifeboat, a wives' choir.

Shona frowned and checked the calls weren't ones she'd missed from last night. She glanced up at the clock on the station wall. It wasn't yet seven, a bit early for a chat about the raffle or a bank holiday barbecue. Her finger hovered over the recall button. She needed to get back to High Pines, change her clothes and make the half-hour journey into Dumfries CID offices.

'Are we done here, Tommy?' she asked the coxswain.

'Aye,' he said. 'You get off. I know you've got your hands full. Call me if I can do anything.'

'You know I'll need a statement from you and Callum?' Shona stopped at the door. 'I'll send someone over. You'll both be around for a while?'

Callum nodded. Tommy gave her a thumbs up. She hit redial and started down the stairs.

'Hi Laura, I haven't got time to chat this morning. Everything all right?'

'It's Jamie. I can't find him. His bed hasn't been slept in but his phone's here.' Laura's voice was high and strained.

'Have you asked Tony? A sleepover he didn't tell you about?'

'I can't find Tony either.'

'Hang on, I'll see if he's about.' Shona turned, then ran back up to the mezzanine level. Tommy looked over his glasses at her as she came through the door.

'Is Tony Carlin here?' Shona asked.

The shore crew around the table shook their heads, so she crossed to the waist-high handrail, hung with drying immersion suits that separated the crew room from the boat hall. Below, Graham Finlayson, the landlord of The

Anchor pub in the next village, was sluicing down the concrete floor with hose and broom.

'Tony Carlin?' Shona asked again, but Graham shook his head. She put her phone back to her ear. 'Laura, when did Tony go out?'

There was a pause. 'I don't know.'

'Could Jamie be with him?'

'Tony's stopped carrying his phone, but he never answered it anyway.'

Shona caught the edge of irritation in her friend's voice. 'Go to Jamie's room,' she said. 'Check if any clothes, bags, money are missing.'

'I've looked. Only his jeans and Gap hoodie.'

'Colour?'

'Blue,' said Laura.

Shona's eyes met Tommy's. He saw her expression and stopped writing. She thought of twelve-year-old Jamie Carlin. Small for his age, dark-haired like his father. A sensation like an army of ice cold ants was climbing up her spine. The clothing described matched the boy on the beach.

'Why?' Laura said, the panic in her voice clear now. 'Do you think I should call Dumfries police office? Report him missing? He's been in trouble at school. I don't want Social Services round.'

'I'll have a word with the control room,' Shona said evenly. 'Then I'll come over.'

She ended the call and saw Tommy still watching her from his desk in the corner. She crossed to him and said quietly, 'D'you know if Tony Carlin had a haaf-net?'

'He worked on the scallop boats, but aye, I think I've heard him talking about it,' he replied in a low voice. 'Is he our man, d'you think?'

'Let's keep this between us until we're sure.'

Shona left the lifeboat station by the open boat hall doors and jogged across the seafront to the Audi. When she reached the car, she took out her phone again.

'Murdo, I've just had a call. Possible ID on the victim. It's local to me. Can you send Kate my way? I'll text her an address. Tell her to meet me there.'

# Chapter 3

Back at High Pines, Shona quickly showered. The MoD had used a detergent mix to wash down their immersion suits and helmets and she still felt it sticky in the roots of her hair. The more she thought about the victim, the more convinced she became that it was Tony Carlin. Soon, the incident would be all over the news – TV, local radio and internet – and it wouldn't take long for her friend Laura to put two and two together. And Jamie? Shona couldn't imagine how Laura would react to the news he was critically injured.

Shona walked into the kitchen wearing her charcoal grey Hobbs trouser suit, a white blouse and low black heels. Her eyes still stung, and it looked as if she'd been crying, despite her quick application of make-up.

Rob had made her a coffee. It sat on the counter next to a home-baked flapjack. When she'd arrived back and given him the news, Rob's face had fallen. It was the last thing they needed, he'd said, as if Shona required informing of that fact. Now, she heard him on the phone in the small office next to the kitchen calling the guests they had booked in to explain the situation. It would be a long day. She forced herself to eat and the sugar and caffeine boosted her energy levels. Murdo called with a quick update as she left the house. Her DCI, Jim 'Robocop' Robinson, had also called and, with one eye on his budgets, made it clear he wanted this death wrapped up as quickly and efficiently as possible.

Ten minutes later she was outside the Carlins' single-storey granite cottage, set back from the road. The garage to the side of the house was open and Shona saw a jumble of fishing nets piled next to a small dinghy. DC Kate Irving was parked a few doors up.

'Boss.' Kate strode towards her on long legs, fair hair smoothed back into a high ponytail. Shona collected her handbag containing phone, notebook and tissues from the passenger seat.

'There's a good chance our victim is Tony Carlin. We'll need ID confirmation with Laura.'

'Does that mean the boy is likely his son?' Kate asked.

Shona nodded. 'No one's seen Jamie since last night. Clothing description is a match. I'd like you to take on family liaison. You up for that?'

Kate's grey eyes widened in eager surprise, but she quickly recovered herself. 'Yes, boss. Thank you.'

Shona thought she also saw a hint of triumph in Kate's expression. Her two detective constables, Kate and DC Ravi Sarwar, were locked in an ambitious tussle for dominance that wasn't always good-natured. Promotion out of Dumfries – to Ravi's hometown of Glasgow or Kate's in Edinburgh – would probably come soon for both of them. They were excellent officers and their complementary strengths meant Shona didn't want to lose either. Ravi would normally be her first choice for this role, but she was careful to spread opportunities around.

'There's a younger brother, Jack.' Shona lifted her hand to knock on the peeling yellow paintwork of the front door. 'I should have recognised Jamie, but his face was so swollen. Did Murdo tell you I know the family?'

Kate gave a quick nod. The door flew open.

Laura Carlin's eyes darted from her friend Shona to the unexpected extra visitor. Her smile moved from relief to uncertainty. A dark-haired boy with pale skin and deep blue eyes stood in the hallway gripping a games console handset and peering shyly past his mother. It struck Shona just how much he looked like his father and brother.

'Laura, can we come in? This is my colleague, DC Kate Irving.'

'What's happened?' Laura's smile became fixed.

Shona stepped in, taking her friend's elbow. 'Let's go into the front room. Hello, Jack. Not at school?' The boy stared back without answering.

'Jack? Say hello to Auntie Shona,' his mother chided. 'He's not well. Stomach pains. I think he's worried about Jamie,' Laura added in an apologetic whisper.

'What are you playing?' Kate pointed to the white steering wheel in the boy's hand. 'Wii, right? I'm ace at Mario Kart. Want to race me?'

'It's Jamie's.' The console was old, already a hand-me-down when it had come to his older brother, but Jack was ready to defend it.

'I'm sure he won't mind if we have a quick turn,' Kate said gently. 'What d'you say, pal?'

The boy looked at his mother, who nodded her permission.

Kate followed the boy down the hall. 'I'll even let you be Princess Peach. No? What's wrong with that? Well, I'll be Princess Peach. You can be Luigi.' Shona heard a burst of music and a cheering crowd as the game started.

'Come and sit down, Laura,' Shona said gently.

'What is it?' She studied Shona's face for clues. 'Have you been crying? Is this Rob again?' Laura gave her a look of sympathy and perched on the edge of a modern sofa in a room otherwise crowded with the dark wood of old family furniture. She had on jeans and a navy blue fleece and looked like she'd slept in them.

Shona moved a magazine from a chair and sat down opposite. She shook her head and took a deep breath. 'Listen, Laura. The lifeboat was called out early this morning.'

'Is that where Tony is? I thought he didn't go out now. What's that to do with Jamie?'

Shona had no choice now but to press on. There was no kinder order in which she could deliver the two pieces of news she had for her friend. She edged forward in her seat.

'We found a man's body on the shore at Kilcatrin. We need to confirm his identity, but you should prepare yourself that it could be Tony.'

'What? No, no!' She covered her face with her hands.

'We also recovered a boy. He's in the DRI. From the clothing description you gave me, I think it's Jamie.' Shona let Laura process the information.

Laura's hands fell, and she blinked at her. 'In hospital? Is he badly injured? Is it a road accident? I told him to wear a helmet on his bike.'

'I'm sorry, Laura. He's come into contact with chemicals that burned him. He's stable but quite poorly.'

'How's that possible? No... no.' The last note strung out into a howl.

Shona moved forward onto her knees in front of her friend and took her shaking hands in her own. 'We'll get you up to see Jamie as soon as we can. Kate is going to stay with you and support you.'

'Why can't it be you?' It came out like an accusation.

Shona took a tissue from her bag. 'Kate's a really experienced officer. She'll concentrate on you and Jack. I'll be in charge of the investigation. We'll all support you. The lifeboat family, too.'

'Jamie! I want to see Jamie.' Laura's eyes were wide, a mixture of incomprehension and panic as she gripped the tissue.

'We'll check with the hospital again in a minute.' Shona knew she must get her friend to focus on practical steps to keep the shock from overwhelming her. 'I'm going to tell you what will happen next.'

'My head's full to bursting. I'm not sure I can take anything in.'

'It's okay, you don't have to,' Shona said calmly, keeping eye contact with Laura. 'Kate will take you over to DRI in a wee while. First, I'm sorry, I've a couple of questions about Tony. Can you tell me if he has any distinguishing features? Birthmarks, tattoos or scars?' Shona remembered the face and arms burned beyond recognition.

'Will I have to look at him?' Laura said, her voice barely a whisper.

'It wouldn't be fair to ask you,' Shona replied. 'We can use DNA. I'll take Tony's toothbrush, if there's nothing…' She let the sentence trail off, knowing the full horror of Tony's death would soon dawn on Laura.

'Oh, God,' Laura swallowed. 'I… yes, tattoos?' She nodded vigorously, as if convincing herself of what she was about to say. 'He has a swallow on his left forearm, and… I can't think.'

'What about on his body or legs?' Shona noted her friend's uncomprehending stare and hoped she wouldn't ask for more details.

'He's got an anchor on his calf. He had his appendix out as a kid. Oh, and a scar that runs right down his knee,' she motioned across her left knee, 'from an accident on the boat.'

'That's fine, Laura. You're doing great.' Shona mapped the injuries in her mind. His jeans protected his lower torso, calf and knee, and might be enough. 'Have you a photo of Tony I could take with me?'

Laura nodded, handing Shona her unlocked phone. The most recent pictures were all of the boys, but Shona found two clear shots of Tony Carlin and texted them to herself. She handed the phone back to Laura, who sat staring at the switched-off TV in the corner.

'I used to get scared. I'd worry every time he went out on the boats,' Laura whispered. 'You always think something's gonna happen, but now it's real, it's so much worse. You're not prepared, you're never prepared no matter how many times you live it in your head beforehand.'

'Laura? Is there someone who can mind Jack?' Shona took her hand again. 'What about Karen?'

Shona remembered that Karen, another of the lifeboat wives, had a boy about Jack's age and the two might even be in the same class at school. Laura looked at her as if she couldn't remember who Karen was.

Shona took out her phone. 'Is it all right if I call her? I'll ask...'

There was a crash at the front door. 'Mamie?' a thin voice cried out.

'Oh no.' Laura jumped to her feet.

An old man with a thin wisp of upstanding hair, his shirt hanging from below his sweater and tartan slippers on his feet, stumbled into the room. He glared at Laura. 'Who are you? Where's my wife?'

'Dad, it's okay. It's Laura. Remember?' She put out a placating hand, but the man scowled at her.

This must be Tony's father. Shona knew he'd moved into the smaller cottage next door when Laura and Tony married and was, in Laura's words, a bit of a handful, but she didn't realise James Carlin senior was so frail and confused.

'Hello Mr Carlin, I'm Shona Oliver.' He shook the hand she offered with surprising strength.

'James Carlin. Fisherman,' he said. 'Are you here about an order? I can do you five boxes of crab and a couple of stone of plaice.'

'Dad, Shona's here about Tony.'

'What's he been up to now?' James Carlin looked Shona up and down, taking in the suit and notebook. 'You the truancy officer?'

Laura shot her a desperate glance.

'No, Mr Carlin,' Shona smiled reassuringly.

'He'll be joining me at the creels soon enough.'

'Dad, have you had your breakfast?' Laura said, wiping her eyes and taking his arm. The old man didn't seem to notice she was crying.

'I'll just settle him next door,' Laura said to Shona.

'I'll call Karen, shall I?' Shona replied.

'No, no, it's fine. I can ask Tony's brother Fergus to come down. Someone will be in at lunchtime and then…' she trailed off, the enormity of keeping all the plates spinning set to overwhelm her.

'I'm calling Karen to take Jack,' Shona said firmly. 'You settle your father-in-law and call Fergus. Then Kate will get you up to the hospital.'

While Laura was next door, Shona relayed the identification info to Murdo along with the photographs of

Tony Carlin. A short while later, Laura returned and after breaking the news to Jack, she came into the living room. Shona could hear Kate's calm voice talking to the boy in the other room.

'Fergus is on his way,' Laura said, knotting a paper handkerchief to ribbons in her hands, but otherwise calm.

'I have to go now, but Kate will be here,' Shona said. 'I'll call you later. Okay?'

Laura nodded mutely and followed Shona to the front door.

'I can't take it in,' Laura said. 'Tony could be a tosser sometimes, but he was young, not like…' She jerked her head to the cottage next door where her father-in-law sat in the window, his gaze fixed on the sky. 'It's so unfair.'

'I know it is,' Shona replied, hugging her friend. The MoD may try to call this an accident, but those phosphorous grenades should never have been on a Galloway beach to rob a family of a father and blight the life of a boy. Someone was responsible. 'I will get to the bottom of this,' she said. 'You can be sure of that.'

# Chapter 4

Shona met Murdo as she reached the top of the stairs at Cornwall Mount CID office in Dumfries.

'You okay, boss?' Murdo said, taking in Shona's pallor. 'Rough night, eh?'

'I'm fine, Murdo. Thanks.'

'MoD doctor out at Kilcatrin who certified the death confirmed the tattoo and scar on the victim,' he said.

'So it's Tony Carlin.' She handed Murdo an evidence bag containing a battered blue toothbrush. 'Better run this for DNA, just in case.' She handed him a second bag containing a smaller red toothbrush. 'Jamie Carlin's. With his injuries I'm not sure it'll be possible to get a cheek swab for a while and I want belt and braces on this.'

Murdo nodded and his features softened as he took the bags from her. 'I'm sorry. Did you know Tony well?'

Shona gave him a small smile and shook her head. 'Thanks, Murdo. He's been with the lifeboat for years, but I didn't see much of him. His wife's a friend.'

'How's she taking it?'

'What you'd expect. Shocked. First thing I need to do is talk to the MoD about moving the body.'

'They've said…'

'I can guess what they've said, but a sudden death on our patch is our concern.'

Shona's phone rang. Detective Superintendent Malcom 'Mars Bar' Munro's name flashed up. A kirk elder and teetotaller, he'd earned his curious nickname by celebrating the conclusion of big cases not with drinks down the pub, but by handing around bars of chocolate to his team. Shona waved Murdo to go on ahead of her and answered the call. 'Morning, sir.'

'Morning, Shona. All under control?'

'Yes, sir. We've an ID on the victim.'

'Good work.' Superintendent Munro had appointed her and never missed an opportunity to congratulate himself on his foresight. 'Small point. The MoD police are sending you an Inspector Wallace.'

Shona stopped in her tracks. The Ministry of Defence Police, or MDP, were a highly trained civilian specialist force whose key priorities were protecting UK nuclear assets and military housing. Occasionally, they'd work with territorial forces such as during the Ipswich Sex Workers Murders when they'd provided a hundred officers and an Operational Support Unit for searches and enquiries. She knew they'd also deployed with the Met for the Extinction Rebellion protests. 'I don't recall requesting any assistance with this case, sir.'

'Not negotiable and no reflection on your abilities, Shona,' Munroe replied. 'It's within standard protocols for serious incidents of this nature. He'll be there to provide liaison. You might find a use for him. Just keep him in the loop.'

Munroe ended the call with the affirmation that the case was in safe hands.

Shona caught up with her sergeant. 'They're sending an MDP officer. What's that about, d'you think?'

Murdo pursed his lips and shook his head. 'Mibbae just procedure. Might be tricky if we uncover something that points to MoD culpability, though.'

'That's just what I was thinking.'

'Do you want me to get everyone together?' Murdo gripped the doorhandle.

'Give me twenty minutes.'

Shona passed through the CID room and into her own office. She hauled out the folder of briefing notes they had handed her when she first arrived two years ago, and searched the list of responsibilities that came under her remit. It ran from potential terrorist attacks on Robin Rigg wind farm, through crimes against the person to badger baiting and everything in between. Anyone who thought moving out of London to the country meant a quiet life wasn't a senior police officer. Beaufort's Dyke merited a whole page on its own.

Twenty minutes later, Murdo tapped her open door and held up her Charles Rennie Macintosh mug full of black coffee. 'Ready, boss?'

Shona's phone was tucked against her shoulder as she flicked through her final ring-binder of briefing notes. She gave Murdo a thumbs up while preparing to end her daughter's list of grievances.

'I'm nearly sixteen,' Becca shouted. 'Why do I have to wait? Can't you just give me the permission letter now? Say it's a pre-birthday present.'

'Becca, I need to go. We'll talk about this later.'

Shona ended the call and saw Murdo's enquiring expression.

'Becca wants a nose piercing, and another set of holes in her ear lobes. To be honest, it doesn't bother me that much. I get that it's a self-expression thing.' Her own ears were pierced at thirteen in the school toilets by a pal with a scalded needle and a cork, and her hair went through the entire rainbow before she joined the police. 'But Rob's convinced Becca wants to turn her face into a tea strainer and he's dead against it. Course, once she's sixteen it's out of our hands. She doesn't need parental permission.'

'How long till her birthday?'

'Too long to be dealing with phone calls like that every five minutes.'

In the conference room, Shona looked with some satisfaction at the attentive faces that greeted her. She knew they called her 'Wee Shona' behind her back, but their respect was sufficient that none would dare say it to her face. In addition to DC Ravi Sarwar, Murdo had gathered the six civilian aids, a constable from uniform to act as liaison and a couple of volunteer special officers, young lads with an eye on joining the force.

'Sorry to mess up your bank holiday plans.' She took a sip of coffee and sat down at the head of the large, oblong table that crowded the room. 'Kate will be FLO so run questions by her. She's up at the Royal with Laura Carlin, who's confirmed the boy is her son Jamie.'

'Do we know if they're likely to move him to Glasgow?' Ravi said. He had on a bright yellow cashmere sweater and expensive jeans that might have looked too casual for the office on anyone less groomed, his dark hair smooth and impeccably cut.

'The doctor says the proximity of Kilcatrin Range means the DRI is prepared to treat casualties,' Shona said. 'But I think they're also concerned about spreading contamination.' It's one small mercy. She didn't fancy Laura having to make four-hour round trips to Jamie's bedside with everything else on her plate. 'Murdo,' she said, giving her sergeant a nod.

'Right folks,' he began. 'This morning the body of a man was discovered on Kilcatrin Island.' He got up, unfolded an A3 printed map, and attached its corners to the magnetic whiteboard behind him with four small metal discs. He pointed to a fingernail of land lying close to the shore. 'It can be reached by a tidal causeway.' His pen traversed up the short distance to a large promontory of fields and woods covered with red crosshatching and the words *Danger Area*. 'It's part of the Kilcatrin MoD firing range and our victim appears to have suffered chemical burns.'

'Now,' Shona said. 'The coastguard estimate five thousand phosphorus bombs wash up on the beaches around south-west Scotland and Northern Ireland every year from Beaufort's Dyke, a deep trench in the sea bed which is midway between Scotland and Northern Ireland. It's thirty-two miles long and two miles wide and it goes down about a thousand feet.'

'It's like being back in a geography class,' one of the young Specials, Rhys Marshall, muttered. He was a stocky lad who looked like he spent a lot of time at the gym.

'Well, here's some history to go with it.' Shona glared at the offender over her glasses as Rhys turned pink to the ears, his card well and truly marked. 'Since the end of World War One, at least a million tons of munitions have been dumped in it. About a quarter of that is nerve gas plus a hundred and twenty thousand tons of mustard and phosgene chemical weapons. There are also a couple of tons of nuclear waste in there but no one's sure exactly what because although it came from private companies, much of the paperwork is covered by the hundred-year rule.'

'Fuck's sake,' Ravi tutted. The two silver bracelets on his wrists clinked softly as he pushed back his hair in manner that Shona recognised as a gesture of deep annoyance.

Murdo nodded. 'Aye, there's been incidents where kids have picked up stuff on the beach and sustained injures to their hands and eyes. At Cairnryan, just after the war, a wagon on the train bringing the stuff to the coast blew up. Killed eight men and destroyed the pier. It was kept quiet from the public.'

'If this dump is a thousand foot deep, how are they coming to the surface?' Ravi leaned forward, his face serious.

'The British Geographical Survey has been monitoring disturbances and thinks detonating hand grenades are dislodging other items,' Shona replied.

'Is this what caused our victim's injuries?' Ravi jotted a line in his notebook.

'It's too early to say. Anthrax and Sarine are thought to be among the items dumped. They were sealed in metal drums or encased in concrete but after fifty years in salt water, who knows what condition they're in.'

'Is anything being done to find out?' Ravi asked.

'There's due to be a camera survey in the area but nothing's been fixed.' Shona sighed. 'I think what we're seeing here from the MoD is a drip-drip strategy. When they release a new piece of information, they immediately follow it with an assurance that everything is safe. Truth is, we don't know what's down there, or how stable it is.'

'Does that mean there's more to come? That's a major public safety concern for us,' Murdo said.

'It's a primary concern, Murdo. The beaches will stay closed till after the clean-up but, according to the MoD, that could take a fortnight. We need everyone, including ourselves, uniform, the Specials, getting this message across. Don't sneak onto the beaches, and for the love of God, don't pick anything up. It could kill you.'

A murmur of low, uneasy chatter sprang up around the table as the police officers and civilian aids processed the ramifications of what they'd just heard.

'Meanwhile,' Shona said loudly, bringing everyone's attention back to her, 'we'll do DNA to confirm, but we currently have an assumptive ID on our victim. Murdo?'

'Anthony James Carlin, thirty-five years old.' Murdo read from his notebook. 'He's a fisherman and co-owned a boat with his brother, Fergus, but like most of these fellas he also worked on the scallop dredgers out of Kirk-cudbright. He was a long-serving member of the lifeboat crew at Kirkness and was married with two sons, one of whom appears to be the lad at the Royal.'

Shona raised her pen to interrupt. 'Did he have a haaf-net licence?'

Murdo nods. 'Aye. He's registered, but not for that stretch of shore.'

Shona turned to the faces around the table. 'We need to establish what Tony Carlin was doing and how he got out there. There're no reports of a drifting boat from the coastguard, and there was a dinghy parked in the garage at the house. Murdo, get someone to call Fergus Carlin and ask him to check the boat he owned with his brother is still on its mooring.'

'Yes, boss.'

'We're treating this as an unexplained death,' Shona continued. 'At present, our only witness is in a medically induced coma. Forensics are going to be vital.'

'Think we'll recover much?'

'We're in neap tides, so it's possible.' Shona saw the blank looks. 'The distance between the high and low water mark is less that on spring tides. The sea doesn't come so far up the beach.'

'Can't see the crime scene being preserved with the army boys walking all over it.' Murdo said.

'True. They've instructions to clear the phosphorous shells, but that doesn't mean an over-zealous squaddie won't decide to do on an impromptu litter pick. I've instructed them to set up a five-metre cordon around where Tony Carlin was found, but they've tramped through there to recover the body, not that I'm thinking footprints.'

'What are you thinking?'

'I'm thinking this is going to be high profile. If it turns political, I don't want the finger pointed at us, that we didn't do the best job we could.' She looked at everyone around the table in turn. 'Murdo will allocate you tasks. While I want you to warn and reassure people, I trust you not to divulge any details from this enquiry. We don't want a panic on our hands.'

As they packed up, Murdo came up beside her and said in a low voice, 'We'll get flak from the tourist trade. What's your man saying about it all?'

'Well, we're not banning folk from coming, but it's bound to put a dampener on things. Rob's been ringing trying to work out if our insurance will cover us. It might come under act of God.'

'Well, the way the MoD have been acting,' Murdo replied, 'they certainly think they're on a par with the almighty.'

# Chapter 5

On Saturday morning, Shona woke to the scent of bacon drifting upstairs. Rob must already be cooking the guests' breakfasts. She'd slept deeply. Her phone showed a stack of texts from Murdo starting at five a.m. The army and navy personnel had arrived and clean-up operations were underway. There was still no news from the MoD about releasing the body, but Murdo expected an update later this morning.

Shona pulled on her running gear, more in hope than expectation. The five miles out to Knockie Point and back was a favourite hour's run she often did with Laura Carlin, even if they undermined all their good work with lattes and the leftover Danish pastries from Rob's guest breakfasts when they came back to High Pines. She wanted to clear her head, prepare herself for the challenges ahead, but knew there was little chance she'd get out this morning. Laura would be at the hospital. How long it would be before it hit her that her life was utterly changed? In the present, as her son hung between life and death, all time would be suspended. The clocks stopped. The outside world would blur into the background as it did for Shona when Becca had been injured in a hit-and-run. Everything shrank to each creeping second in which her child still clung on to life. It filled her consciousness. Only after Jamie's recovery or death would Laura wake to the realisation that Tony was gone. He'd taken his fishing boat to a far shore from which he would never return, and she could not follow.

What would Shona do if faced with a similar life-changing event? She couldn't imagine being without Rob. Even with his troubles and impulsiveness, he was still her funny, loving soul mate, a good and attentive father to Becca and she didn't doubt for one minute that he loved his wife and daughter with his whole heart. But she'd also realised Rob's choices often served his own needs and those closest to him could be caught in the crossfire. She was committed to saving their marriage, but at what cost? She might forgive him for his frailty, his stupidity, his pride. For the financial mess his gambling had left them in. But you cannot wipe the past clean, no matter how much you might wish to.

When she entered the kitchen, Rob had his back to her at the cooker, an apron over his shorts and T-shirt. Although his cropped dark hair had gone prematurely grey in his thirties, he was still lean and tanned and somehow it suited him. The silver fox look, Laura called it, with what Shona thought was a hint of admiration.

'What time d'you call this then, Sleeping Beauty?' he said, not turning round.

She hugged him from behind and peeped on tiptoe over his shoulder at the scrambled eggs and smoked salmon in the pan. Warmed bagels sat on two plates nearby.

'You looked spark out. I didn't want to wake you,' he said. 'Sit down. The guests have already gone. This is for the workers.' He smiled as she squeezed him and planted a kiss on his shoulder. He turned to look at her. 'Sure you're okay?'

'I'm fine.' Shona felt her stomach rumble and realised she'd skipped at least one meal yesterday. She pulled out a chair. 'How are the bookings? Many cancellations?'

'A few. I've persuaded most to re-book, but I've had to give them a discount on the peak summer rate. That'll hit out margins.' He spooned out the scrambled eggs, sprinkled over a home-grown mixture of fresh herbs and set the plates on the table. 'You got any idea when the beaches will open again?' he said casually.

Shona reckoned it was the number one topic of conversation in the calls and texts he'd received from fellow members of the B&B owners association, all of whom knew his wife was with the police and were keen for the inside track.

'The beaches will open as soon as it's safe,' Shona replied. 'I know it's the holidays. I'm not in the business of pissing on anybody's chips.'

'Is that your soundbite for the lunchtime news?' Rob raised an amused eyebrow.

'Pretty much.' She tried to smile. She didn't want to think about the state of Tony Carlin's body and how that might be repeated if the warning to holiday makers, fishermen or dog walkers went unheeded.

Rob took a bite of his creation and nodded his approval, then his handsome face turned serious. 'I had a call from my solicitor.'

'What did he say?' Shona concentrated on her breakfast, but she felt her heartbeat skip up a notch. 'Will you be charged?'

Rob, a former merchant banker, had been caught up in an enquiry into financial irregularities at Milton McConnell, the employer he'd left under a cloud which had, partly, prompted the family's move back to his home turf on the Solway two years ago.

'No decision yet.'

Shona knew from her time as a City of London cop the likely penalties he faced: a prison sentence of four to five years, ten-plus in serious cases. Rob had, unwittingly, he claimed, overseen a team where fraudulent financial transactions were mixed with legitimate ones to buy gold for export. Co-mingling, it was known as in banking circles. To Shona and everyone else, it was more familiar as money laundering.

'Milton McConnell faces a huge fine. Could be millions,' Rob continued. 'They'll try to blame the whole thing on individual rogue dealers.' He shook his head. 'Once I saw what was happening, it was too late. I wanted to protect you and Becca. Going quietly seemed the best option.'

'Have they established who the gang was behind this?'

'You know what it's like. Ironically, once you turn wealth into something tangible – gold or stolen art – it can be harder to trace. The electronic trail goes cold. Exported gold gets recast abroad, a legitimate clone of itself, then converted back into stocks, bonds or cash.'

Shona wondered if Rob's realisation that he'd been fooled had fired his taste for gambling, a desire to show he was not a failure, that he could still work the numbers and come out top. At heart, she knew he was a risk-taker. His privileged upbringing of private school and city job taught him to weigh the odds, but ultimately life had always been good to him, so why would anything change?

'Just tell the truth.' Shona realised her voice had an official tone. For a second she caught a hint of mischief in Rob's expression and thought he might make a joke of it, but if he was intending to, one look at her face made him think better of it.

'Make sure you tell your solicitor every detail,' she continued. 'No matter how incriminating you think it is. Don't let the bank turn the tables on you with something you haven't admitted to. Every fake taxi receipt or fly delve into the stationery cupboard, tell him. Understand?'

Rob nodded, all trace of humour gone. They both knew this was about more than a tactical divulgence. The rebuilding of their relationship had to be based on truth and a sense they could trust each other again after a dragging out of secrets both would prefer to have remained hidden.

'Where's Becca?' Shona said, changing the subject. Arriving home late last night, her daughter's bedroom window was unlit. Shona guessed she was asleep.

'She went to Ellie's,' Rob said, polishing off his bagel and getting up to make coffee. 'She's worked hard this week. I said she could stay over.'

Their move from London had also been influenced by a sense that Becca was spiralling out of control. Her suspension from school for cannabis possession had sealed the deal. But Becca hadn't settled, calling out her new classmates for what she saw as their small-town homophobic and racist attitudes, and eventually going head-to-head with bullies in a way Shona recognised, with some embarrassment, as a reflection of her own younger self. When Becca had opted for home schooling, managed by Rob, it seemed the best compromise. She was doing some volunteering with a heritage and countryside charity, but Shona was glad that the close friendship with Ellie, one of the few new friends she'd made, hadn't seeped away as Shona had feared.

'How's her studies going?' she said.

'I've got her booked in at Austin Friars in Carlisle. She'll do her IGCSE exams as an external candidate next month.'

'And you're sure those will help get her into a Scottish university at the home fees rate?' It came out as more of an accusation than Shona intended. The education fund they'd set up had disappeared into the abyss of Rob's gambling.

'I've looked into it,' Rob replied stiffly. 'She'll need Highers or A-levels, but she qualifies on residency. International GCSEs were the only option. It's impossible to find coursework supervisors. She just needs to study online and sit the papers in person. There's nowhere in Scotland south of Glasgow.' A hint of peevishness crept into his voice. 'Don't worry, I'll be the one driving her back and forward over the border for seven different exams.'

Shona felt a pang of guilt. It was true the B&B was Rob's business, but he also now shouldered the bulk of Becca's education, although Shona pitched in with her valuable but not always immediately appreciated insights on the importance of time-management, the validity of moral versus legal arguments, report writing and interrogating the evidence. Rob went to a posh boarding school in Perthshire while she'd battled her way through a state education in one of the most deprived parts of Glasgow. Although she matched him for intelligence, and her police career had deepened her skill set and empathy, some of the topics thrown up by Becca's IGCSE in Classical Civilisations, a necessary precursor to her current ambition of studying archaeology at Glasgow University, were definitely beyond Shona's experience.

'I'll take her if I can,' Shona said. It sounded like the poor concession it was, but if their roles were reversed, and Rob was a DI shouldering the responsibility Shona had, it wouldn't even have come up.

Rob had his back to her, measuring coffee into the espresso machine. 'It's fine. I know you're busy.' She could feel him mentally rolling his eyes. 'You off into the office today?'

'I'm waiting for them to release the crime scene and Tony Carlin's body. The uniform super is managing the clean-up and public information aspects. Murdo will bell me when we can get over to Kilcatrin Island.' She picked up her phone and opened the tide times app. Low tide had just passed. Shona sighed, frustrated at the missed opportunity. High tide would be ten past three this afternoon, covering the causeway. The next opportunity to cross to the island would come after dark. It was possible, but not ideal. A more likely opportunity was tomorrow's low tide at 9:57 a.m. She'd continue to press the MoD for access but she knew they marched to their own drum and she needed them onside. Having the forensics team waiting in a van at Kilcatrin Ranges' gates would do nothing more than eat up her budget.

'How's Laura?' Rob sat back down, pushing her coffee towards her.

'Kate's with her at the Royal.'

'You going over?'

'Kate's dealing with it for the moment,' Shona said, absently scrolling through her messages.

'It?' Rob raised an eyebrow. 'Thought you and Laura were good mates.'

'We are,' Shona said. 'I'm also SIO on her husband's unexplained death. The best way I can help her right now is by getting a quick and thorough explanation of what happened to Tony.'

'No room for sentiment, then?'

She knew he was goading her, payback for her official earlier tone. 'Plenty of room, but it won't get in the way of me uncovering what happened. Just remember who found his body.' Shona pushed back her chair and crossed to put her empty coffee cup in the sink below the window with its panoramic view of the estuary.

Rob got to his feet and held up his hand. 'I know, I'm sorry. Laura couldn't have a better person to fight her corner.' He stroked her hair back from her cheek. 'Just go careful, darlin'. The MoD have fucked up and around here people have long memories. I don't want them wondering whose side you're on.' He wrapped his arms around her, and she leaned into his comforting solidity and warmth.

'Right now the case has to be my priority,' Shona said, hugging him back. 'But yes, Laura's going to need everyone to pitch in.' Shona admired Laura's strength and no-nonsense approach to life and her ability to have a laugh. She recalled that although Laura's job as a part-time receptionist at the local doctor's didn't come near Shona's in responsibility, they'd both sounded off over crappy bosses, difficult customers and laughed about it. 'I need to talk to Tommy anyway. I'll see what the lifeboat family can do to help. I'll go in on my way back from my run.'

'Sure you don't want to stay and help me clean the guest rooms?'

'I'm not sure I'm suitably qualified.'

'I'd offer you an apprenticeship but I doubt there's anything I could teach you.' He grinned. 'Mind you, everyone's out. We could just both skive off and go back to bed.'

Shona groaned. 'There's nothing I'd like better.'

'See this apron? It means I'm my own boss.'

'I'm not. I'm a public servant and right now I'm not in their good books.'

'I'm one member of the public whose good books you could definitely be in.' Rob pulled her close again and began kissing her neck.

But just as Shona felt her resolve slipping, her phone rang. She wriggled free of Rob's grasp.

Murdo reeled off another update as Rob stuck out his bottom lip in tragi-comic disappointment. She mirrored his expression, then blew him a kiss and mouthed, *later*. Shona headed back upstairs to change into her suit. The list of tasks was piling up. This morning, there would be no time for anything but work.

## Chapter 6

It was barely nine a.m. when Shona drove along Kirkness seafront, but the visitors' parking bays were already full. She reached the lifeboat station and pulled in. Tommy was standing in the empty boat hall, looking as if he wasn't quite sure what to do with himself. A couple of the shore crew were going over an inventory that Shona was convinced they'd checked yesterday. Tony's death had left everyone subdued but in the back of their collective mind was also the concern about the consequences of the *Margaret Wilson* being out of action. When an emergency came in, it would be their fellow volunteers at Kirkcudbright or across the Solway in Silloth who would answer the call. Shona shared their frustration.

'Any update?' she said to Tommy, nodding at the empty hall.

'I'm bringing her back this afternoon. We'll check her over for damage from thon chemicals, whatever they are. I doubt we'll get the full story from the MoD.'

'You still think the phosphorous grenades came from Beaufort's Dyke?'

'Aye. I'm sure of it. There's an active marine guidance note for an undersea cabling company working just off the Rhins of Galloway. Pound to a penny they've a hand in this.'

'Thanks, I'll chase that up.' Shona made a note on her phone. 'Tommy?' she said, a new idea forming. 'If they were still dumping in the 1970s, do you think there's anyone still around who remembers what went out on those boats?'

'Aye, mibbae. They'd be in their seventies at least now.'

'So who do I ask?' Shona said. Tommy had taken over the boatyard next door from his father, the family business going back into Kirkness's boatbuilding heyday in the last century.

'If I mind right, the dumping boats all came from Cumbria. You'll no' find anyone local.'

Shona nodded. She wasn't sure how it would help, but with one man dead, it would be good to build a picture of the likely ongoing threat from as many different sources as possible.

The shore crew had propped a whiteboard up outside the station. In addition to the usual tide times was a stark warning to avoid the shoreline, stay vigilant and call the coastguard if you spotted 'military ordnance or discarded pyrotechnics'. A tourist in expensive trainers approached the open doors of the lifeboat station. Shona hoped he wasn't about to complain about the lack of beach access, but as he came closer, he extended his hand and Shona saw the recognition on Tommy's face.

'Fergus. My condolences,' Tommy said formally, taking the man's outstretched hand in both of his.

'I just wanted to thank you all for what you did for my brother and Jamie,' Fergus Carlin said quietly, dipping his head. He was as fair as his brother was dark, with the reddish blond hair and light blue eyes that reminded Shona of the Viking genes that pervaded much of the Solway's population.

Shona had considered jogging to the station but was glad she'd abandoned that plan and that her first meeting with the deceased's brother saw her dressed in a suitably sombre suit, the mark of diligent authority, not as a park runner.

She straightened her shoulders and gave him a sympathetic smile as she shook his hand. 'Hello, Mr Carlin. DI Shona Oliver. I'm the Senior Investigating Officer on your brother's death. I'm very sorry about Tony, and your loss.'

'Thanks. I spoke to your fella. Ravi, is it? I told him the *Arcturus* is still tied up.'

'Thank you. We'll keep in touch. And remember, we're all here to support you,' Shona said as Tommy nodded in agreement. 'DC Kate Irving can tell you about the investigation. The lifeboat station is only at the end of a phone. Please, call on us if there's anything at all we can do.'

'I will. Thanks.'

'You coming in for a brew, Fergus?' Tommy said.

'No, I better get back. Just wanted to say thanks for going out. I know the lifeboat meant a lot to Tony.'

'How's Old Jimmy doing?' Tommy asked.

'My dad's okay, thanks. He doesnae really know what's happening most of the time. I've got the carer sitting with him while Laura's up at the hospital.'

As they watched Fergus walk away, his shoulders stooped as if he carried the weight of the world, Tommy said, 'Is Tony Carlin's body still out at Kilcatrin?'

'Yes. The MoD should release it today.'

'Don't suppose there's any way we can bring him back on the lifeboat?' Tommy looked at her keenly. 'One of our own, Shona.'

Shona bit her lip. 'I'd love to say yes, Tommy, but the possibility of contamination… plus I doubt the fiscal would agree.'

'Aye. It was just a thought.'

'It was a good one, Tommy. You can leave it to me now.' She patted his arm. 'I better get on.'

Shona returned to her car and made two calls. The first was to the MoD at Kilcatrin, informing them they needed to get Tony Carlin's body ready for collection. Failure to do so would leave them open to a charge of obstructing a police investigation. The second was to DC Dan Ridley over in Cumbria CID. It may have been fifty years since dumping in Beaufort's Dyke was halted, but it was high time someone had a look at exactly what had gone on there. If the dumping ships left from Cumbria, he was best placed to follow it up.

She sat tapping one finger on the steering wheel of the Audi. While Dan had been helpful, the MoD had given her the run around. She pulled up her detective sergeant's number.

'Murdo, what's the contact info for the MDP police officer they've brought in?' She noted the details and ended the call. Some jobs were better done in person.

Half an hour later, she slowed as she approached the entrance to Kilcatrin Ranges. A small group of protestors brandishing placards was already there. *Climate not Trident. Kilcatrin is State Terrorism. Bairns Not Bombs.* A couple of uniforms were keeping an eye on them. One had his notebook open, jotting down the details of an unroadworthy-looking van parked on the verge. As Shona approached, the other police officer stepped out into her path and held up his hand. She fished out her warrant card and pressed it up against the windscreen and he immediately waved her through.

The next line of sentries were armed and less obliging but eventually directed her onto a pale concrete road that led to a high wire fence and a guard post. There was a barrier pole across the entrance. A red flag flew above it to indicate the ranges were in operation. She showed her warrant card to the young soldier who returned to his green Portakabin to phone. A few minutes later, a Land Rover drew up at the other side of the barrier.

Inspector Simon Wallace was a man so purposefully bland, Shona reckoned it would always take a second or two to confirm you actually recognised him each time you met. Perhaps that was the point. His slim face had a polished look, the skin stretched tight across the cheekbones. He wore neutral coloured zipped activity trousers, neither beige nor green, and a fleece of inde-terminate colour between blue and grey. Both had a starched quality, as if nothing would stick to him. His rank within the Ministry of Defence Police was equal to her own. Shona concluded he was a police officer who'd shed his uniform but couldn't quite bring himself to dress as a civilian.

'You need to leave your car in the car park.' He indic-ated an empty patch of tarmac by the gate. 'We use civilian cars as targets on the ranges. I wouldn't want you to get blown up,' he said without the hint of a smile.

Shona parked the Audi. They shook hands. She couldn't place his accent, which could have been anything from educated Edinburgh to southern England.

'Get in.' He moved towards the Land Rover. 'I'll take you down to the op area.'

'First, I need to know when Tony Carlin's body will be released.' Shona wanted a few things straight before he got into the driving seat. She opened the boot of her car and took out a waterproof jacket and pair of wellingtons.

'There's significant risk of secondary contamination.'

'I'm aware of that. You have the deceased in a hazardous materials container? Inside that are two body bags, the inner one gas-tight and chemically resistant?'

'That's correct.'

'Then it's safe to transport.' Shona was aware the Ministry of Defence Police had their own forensics teams and CID department but there was no way she was letting them run the show.

When she'd gone through the briefing notes yesterday, the first person she'd called was Professor Sue Kitchen, head of Forensic Pathology at the University of Glasgow, which held the Crown Office contract to perform post-mortems for the Procurator Fiscal's office, and one of Scotland's most senior pathologists. Her nickname of 'Slasher Sue' was partly due to the speed at which she conducted her post-mortems and also her ten-year stint as Scottish National Fencing Champion (Epee). She'd hung up her blade, in that capacity at least, and now sat on the sport's governing committee.

'A refrigerated vehicle will be needed, not an ambulance,' Inspector Wallace said.

'It'll be here this afternoon from the Queen Elizabeth.' Shona shut the boot of her car and turned to face him.

'You know, I remember an incident in Suffolk,' he said in a conversational tone, indicating again that Shona should get into the Land Rover. 'Home Guard had buried just such items in a field after the war. A tractor team dragged them up and ended up in the local A&E. It took four days to decontaminate the hospital and wrote off a couple of ambulances.'

Queen Elizabeth University Hospital Mortuary in Glasgow was equipped with the ultimate biosecure facilities partly due to the proximity of a nuclear submarine base at Faslane on the Clyde. Inspector Wallace would be aware of that fact. Why he had chosen not to acknowledge it to Shona spoke volumes.

'I'm sure Professor Kitchen's team is up to it,' Shona replied. 'How far on are you with decontamination? My forensics people need access as soon as possible.'

'Then you'll be keen to see for yourself.' His expression was just the right side of professional, no more.

They passed through open green fields pockmarked with large craters that had been quickly reclaimed by nature. Here and there were ponds, perfectly round in the shell holes, and grass-filled hollows where clusters of young rowan trees had sprung up in the centre protected from the wind.

Further on, the land was cloaked in ancient woodland where it fell away towards the firth. Bluebells hung like an azure mist above the grass. Wallace pulled into a layby and they got out. Wild garlic flowers, an explosion of tiny white fireworks, lined the lane, adding their own scent to the heady mix. Despite the beauty around her, it was the busy shoreline and low grey sky that matched Shona's mood. Troops in plastic suits and masks were buddied-up in pairs, carrying metal bins filled with the glass incendiaries between them.

'How will you dispose of the grenades?' Shona said.

'Open burning on a remote site.'

'Somewhere around here?' Shona was already calculating the potential bang several thousand phosphorous bombs might make.

'We'll let you know,' he replied.

Shona watched the soldiers on the beach as Inspector Wallace reeled off a string of reassurances about collaborative working and ensuring public safety.

The causeway to Kilcatrin Island was covered by the sea. There was little Shona could do until the tide turned. Professor Kitchen's assistants would begin their job this afternoon in Glasgow and a forensics team from Police Scotland's crime campus at Gartcosh would arrive on site first thing tomorrow. But there was a question Inspector Wallace still hadn't answered. What exactly was he doing here?

'Watching squaddies sweep up. Isn't this a bit below your paygrade?' Shona smiled and cocked her head at the beach.

'Always nice to get out of the office,' he said. His mouth turned up at the corners in an approximation of a smile. 'And at least it isn't raining.'

# Chapter 7

Inspector Wallace returned Shona to the guard post. He showed no hint of relief, but she felt he must have accomplished his morning's tasks. Liaise with local constabulary. Tick. Deliver obscure, hand-patting reassurance. Tick.

Shona calculated she'd be back at Dumfries CID in around forty minutes. In defiance of Wallace's weather assessment, a thin mist of raindrops had begun to coat the Audi's windscreen. She set the wipers going. It wasn't an entirely wasted journey. Tony Carlin's body would be released, and it was a useful opportunity to size up Inspector Wallace. A catch up with Murdo and with Kate at the hospital were her priorities. There'd been no further update on Jamie Carlin's condition since first thing this morning. No news was definitely good news on that score.

At the junction of the concrete entranceway and the main road, she slammed on the brakes. The protestors she'd passed on the way in had multiplied. Behind her, the sentries closed the security gates and a lorry pulled up. A dozen soldiers, their personal weapons slung across their chests, jumped down.

Shona got out of her car. A group of protestors surged forward and sat down on the main road to her left, locking arms. Whistles and drums started in an attempt to disrupt police comms. Shona studied the human wall for motorcycle wire locks or handcuffs that would make the protestors harder to remove.

'Can you clear the road?' Shona said to the police sergeant in charge. She didn't want anything stopping the removal of Tony Carlin's body.

'Question of numbers, ma'am,' he replied. 'The traffic management plan calls for a couple of lads up at the cross-roads, putting up a diversion. What wi' it being the bank holiday 'n'all.'

Stuck in a jam or exercising your democratic right to protest in a drizzle. Neither was high on Shona's bank holiday to-do list. 'Push them back. Tell them they'll be arrested.'

'Probably what they want. Not sure we should tie up officers processing them.'

He had a point.

'Look,' Shona said over the rising din. 'There's a refri-gerated unit coming from Glasgow to collect a fatality. It'll have an escort. It's a priority. Make sure it gets through.'

'Yes, ma'am.'

A second group of protestors were moving away, intent on blocking the road in the other direction to Shona's right. Officers held them back, their arms wide, heads shaking, doing their best to calm the situation. A few scuffles developed. Shona saw an officer reach around his belt for his cuffs. Arrests were inevitable.

'If you need to get out, ma'am, I'd do it soon. We have them here regular, it'll blow over by teatime.'

'Familiar faces?'

'Aye, a few.'

The jostling became outright pushing and shoving, a show of force. A few protestors were brought to the ground and held there. Shona scanned the crowd and saw a familiar face of her own. 'What the—'

She jumped into the Audi and pulled out onto the main road. She squeezed through the crowd and stopped, her window down.

'Get in,' she ordered, and for once, her daughter didn't argue.

As they moved off, Shona shot her daughter a look in the rear-view mirror and saw another girl had followed Becca into the backseat of the car. She was a few years older with a nose ring, her blonde hair in tight, cornrow braids bound at the end with small seashells that clinked as she repeatedly turned to study the protest as it receded through the Audi's rear window. Both girls were giggling in a pitch Shona recognised as relief tinged with fear, but it irritated her just the same.

'Seatbelts,' she barked. 'Becca, aren't you going to introduce me?'

Becca's silence told her mother she'd rather not, but the girl herself said, 'Hi. I'm Willow.'

When nothing else was forthcoming, Shona bit back more questions and smiled. 'So where can I drop you, Willow?'

'Bankend. If that's okay?'

'That's fine,' Shona said. She didn't know the girl, but she had the impression any further questions would be met with evasion or one-word answers.

Beyond the occasional whisper and stifled giggle, Becca and her friend were largely silent for the twenty-minute journey.

Bankend was a village on the far side of the estuary from Kirkness, but there could not have been a bigger contrast between the two. On the outskirts, an optimistic small holder had roped off part of a muddy field, advertising it to touring caravans without any takers. The village was a mix of mid-twentieth-century social housing, the grey roughcast crumbling into pebbly, overgrown gardens. Most of the people Shona passed as they entered the village seemed to have taken on a similar appearance, grey, bland and overweight. Here and there, a retired couple had kept their grass trim, a stag garden ornament by a concrete bird bath. The entire village was flat, dull and worn out. Time had passed it by, and it had passed a long time ago. In the village centre a few two-storey granite buildings, the last remnants of a once prosperous market village. The single pub was shuttered and there wasn't a car under ten years old in the streets. The harbour was half silted up with a few rusting trawlers and abandoned-looking pleasure boats sat in the mud, grass sprouting around their keels.

'You can drop me here,' Willow said as they reached a turning that led to the harbour. A hand-painted board announcing the Gaia Collective was propped up by a gate. Repurposed buses, some propped on blocks, clustered between old industrial buildings. Shona went down the lane anyway and stopped by a horsebox painted with a sign offering organic, vegetarian street food. She studied the half-a-dozen faces that showed an interest in their arrival. Becca moved to unbuckle her seatbelt, but Shona stretched back her hand, rested it lightly on her daughter's knee, and gave her an uncompromising look. Becca slumped in her seat and folded her arms.

Willow registered the exchange. She winked at Becca, then hopped from the car, without offering her thanks, and hurried to a group of men and women, all under thirty. They stood silently, arms folded, as Shona put the car in reverse. Halfway up the lane, she did a three-point turn. Willow and the rest of the group continued to watch until she was out of sight.

Once clear of the village, Shona pulled in by the side of the road and turned to Becca. 'Well?'

'Well, what?'

'What were you doing out at Kilcatrin? And get in the front. I'm not your Uber.'

Becca opened the car door and for a moment, Shona thought she might walk off back up the road. When Becca climbed into the passenger seat, Shona floored the accelerator. This was best done on the move, partly so her daughter couldn't leave and partly so Shona couldn't take both hands off the wheel to strangle her.

'Is this the environmental group you've been volunteering with?' Shona said.

The Gaia Collective at Bankend had crossed Shona's radar before. It was mainly issues with untaxed vehicles, but there had been the odd incident that straddled the line between their recycling of apparently abandoned building material and outright thievery. It was certainly somewhere she didn't want her fifteen-year-old daughter hanging about.

'Willow says there should be a public enquiry.'

'Blocking the road isn't the way to make it happen,' Shona replied. 'You told your dad you were at Ellie's.'

'I was.' Becca's heart-shaped face registered outraged. 'She was busy and didn't want to come. Anyway, the protest needs numbers to get on the news. People should know what's being done in their name. You could end world hunger with just ten per cent of what the superpowers spend on weapons.'

'Look Becca, I'm not disagreeing with you.' From the corner of her eye, Shona saw Becca's slightly startled expression and pressed on. 'You want to save the world, I'm all in favour of it.'

'So why did you drag us into the car?'

Shona thought that was a bit excessive, even for Becca. Then she remembered the armed soldiers, the potential for escalation. If she'd had to drag her, she would have.

'Look, I didn't want you caught up in something that would lead to a police or fiscal warning, or worse.' Shona made an effort to lower her voice and slow her breathing. Becca had had a scare at the demo. There was nothing to be gained from bawling her out. 'This is a really important time for you with your exams coming up. Schoolwork is your priority. That's what will give you the skills to move forward and do the things you want to do. Understand?'

Becca let out a long breath. 'Yes. Okay. Thanks, Mum. Will you tell Dad where I was?'

Shona had already decided she wouldn't say anything to Rob. He'd only take it as a dig at his parenting and side with Becca.

'Let's just get you home.' Shona took the right turn into Kirkness. 'But Becca, I want you to stay away from Bankend. Can you do that? There are other ways to pursue your interest in the environment.'

'Suppose.' Becca resumed her slouched position.

Shona had expected an argument. Maybe her daughter really did get a fright.

At High Pines, an unfamiliar red two-door MINI Cooper was in the one of the guests' parking slots. Just beyond, Shona saw a young woman in a long floaty dress, with her back to the sparkling estuary beyond. Her tousled blonde hair was swept over one shoulder as she pouted at a phone held flattering high in front of her for the perfect selfie.

In the kitchen, Rob was washing salad leaves. On the draining board stood a veg box from the co-operative up the road.

'How's my favourite lassies?'

Becca stamped past her father and went upstairs to her room.

Rob raised his eyebrows at Shona. 'It's nothing. I saw her on the road back and picked her up.' It was almost the truth. 'New guest?' Shona pointed out the window.

'Just arrived. Her name's Emma Johnstone. She's a blogger.'

'As in online journalist? You didn't think to run that by me? Who does she work for?'

'Viva Caledonia.'

'Great, that's all I need. Some keyboard warrior. At least the TV and print journalists will take a telling off the press office or cut a deal for an exclusive. The PCC is a bit of a toothless tiger but the legit journos make a show of signing up to it.'

'It's nothing like that. Viva Caledonia's got more than twenty thousand followers on Insta and loads on Twitter. They have a fresh take on travel and lifestyle with culture and current affairs.' Rob sounded as if he'd just read that on their website to back up the decision he'd already made. 'Shona, we need the money. She's promised to give us a good write-up.'

'Promised but not guaranteed. Couldn't you have put her off for a few weeks? Just until things are back to normal.'

'We need some clawback, especially after all this...' he threw up his hands and they fell back to his side,

'…this fuck-up with the beaches.' Shona couldn't escape the feeling that somehow the blame rested with her, but she swallowed a retort that would send the conversation into the stratosphere.

'But you're giving her a discount?' Rob's expression said that he had.

'Well, we can't afford to pay upfront for advertising.'

'With paid advertising, it's less of a…' She bit back the word. Gamble. 'I mean, we've more control.' She needed to get into the office. It wasn't her problem right now. Shona shook her head. 'Just keep her out of my way. If she asks about the investigation, say nothing. And if she disses your décor or the thread count of your sheets, don't say you weren't warned.'

## Chapter 8

From her office window, Shona saw the lights on the bypass come on. The young Special, Rhys Marshall walked into the CID room carrying a couple of sweating carrier bags. A muted cheer went up. Shona dropped her glasses onto a pile of paperwork and followed the smell of fish and chips.

Murdo was dishing out wrapped packets to her detective constables, Ravi and Kate, and the support staff.

'Right, listen up, everybody. There's still reports of fresh grenades coming in on the tide.' There was a collective groan. 'The good news is forensics will be at Kilcatrin tomorrow morning and some of you lucky folk will be joining them.' She helped herself to one of Ravi's chips. 'Low tide is around ten a.m. but I want you there by seven. We'll only have a six-hour safe window unless you fancy spending the night.'

'I'm guessing it won't be like Love Island,' Ravi said.

'Distinctly chillier,' Shona replied.

'Should suit you then, DC Irving.' Ravi gave his fellow detective constable a wink.

'Ha, ha.' Kate glared at him and reached for a sachet of ketchup.

Shona took her wrapped fish supper from her sergeant. An unclaimed packet lay beside it. 'Murdo, did we over-order or is someone just very hungry?'

'The boy's on his way.' He nodded to the door just as DC Dan Ridley from Cumbria CID pushed through it, shaking raindrops from his coat. Ravi shot Kate a look.

'Hi Dan. To what do we owe the pleasure?' Shona said with genuine warmth. 'You got something for me?'

'Yes, boss.'

'That was quick. See,' she addressed the others around the room, 'enthusiasm and efficiency. Take a lesson from this lad. Although, you could have phoned. Saved yourself the journey.'

'Oh, you know.' Dan shrugged, a blush creeping up his neck as he took the vacant chair next to Ravi. 'All quiet in Cumbria.'

'Come to see how a proper CID office is run, haven't you, pal?' Ravi clapped him on the shoulder and flashed him his megawatt smile.

'Put him down, Ravi. D'you want to tell me now, Dan?' She nodded towards her office and he followed her in.

'Subsea UK is the undersea cabling company who've been working in the Irish Sea,' Dan said, as he sat down opposite Shona, who'd set her fish supper on the desk. 'They're laying a new data line, the IRIS Alba,' he continued, 'but deny they're working anywhere near Beaufort's Dyke.'

Shona nodded. It would be easy enough to check the ship's movements with the coastguard HQ in Belfast so there was little point in them lying. 'Anything else?'

'Well, I know for a fact some of the original dumping ships left from Maryport in Cumbria.' Dan shifted in his seat. 'My father worked on them.'

Shona digested the information along with a chip from her packet. 'Is your father still around?'

'No, but some of his mates might be. I'm in court this week. It's quite complex, a group targeting farm machinery, but I'll definitely chase this up.'

'Do that,' Shona said. 'And listen, you have an inside track on this. Don't be afraid to use the family connection. I know it can be difficult to break into close-knit communities and folk might not want to talk to an outsider. Get everything you can get. What was on those ships? Rumour. Conjecture. Sift it fine and you'd be surprised how many people know something others aren't keen to admit. Is your guv'nor happy to let us borrow you for a bit?'

'Yes,' Dan said with no hesitation. His desire to escape his current unhappy posting was no secret. He didn't get on with his DCI, who Shona felt might leave himself open to a constructive dismissal case if he wasn't careful due to the way he treated this keen detective constable. Dan had abandoned his hope of applying to the Met in London after working with Shona on a previous case and now saw his career path north of the border. Shona had told him to work on his micro-credentials and gain experience, but with budget constraints there seemed little hope of a job opportunity with her team opening up soon.

There were grins and back slaps from around the room when Shona announced Dan would be joining them. Everyone except Kate seemed keen to have Dan on the case. Shona wondered if the pair's previous office flirtation had developed into something more. Whatever had happened, they were both studiously avoiding each other's gaze and Kate looked distinctly uncomfortable at the prospect of working with Dan.

'Okey-doke. Briefing in ten minutes everybody.' Shona turned back to her office, beckoning Murdo to follow her. 'Dan,' she said over her shoulder. 'Last in gets the kettle on, I'll have my coffee…'

'…black, no sugar.' Dan grinned.

'Fast learner. You'll go far.'

When the chip papers were binned, Shona called everyone's attention to the whiteboard in the corner of the CID room.

'I've had confirmation Tony Carlin's body was picked up and I've spoken to Professor Kitchen. The initial post-mortem assessment shows the victim suffered from chemical burns and toxic inhalation.'

'When will Slasher Sue get a better look?' Kate said.

'It'll be a day or two. Further assessment is required because it's unclear if the substance was phosphorous, mustard gas or a nerve agent from the bombs or something else the Ministry of Defence won't admit to. They'll do the PM in stages to allow any harboured gases to disperse. The ultimate cause of death could be shock from the skin injuries, or asphyxiation from chest muscle paralysis due to nerve gas, or a combination of both.'

Murdo shook his head. 'Doesnae bear think about. And that poor lad, Jamie. He's our only witness. You know the family. What's he like, boss?'

Shona thought for a moment. Jamie was too young to have played with Becca so what she knew of him came mostly via Laura.

'I think he used to come down to the lifeboat with his dad when he was younger, but that changed when he went to high school. He's not settled well. I'd say, takes after Tony rather than Laura. Quiet, a bit shy maybe. He and Jack are close, they play a lot of video games together.'

'It'll make our case harder but you can't help hoping he'll no' remember too much about what happened,' Murdo said.

There was a part of Shona that agreed with him. 'Any update on Jamie from the hospital, Kate?'

'He's still in an induced coma to help him breathe,' Kate replied. 'I've persuaded his mum to go home for some rest. I'll take her back in tomorrow, although she can't get to his bedside. They won't even let her hold his hand.'

The mood of the room was turning downwards. It was time to galvanise her troops.

'Right, so we need to use the time until a conclusive post-mortem result to nail down Tony Carlin's movements and what he was doing out there. Murdo, what can you tell us about the area he was found in?'

'It's mostly farmland acquired in 1942 to train forces for the D-Day landings, but the range includes a stretch of sea about fifteen by twenty miles off Kilcatrin Airds. What they'll admit to is developing long-range anti-tank weaponry in partnership with the US military.'

'They used depleted uranium shells,' Shona said. 'Thirty-one tons of the stuff went into the sea. The area's marked as a hazard on marine charts. And some of the protestors today had banners about this.'

'Aye, it's a particular sore point. They've been coming down from the Peace Camp at Faslane to protest for years, but it's been quiet recently. Got a feeling that's about to change. An EU ruling back in 2010 told the MoD to stop, but they argued it wasn't covered by the legislation as the shells were *placed* and not *dumped* in the sea.'

'But there's no evidence Tony Carlin had links to the protestors?' Shona looked at Murdo and Ravi for confirmation. Both shook their heads.

'A few years ago there was a mass walk-on by protestors,' Murdo continued. 'Security got tightened up and access became highly restricted. New fences, cameras, with no local consultation.'

'Any word on a vehicle?' Shona said. 'The coastguard has no record of a vessel.'

'We're on the lookout for a silver Nissan Navarra pickup registered to Tony Carlin, currently unaccounted for.'

Shona remembered the open garage door at the Carlins' place with a pickup-sized space among the fishing gear. 'Okay, that's a priority. Moving on, DC Irving is acting as family liaison,' she said, for Dan's benefit, and thought a hint of discomfort passed across his face. 'Kate, has your victim profile gone to the fiscal?'

Kate nodded, eyes on her notebook. 'I've also logged a witness statement from Laura Carlin onto the system.'

'Good. Can you expand on that for us?'

Kate hesitated. Everyone in the room knew the lifeboat connection and Wee Shona's personal relationship with the family and understood Kate's desire not to put a foot wrong.

Shona raised her eyebrows in encouragement. 'Go on. I want to hear your impressions.'

'Okay.' Kate opened her notebook. 'Laura Carlin describes her husband as a hard-working family man, but admits he'd been depressed and drinking recently.' Kate sent her boss a sideways glance.

Shona kept her face blank. It wasn't exactly news to her. She and Laura had been out at the cinema in Annan a few weeks ago but the evening was cut short when Jamie had phoned his mum to say his father was drunk and passed out on the sofa.

'And she doesn't know what he and Jamie were doing out at Kilcatrin?'

Kate shook her head. 'I haven't interviewed Jack formally, but he doesn't know either.'

'Ravi, did Fergus have any idea why Tony was out there?'

'He claimed not to know. Said he hadn't seen him in a few days.'

'Did you ask about the haaf-net?'

'Aye. He rolled his eyes when I mentioned it,' Ravi replied. 'I got the impression Fergus was more into technology. He's got some nice stuff at his flat. A wide-screen TV and a sound system, and one of those fancy mountain bikes. He doesn't have much interest in old fishing practices.'

'It certainly fits with the haaf-net we found,' Murdo said. 'But there's no licences for that stretch of the coast. Could this be a bit of poaching?'

'No record of Tony Carlin being prosecuted or even warned,' Ravi replied.

'We'll need information on any vehicles Tony had access to,' Shona said. 'CCTV from the roads around Kilcatrin in case he arrived there by car. Did someone give him a lift? Murdo, put out an appeal for witnesses, talk to the other haaf-netters. I want to know how he came to be on that beach.'

'If Tony Carlin died as a result of the phosphorous bombs, could we be looking at a corporate homicide scenario against the MoD or the UK government?' Ravi said.

'You'd have to prove recklessness or gross negligence and not all government departments are qualifying organisations. There's also the question of *mens rea*, which is…?'

Shona turned to Rhys Marshall, the young Special who'd interrupted the previous day's briefing and only partly atoned by fetching the chips.

For a moment, he was caught like a rabbit in the headlights of her glare.

'*Mens rea,*' he stuttered. 'Err… it's *the knowledge that one's action or lack of action would cause a crime to be committed,* I think.'

'Thinking is not good enough, Rhys, you should know,' Shona snapped.

'Dumping thousands of tons of explosive and barrels of nuclear waste into the sea without a secure auditing method or accountability says reckless to me,' Ravi muttered.

'I'll not argue with you there, Rav, but that's a view that doesn't leave this room. I'll discuss with the fiscal how they want to play this. Right, early start. You lot get off home.' She balled the fish and chip paper someone had left on a nearby desk and threw it into the bin.

'You can kip at mine if you like,' Ravi said to Dan. 'It'll be tidier than hers for a start.' Ravi, it seemed, had picked up on the vibe and was on a fishing trip of his own. Kate glared at him. Dan didn't take the bait.

'Thanks, mate, but I better get back.' Dan turned to Shona. 'I'll go over to Maryport tomorrow, see what I can find.'

'Great. Thanks, Dan.' She smiled.

The group dispersed. Shona summoned Ravi with a jerk of her head. He came hesitantly into her office. But instead of the expected ticking-off, she said, 'The website Viva Caledonia? Familiar with it?'

Ravi nodded. 'They're mostly lifestyle stuff.'

'Emma Johnstone, one of their bloggers, has just checked in to High Pines.'

'Okay.' Ravi raised his eyebrows in a way that confirmed Shona's doubts about the wisdom of the arrangement.

'Can you check her out for me? What stuff does she do? Any other publications she works with.'

'Sure.'

'Also, a young woman called Willow from the Bankend commune. I'm sorry I don't have a second name. She was at the protest today at Kilcatrin.'

'Think she might be a witness?'

'Just map her connections. I want to know how all these pieces fit together. Tony Carlin, Kilcatrin Ranges, the protestors. I don't want anyone blindsiding us in this investigation. It could be nothing, but Ravi, come to me with what you find, okay?'

'Okay, boss. See you in the morning.' Ravi crossed the office in his customary long strides to say goodbye to Dan, who was talking to Murdo, then swung his jacket round his shoulders, stuffed his notebook in the pocket, and left for home.

The office emptied. Murdo knocked on the glass partition of her office to say goodnight as Dan waved from the door.

Shona started at the photograph on her desk of Rob and Becca. *Semper Vigilo*, Always Vigilant. That was the Police Scotland motto. That was how you kept people safe, and there were two people in her life she was determined, at all costs, to keep safe.

## Chapter 9

Despite the grim task ahead, Shona relished the early start. She was up with the sun just after five and ate her porridge in a golden light that flooded the kitchen at High Pines. Beyond the window, Kirkness estuary lay quiet. Small boats had begun to tilt and slumber as the retreating tide placed them on the shining mud until it returned later that afternoon.

Shona headed west to Kilcatrin along empty roads. This morning, her commute was in stark contrast to her previous hacks across north London from the flat in Camden to the City of London nick at Bishopsgate, which could take twenty minutes or two hours through the canyons of shops and tower blocks. Now, the open sky was mirrored below and sheep were scattered like tiny white clouds on the rich green of the fields. It was a timely reminder that, despite the challenges they faced, the decision to relocate back to Rob's home patch had been the right one.

At Kilcatrin Ranges, the hardcore of protestors who'd lingered overnight at the gates and had been joined by a TV crew and several glum photographers, hands thrust in pockets as they shuffled on the roadside. A police van was parked on the verge. All were under the watchful eyes of the sentries behind the wire.

Forensics were punctual. Soon the convoy of vans, book-ended by military support vehicles with their hazards flashing, crawled along the five miles of access road through the firing range to the causeway. Shona rode in the lead vehicle, Inspector Wallace beside her. Murdo and Ravi, with two regular constables and a couple of the Specials who'd been roped in to help with the search, cadged lifts in the crime scene vans.

'As a courtesy to your investigation, we've priorit-ised the safety of the immediate crime scene,' Inspector Wallace said, his attention out of the window.

*As a courtesy.* That was big of him.

'My team are trained for biological situations,' Shona replied calmly. 'They're not a bunch of kids blundering about picking up shiny things. The priority is securing the scene and collecting evidence.'

They got out and Shona shook hands with a wiry man in his forties, Senior Crime Scene Examiner Peter Harrison from the Gartcosh campus. Slow waves washed semi-circles of froth across the causeway, slick with seaweed, as the Solway gave up the island crossing. Looking at the green mound of Kilcatrin Island, with its nesting birds and spring flowers, Shona couldn't imagine that when Tony Carlin arrived forty-eight hours before he was aware he'd meet his death there.

Peter's team were suited up and ready to go. The crime scene was on the far side of the island. The MoD Land Rovers would go across carrying the required staff and equipment.

'I want the search area extended to the low water mark,' Shona said. 'No boat's been recovered, so the key entry point becomes the causeway. We'll search ten metres on either side of that.' Shona moved down to the water's edge.

'The operation is time-critical,' Wallace said. 'I'm not sure you have the resources to complete it.'

'We'll start with the point where Tony Carlin's body was found and work outwards,' Shona replied. 'And if we're unable to complete the search area on this tide, we'll come back as many times as we need to until we're finished.' It would impact her budget and her DCI wouldn't like it, but she wasn't giving ground to Wallace on operational matters.

'What are we looking for?' Peter Harrison broke in, eyeballing the two inspectors as they faced off on the cockleshell beach.

'Personal items. Anything alien to the locus,' Shona said. 'We haven't recovered a mobile phone, although he had a VHS radio.'

'Much of this stuff will be contaminated,' Peter said. 'We'll need to make a decision about what leaves the site.'

'I'll be here all day, you can run anything you want by me.' Shona glanced at Wallace, expecting a challenge, but he was staring out at the island so she turned on her heel and went to brief the other staff.

Once across the causeway, Shona saw for herself how the tide and the MoD had scoured the beach.

During the rescue, in the half-light of dawn and with a seriously injured child to deal with, she had memorised what she could of the crime scene. There was little for Peter and his team to work on. She retraced her steps where she'd come ashore, then went to find Wallace.

'Where's the shore debris that was by the body?' Shona demanded.

Wallace pointed. A pile the size of a small truckload sat among the low bushes above the waterline. It must have been every scrap of flotsam and jetsam collected during the grenade clearance. Without the context of the place it was found, it would take twice as long to decide what was significant. She could feel a bubble of anger forcing its way up.

Peter raised his arms and let them fall back to his sides. 'Okay, sooner we get started, sooner we'll be finished.' He called two of his assistants over.

'Peter.' Shona indicated the radio she was holding before tucking it in her pocket. Peter gave her a thumbs up. She turned back to the causeway. If she didn't get away from Wallace, there was an even chance she'd take a large bite out of him.

Shona crossed to the mainland and began climbing up to Deadman's Point. She wanted to get the lie of the land, literally. The timeline had worrying gaps. How did Tony Carlin get here? Was there a boat washed into a cove that held important evidence of his intent? She chided herself for leaving her binoculars in the boot of her car, which now sat five miles away by the guard post at Kilcatrin's gates. But the coastguard and the military were still scouring the coast for grenades. She could rely on the coastguard, if not the MoD, for an update if they found a vessel.

St Catrin's kirk was a low building of local stone and farmhouse proportions, hunkered into the soil. Only the small bell tower at the west end gave away its true function. The surrounding graveyard had a few stones, the makeshift wooden crosses for the nameless victims long rotted away, and ran uncontained by a wall or fence to the cliff. Shona zipped up her fleece and walked to the edge.

The earlier sunshine had vanished behind a rampart of cloud sitting low on the horizon. The bank holiday-makers and the protestors at the gate would get a soaking before the day was out. Below, the forensics team in their white suits moved like ghosts across the scene. The wind was a sudden hand at her back. It urged her to the end of the cliff as if intent on harvesting another soul. A shadow moved at the corner of her eye; she turned, half expecting the risen spectre of Tony's ghost, or some long dead sailor, come with a message from beyond the grave.

Inspector Wallace stood watching her. Shona had the sense he was making his assessment. The threat she posed to his plans, how she might be dealt with. If he wanted to do away with her, this was the perfect spot. She took a step back from the cliff edge. At times like these, offence is the best defence.

'Are you worried we'll find something we shouldn't?' she said. 'Something inconvenient that'll turn up in a forensics report? It's a bit late to worry about bad publicity. That ship has sailed.' She regarded the blank page his face presented for a moment. 'If there's another reason you're here, beyond babysitting the local constabulary, this would be a suitable moment to share it. Then we can both get on with our day.'

Inspector Wallace's thin smile didn't reach his eyes. 'Perhaps it's best we chat here, where we're not overheard.' He glanced casually at the headstones as if to confirm none of the occupants were eavesdropping. 'You're acquainted with Tony Carlin personally, I believe?'

Shona nodded. He'd have done his homework; she needn't bore him with details.

'And have you established what brought him to Kilca-trin Island?'

Shona had already updated her DCI, Jim Robinson, and taken a phone call from Mars Bar Munro. Her lack of a solid timeline wasn't a secret, but forty-eight hours in it felt like momentum was already slowing. If she couldn't make progress soon, there was a real chance she'd be pressured to hand it over to the MoD police.

Instead of gloating, Wallace nodded and said, 'Just between you and me, I may be able to help you out.'

'Okay,' Shona said, carefully. 'I'm listening.' Anything Wallace offered her was probably a poisoned chalice.

'You'll be aware our CID officers handle defence-related crime. We could offer Police Scotland one of our Central Support Groups to work on this, but I'm not sure that will be necessary,' he said, and Shona recognised it for what it was, a compliment wrapped around a threat.

'I'm currently looking into information received,' Wallace continued. 'Chemical weapons are being offered for sale for the purposes of terrorism. It's possible they were recovered from Beaufort's Dyke.'

Shona blinked. 'You think Tony Carlin's death had something to do with this?'

'I'm anxious to hear your thoughts about what he was doing here.'

'Would anything they recovered be viable?'

'For a dirty bomb? You'd need to think carefully how you handled it, but you and I, here in this place, are evidence of the material's efficacy. There's also the added advantage that casualties are more difficult to treat. We don't know what's in the cocktail.'

'You think he came fishing with his haaf-net for phosphorous bombs?'

'I'm hoping you'll convince me otherwise.'

The coastguard had no warning about the deadly tide leaking from Beaufort's Dyke, but Tony Carlin knew the currents. Deadman's Point had been a final resting place for centuries. Tony was an experienced fisherman and raised on this coast. He had local knowledge. Was that why he was there? She couldn't reconcile this with the man she knew. A lifeboat man who put his life on the line for others. And what about Jamie? Would Tony have brought his son on a trip so dangerous it got him killed?

'Don't think because he was an ordinary fisherman that he was incapable of this,' Wallace continued. 'Terrorists *are* ordinary and from every background. The Glasgow Airport attackers were a doctor and an engineer.'

It was ridiculous. Laura's husband a terrorist? Shona shook her head. 'I can't see it.'

'Tomorrow I'm applying for a warrant from the fiscal to search the Carlin home, and the boat too.'

'Not Fergus Carlin's flat?'

'It's an unlikely venue when you have a quiet cottage and a number of outbuildings at your disposal, but I'm not ruling out a later visit.'

'I think the MDP turning up mob-handed would be a very bad idea,' Shona said. 'A fisherman's widow with a son in a coma, the press will jump on this.'

Wallace stared at her.

'This is a close community. It'll be all round Dumfries and Galloway before you're through the door. Anyone else implicated will scatter. Let my team do the search. Laura will agree. I doubt we'll even need a warrant. The minute we find anything linked to Beaufort's Dyke, I'll be on the phone to you. And I can check the *Arcturus*. I'll know if there's anything amiss.'

Rob's words in the kitchen yesterday came back to her. *The MoD has fucked up. People have long memories. I don't want them wondering whose side you're on.* It was a gamble but the only other option was to let Wallace run the show.

'You were with the City police, weren't you?' Wallace had turned to face her, hands deep in his pockets, his posture challenging.

Was the spectre of DCI Harry Delfont, the boss she'd thought corrupt and who'd paid her suspicions back with interest, going to follow her forever?

'So you'll know the damage that can be done,' he said. 'Imagine that happening with a dirty bomb.'

So it wasn't Delfont he meant, and she did know. The Bishopsgate and Canary Wharf bombs were just before her time, but the 7/7 tube and bus bombings had left their mark on every London cop. Fifty-two killed, hundreds injured. A profound shift in how forces operate and co-operate. His meaning wasn't lost on her. If she got this wrong, the results could be catastrophic.

Wallace hadn't waited for her answer but started back down the hill. She watched him go, then took out her phone and updated Murdo.

'Our MoD friend, I think he's with the Force Intelligence Bureau,' Shona said. Wallace's deployment made sense now. A covert intel gatherer and counter-terrorism specialist. He wasn't here because some military munitions washed up on a beach, even if they killed a man.

'Aye, I was wondering if he might be FIB. At least he's not MI5.'

'Yes, small mercies.' A full-blown spook might push the enquiry in any direction he chose and she'd be powerless to stop him. Shona updated Murdo on what Wallace had told her and her sergeant gave a low whistle. 'Let's keep this between ourselves for now,' she continued. 'I'll ask Laura Carlin for permission to search the house. We'll brief the team later this afternoon.'

Tony's death was in danger of falling into that over-lapping area patrolled by the Ministry of Defence, the security services and the territorial police forces. She didn't believe for one minute that Tony and his brother had links with terrorism. Her own team were the best placed to get justice for the Carlin family.

Back at the beach, forensics had bagged a range of items that may or may not have belonged to Tony Carlin. A jacket. A bait box. An empty wallet. They headed back over the causeway, the tide lapping hungrily on either side.

As she got to her car, an update came in from the lifeboat station. While she'd been on the island, coxswain Tommy McCall had come to Kilcatrin mob-handed with three of the Kirkness crew, an RNLI regional manager and a marine safety engineer who'd run everything including a Geiger counter over the *Margaret Wilson* and decided she'd need repairs. Tommy wasn't having any better luck at this cursed place than she was.

# Chapter 10

Murdo picked Shona up the next morning from High Pines. When they arrived at the Carlins' house, the search team led by Ravi were already there. Laura was at the hospital, her younger son Jack at Karen's. James Carlin senior was on his way to the day centre in Dumfries, after his carer handed over the keys to the main house and its smaller neighbour. A couple of reporters and photographers were stationed across the road. Shona gave them a brief statement that no warrant had been applied for and this was a routine search with the family's permission.

'Are you staying, boss?' Ravi asked. Shona had gone through the search strategy with him the night before. Kate was also present. When she'd informed them of Wallace's suspicions, a small crease had appeared between Ravi's eyebrows and Kate had visibly paled. Given Tony Carlin's death, it was legitimate to list biohazard as a health and safety consideration for the search, but Shona had stopped short of calling it an active line of enquiry. Basic gloves and masks would do. Full hazmat was unnecessary at this stage and would alert the journalists and she didn't want this on the front pages.

'We'll get off,' Shona said. 'Murdo and I are paying Fergus Carlin a visit. Remember, I want Tony's mobile and laptop and anything that indicates why he was at Kilcatrin. Check the dinghy in the garage and any vehicles on the property that aren't registered.' She took a step closer and lowered her voice. 'You get even a hint of a suspicious substance, stop the search, secure the area and bell me.'

As they headed out to Kirkcudbright, where the Carlins' boat was moored, Shona considered whether she should feel a twinge of guilt. A search of the home was within the remit of the case. Fergus lived alone in a one-bed rented flat overlooking the harbour, which she agreed with Wallace was a less likely venue for anything underhand than the Carlins' cottage, with its quiet setting, parcel of land and garage. If Wallace had hard evidence of terrorism, he'd have been through the Carlins' door before Tony's body was cold. She knew he was using her to flush out confirmation. Against this, she balanced her desire to protect her friend from unnecessary trauma. That Laura had agreed to the search without hesitation told Shona she knew nothing. Her decision not to alarm the community was the right one and not at odds with her responsibilities as SIO, or her desire to get to the truth. This was about one thing, getting justice for Tony, for Laura and their sons.

On the outskirts of Kirkcudbright, they passed signs for the bank holiday Monday fair and joined a queue of traffic.

'I'll just get an update from the coastguard,' Shona said, as Murdo cruised the streets for a parking place. 'I want to know if they've found a boat.'

At the harbourside, stalls clustered around a raised area by the tourist information centre as a giant wicker man stood guard over the craft market. Beyond, scallop boats lined the quay. Murdo slotted the car into a recently vacated space and set off for the ticket machine.

'No boat wreckage has been found,' Shona said when he returned. 'But the fella I spoke to was on duty recently and remembers a note in the log. The *Arcturus* has been disappearing from the charts.'

Murdo leaned through the driver's door and fixed the ticket to the windscreen. 'The brothers say why?'

'When they were warned about it, they said their GPS chart plotter was faulty.'

'That sound likely?'

Shona pressed a finger to her lips as she considered. 'Maybe. For most fishermen, the boat's their biggest asset. A faulty location device is a safety issue. They're part of the automated collision avoidance system. It stops bigger vessels running into you in the dark or while you're trawling. And if you get into difficulties, where do they send the lifeboat? Unless you don't want to be found, of course.'

'Where did they go missing?'

'Out in the North Channel.'

'Near Beaufort's Dyke?' Murdo let out a long breath. 'Well, that needs further explanation.'

'Agreed,' Shona said, getting out of the car. 'Let's see what Fergus has to say.'

A chain was hung across the quayside, separating the tourist area from the working port. Shona and Murdo stepped over it. Beyond, the air was rank with the smell of salt and waste oil. Four muscular, thirty-metre-long scallop boats sat moored up, the heavy beams of their trawl arms reaching up towards the grey sky. Rusty, chain-mail dredging panels were looped over their sides like drying tea towels.

At the end of the quay, dwarfed by her companions, sat the nine-metre-long *Arcturus*. Everything was old but neatly stowed. Rubber hoses wound in flat spirals on the chipped blue paintwork of the scrubbed deck, hawsers coiled neatly. Salt spray had battered the wheelhouse windows almost opaque. In contrast, bolted to the mast above them were the white plastic globes, expensive and new, housing the radar and GPS kit.

Fergus Carlin nursed a mug of coffee. An electric sander and toolbox lay at his feet. Shona introduced Murdo and repeated her condolences.

'Getting her lookin' her best?' Murdo said.

Fergus Carlin shrugged. 'Just a bit of a paint up. She'll get a better price if she's tidy.' He placed the mug on the deck and rolled down one sleeve of the plaid shirt he wore untucked over his jeans. 'I'm a bit busy. Not sure what else I can say. I've given your fella Ravi a statement.'

'You're not carrying on the business?' Shona asked.

Fergus shook his head. 'We'll have to sell. I know you're a friend of Laura's so she must have told you.' He gave Shona a shrewd look. Fergus's gratitude for her service with the lifeboat didn't extend to her as a police officer, even if she was a friend of the family.

'You've got a Facebook page,' Shona said. 'Free delivery over £30, isn't it? We've had crabs and lobsters from you for the B&B guests. Rob said they were really good.'

Fergus looked a little mollified. 'Laura set that up.'

'She mentioned you were thinking of doing ready meals too?' Shona remembered a discussion between Rob and Laura about recipes and bulk freezing. 'Fergus, is it all right if I come aboard?' She smiled. 'I just need a quick chat. Fill in some gaps. I'm gasping for a coffee.' She turned to Murdo and nodded to the cafe across the road. 'Murdo, would you? And get Fergus a refill.' She fished in her pocket and handed Murdo a £10 note.

'Sure, boss,' Murdo said, correctly interpreting Shona's expression. Don't hurry back. The lack of a second officer meant anything Fergus said now would lack corroboration and be inadmissible in court. Despite Inspector Wallace's view of the brothers, what Shona wanted most now was Fergus's trust and an insight into Tony Carlin's mindset.

Fergus looked like he was about to argue but then he shrugged. 'Be my guest.'

Shona climbed down the wrought-iron ladder fixed to the quayside.

'I'm sorry if you think my questions are intrusive,' she said. 'I'm just trying to build a better picture of Tony and his life.' She pointed to a sanded down area of the deck. 'How did that happen?'

'Electrical fault,' Fergus said. 'Thankfully, we didnae have to call out the lifeboat.'

'I can see how Tony would have found that embarrassing.' Shona smiled. 'D'you mind if I have a look around?'

'Thinking of buying?'

'I'm sure Tommy McCall will help you sell if you decide to go ahead.' She pointed to the scallop trawlers. 'I went out to *Jennifer* with the lifeboat couple of months back.' It was disorientating working at night, in high water, the metal scourgers swinging overhead and the deck in constant motion. 'I know it's the most dangerous job in Britain and it takes a certain kind of courage to be a fisherman.' She stopped and looked Fergus in the eye. 'I just want to understand what took Tony out to Kilcatrin. I'm not here to judge him. Or you.'

Fergus considered her for a moment, then he sighed.

'I don't know how much longer we'd have lasted but, truth is, Tony's death has left us in a right mess. We used to go after king and queen scallops, lobsters and crabs, but there was too much competition. These boats,' he indicated the line of trawlers, 'Cumbrian operations, the Isle of Man vessels, foreign boats. You name it, everyone was on our patch.'

'It must be a hard business to make a living.' Shona opened the wheelhouse door, running her eyes over the open lockers and piled up papers.

'We've tried everything. Fishing trips. We even looked at going into business recycling shells. You know, for every fisherman there's seven shore jobs? Brexit isn't going to help the sub–ten–metre boats. We need support from the government.'

'What happened with the ready meals idea?' Shona said.

'The additional overheads cost a packet. It just made things worse.'

'The coastguard mentioned your GPS was faulty.' Shona watched Fergus carefully.

'We tried to fix it ourselves. Couldn't afford a new one.' He caught Shona's glance up to the new kit on the masthead. 'Just got that second hand. Doesn't look like I'll be needing it now.'

She saw no evidence of a lie, but she didn't know Fergus well enough to be sure. 'Fergus, why might Tony have gone out to Kilcatrin?' Shona moved methodically across the deck to the back of the boat. She couldn't see anything to indicate the *Arcturus* might hide any secrets.

Fergus shook his head. 'The phosphorous shells killed him. Does it matter why he was there? The MoD is behind this. They're trying to dodge the blame and you're helping them.'

She could come down hard on him. Ravi had noted the expensive technology he had at home. She could get that warrant to search his flat. Given the precarious nature of their finances he painted, did he have receipts for everything? Did he want the Vatman paying a call?

Instead, she swallowed the sting of indignation at his words. 'Tony was part of the lifeboat family, and I'll do everything in my power to see he gets justice. But, know this Fergus, until I'm satisfied, the questions will just keep coming. It's better you talk to me.' When he didn't answer, she continued. 'We found a haaf-net on the beach. I've a team searching the house.' Shona saw his look of outrage. 'It's just procedure and Laura's given us permission. Your father's at the day centre. Are we likely to find Tony's net at home?'

Fergus's mouth set in a firm line. He folded his arms, his eyes on the scallop trawlers which had simultaneously offered a lifeline of shift work, but ultimately put their small operation out of business. The silence stretched between them. A burst of music came from the fair behind, and Shona glimpsed a stilt-walker making his way among the crowd. At the end of the quay she also saw Murdo, coffee cups balanced before him, in conversation with a man in a white shirt, epaulettes on his shoulders.

'To be honest, I don't know why Tony bothered with it,' Fergus said, eventually. 'That's no' true, I do know.'

He looked Shona in the eye for the first time and she could see there were tears.

'For my brother, it was about more than the fishing. D'you know the family used to have the farm at St Catrin's? We went back generations. My father grew up there as a boy. They got moved off by the MoD years ago. A pittance in compensation. That's when Dad started fishing full time. Tony thought it was his hereditary right. He had a haaf-net licence, he didn't see how he was breaking the law.'

'So was he poaching?' She thought of the financial strain the Carlins were under. Rob had recently told her a wild Atlantic salmon could fetch £100, a bit less on the black market. A few of those now and then would help out with the weekly shopping bill or fill a tank with diesel.

'Tony just wanted to turn back the clock,' Fergus said. 'He'd always return any fish he caught. Walking out into the tide. Just standing there freezing your balls off with nothing to show for it. Why bother?'

Murdo came over with the coffees, handing one down to Fergus who took it with a small smile of thanks. They talked through the likely arrangements to return Tony's body to the family and why there was a delay with the post-mortem until Fergus decided he needed to head back to his flat. He gathered up his tools. Shona climbed up to the quayside.

'Can't be doing with all this tourist guff,' Fergus said, as the noise from the fair climbed another notch.

Shona and Murdo shook his hand and watched him walk away. Murdo stood looking down at the boat.

'Boats,' he said. 'Can never see the appeal myself.'

'Holes in the water you pour money into,' Shona replied. 'It's what some people say. If you're born into fishing, it's harder to leave them behind, though.'

'You weren't born into this boat stuff, were you?'

'No.' She smiled. 'Not many boats on the schemes in Glasgow.'

'I was talking to the harbour master. That's the fella with the...' Murdo pointed to his shoulders.

'Yes, I saw. What did he have to say?'

'Seems that wee repair job Fergus was doing? Something burned a hole in his boat. Electrical, apparently.'

'Fergus told me the same thing.'

'Well, the harbour master wasn't convinced that was the whole story. Should we pop up to Fergus's flat and ask him about it?'

Shona thought for a moment. 'It might explain the issue with the GPS. If he's selling the *Arcturus*, he'd want to play down problems. The harbour master expand on his suspicions?'

'He didn't. But I also got the idea he wasn't a big fan of the Carlin brothers in general and was eyeing up the mooring for a new customer.'

'Interesting. Well done, Murdo. I'll update Wallace, but I didn't see anything on the boat that supports his theory.'

A ping alerted Shona to a text message. It was from Professor Kitchen. The post-mortem would take place tomorrow afternoon in Glasgow. It was fortunate timing. Shona had a long-standing appointment in the city that morning that she'd been on the verge of cancelling.

'Slasher Sue's on for tomorrow,' she relayed to Murdo.

Murdo swallowed the last of his coffee. 'Head back?'

'Yes. You can drop me at the hospital.' Shona didn't want Laura to think she'd abandoned her and she needed an update on Jamie. 'I'll get a lift with Kate.'

On the way back to Dumfries through the rolling Galloway landscape, she thought of what Fergus told her about Tony and his haaf-net. How much nerve would you need to walk out a mile across the Solway's shifting quicksand and stand chest high in the water? The treacherous nature of the estuary still made her uneasy on shouts, even with the lifeboat nearby. You cannot see it, only feel it. The mud looks solid, but the sea runs beneath it, a hidden current. In a single step, the solidity melts, land becomes water. It waits for you, but you cannot see it until it's too late.

It seemed a cruel irony that Tony, who brushed past death on the scallop boats, avoided being washed away by the tide, or swallowed up in a sink hole in the Solway mud, fell prey to a phosphorous shell made seventy years ago, dumped and long forgotten, a thousand feet down at the bottom of a sea. Did he bring it on himself, or was he the unlucky victim of fate? The truth was slipping through her fingers like the retreating tide. Fergus's explanation for his brother being on the beach that night made sense, but she still had the feeling there was a lot he wasn't telling her.

# Chapter 11

The car park at Dumfries Royal Infirmary was more than half full, despite it being a bank holiday. Shona could imagine the customers who were coming into casualty. RTAs, gardening accidents, falls from trampolines, perhaps the odd barbecue injury. She hoped none of them were related to the deadly tide still sweeping around her area's 200 miles of coast. Murdo dropped her outside the main door, then he headed off to check with Ravi and the rest of the team's progress. A small group of protestors were outside holding a vigil for Jamie, their banners echoing those she'd seen at Kilcatrin Ranges.

Shona showed her badge to the woman at the desk, whose face seemed to settle into a deeper shade of sombre as she issued directions. The isolation ICU ward had No Entry signs and a swathe of plastic across the doorway. Shona pressed the bell. Eventually, a nurse in protective clothing and a face mask gave her an update on Jamie's condition. He was still in the induced coma but his breathing was better. They were taking care not to talk about his father's death around him, unsure exactly how much he could hear. The nurse directed her to the family room.

Laura and Kate sat in silence, their heads bent over their respective phones, paper cups of tea on the low table in front of them. Both were dressed in subdued tones, Kate in her grey suit, Laura in black jeans and a purple top the colour of an old bruise. Both seemed out of place with the forced jollity of the room with its flower-filled meadow mural and the bright cushions. Laura jumped when Shona opened the door.

'Oh my God, Shona.' Laura threw herself into her friend's arms.

Shona could see the toll that recent events had taken. Always slim, Laura had become more bird-like, her bones a little nearer the surface.

'How y'doin', darlin'?' Shona hugged her back. *Everything okay?* she mouthed over Laura's shoulder to Kate, who gave her a small nod.

'Have you any news about Tony?' Laura said.

'The pathologist is taking a look tomorrow,' Shona replied gently. 'We'll know more then.'

'When can we have him home? People are asking me about the funeral.'

'We'll know more tomorrow,' Shona repeated. 'How are you coping?'

'I'm okay most of the time and then I just remember what's happened and Jamie and everything…' Tears sprang into her blue eyes.

'Here, sit down.' Shona guided Laura back to her chair.

'Jamie's gonna be okay, isn't he?' Laura said. 'Shona, what was he doing there?'

Shona squeezed her friend's hand. 'I know you've given Kate your statement. Is it okay if I ask you a couple more questions?'

Laura wiped her eyes and nodded.

'I've just seen Fergus,' Shona began. 'He thinks Tony was out at Kilcatrin with his haaf-net.'

'I suppose. But he's got a licence for the shore at Kirkness.'

'Did Tony's family live at Kilcatrin?'

'His father did when he was wee.'

'Fergus also said Tony believed he had a claim to the place. Is that right?'

'I suppose. Old Jimmy talks about it all the time now he's unwell. The MoD just turfed them out. It was after the war so they could do what they liked. Tony wasnae happy about the testing, the pollution. He used to complain about what they were doing to the land but saying it's a nature reserve. Greenwashing, that's what he called it.'

Shona nodded. 'Thank you, Laura.' She took in the dark circles under her friend's eyes. 'Listen, you should go home.'

'But I can't. What if he wakes up and asks for me?'

For a moment the image of Jamie, on the beach and in the lifeboat, calling for his mother, rose up in Shona's mind. She bit her lip and forced herself to smile.

'They'll ring as soon as he stirs. You're only twenty minutes away.' Shona got out her phone. 'I'm ordering you a taxi. We'll take you out the back so you don't need to go past the protestors. Karen's on her way with Jack and she'll do tea for you all. She's picked up some meals Rob's made to go in your freezer. Get some rest. Kate's coming to the office with me but call if there's anything you need.'

When Laura was safely in the taxi, Shona shook her head. 'She looks worn through, Kate. Try to persuade her to take care of herself. Get the rest of the family, neighbours, support services involved. Make sure she's not carrying the burden of this on her own.'

'I've tried. She's not listening to me. She'd much rather talk to you.' Kate sighed as they crossed the car park. 'And really, is that why I'm here? I'm not a social worker.'

Shona stopped and stared at Kate. 'No, you're not. See, this is something you could learn from Ravi. Build empathy. Gain trust. See the complete picture. It's all relevant to the investigation.'

Kate flushed, then turned on her heel and stalked off, leaving Shona open mouthed behind. Perhaps she shouldn't have used Ravi as an example. They were still nipping at each other like squabbling bairns. Kate was an only child, like Shona herself, but Ravi had three sisters, hence more practice. Shona's money was on him to go the distance.

She caught up with Kate, who rounded on her. 'Why's Ravi always the blue-eyed boy? Why not me?'

'Well, this for a start,' Shona said. 'Why not me, *ma'am*, is the question you should be asking yourself. Nobody's out to get you, not even Ravi, so just turn it down a notch and we'll let it pass that I'm your senior officer.'

Kate stared at the ground. 'Sorry, ma'am.'

'Look, Kate, you've the potential to go far and you're family liaison on this because I want you to work on those key skills of listening, observation and empathy. I'm happy to discuss the investigation's FLO strategy if you think adjustments are needed.'

'I'm useless at this, aren't I?' Kate unlocked the car.

'You're not useless.' Shona got into the passenger seat. She put her hand on the steering wheel until Kate turned to look at her. 'The family are also victims,' Shona continued, 'and it can be hard building a rapport.' Laura had a stubborn streak and Shona could only image how

Jamie's condition must be gnawing at her hopes for his recovery, making her short-tempered and irritable.

'It's not like the courses.' Kate sighed.

'Look, you just need to keep talking,' Shona replied. 'Explain the support services and that the Victim Information and Advice officer at the fiscal will take over from you. The family will not be left high and dry. Be non-threatening, but remember your primary role is as an investigator. You're the conduit to enable the flow of information both ways.'

'What if she won't talk to me?'

'There will be hard questions that Laura will find difficult. If you meet resistance, apologise and remind her it's procedure. I've known cases where something from the family turns everything around and we'd never have learned it without the FLO.'

Kate sighed and Shona could see she was only partially convinced. There was no point in bringing Ravi in as her replacement. It would set the investigation back, be confusing for Laura and potentially prompt Kate to look for a transfer. She would just have to see it out. It was tough being a police officer and not always in the ways people expected.

'Look, it's a different skill set worth working on. I've no worries about your performance and you'll only be there as long as the initial needs of the investigation and the family require. Then, we'll discuss your exit strategy. Okay?'

Kate nodded.

'Right, let's get back to base.'

As they drove out of the car park, Kate turned on the radio, filling the lingering silence between them and giving each space for their thoughts. The local station was just heading to the news. Shona went through her mental checklist of the next steps that needed initiating when they reached Cornwall Mount. Search update. Revise witness statements. Timeline. Prep for the trip to tomorrow's PM with Professor Kitchen in Glasgow.

'*The unnecessary closure of the regions' beaches by the police is heavy-handed and shows a lack of concern for local businesses and risks tarnishing the region's reputation as a safe, family-friendly destination.*'

Shona froze. Division had issued a press statement and the local uniform super dealt with ongoing enquiries. The familiar voice continued. '*Officers who took this decision need to look at their conduct and I'll be pressing for an enquiry.*'

Kate glanced at her DI in the passenger seat. 'Is that Nicola Baird? She's got some cheek.'

Nicola Baird had been elected to her seat as a Conservative MSP in the Scottish Parliament at a recent by-election. She was a former councillor, but it was her position as the widow of a senior police officer, Shona's former boss DCI Gavin Baird, killed in the line of duty, which had brought her votes. That she and Shona didn't see eye-to-eye was an understatement. Shona had no doubt that the accusation of incompetency was aimed at her.

'It's a politician's prerogative,' Shona said, 'talking shite.'
She saw Kate stifle a smile.

'But learn from this, Kate. We need to get this investigation right. Someone at the back of the class will always stick their hand up and tell us we're doing it wrong.' And it'll get worse before it gets better, she refrained from adding.

## Chapter 12

When Shona entered the reception at Cornwell Mount, it looked like her prediction was coming true sooner than even she expected. Acting DCI Jim Robinson waited, foot tapping in irritation.

'Shona, there you are.' He had a squat, bullish quality beneath his dark navy raincoat, which seemed at odds with the high pitch of his voice.

'Kate, you go on. Tell Murdo I'll be there in a minute. Sir?' Shona turned to Robinson. 'Good to see you.'

'Are you sure you wouldn't rather hand this over to the Ministry of Defence? It'll eat up resources,' he said, dispensing with the niceties.

'It's an unexplained death on our patch, sir,' Shona said evenly. 'If we look like we're shirking our responsibilities, it won't sit well with the community or the press.'

'What about the Marine Accident Investigation Branch then?' he said with an air of desperation. 'It's in all our interests to resolve this quickly.'

'I doubt MAIB would see it as within their remit,' Shona said. MAIB was an independent unit from the Department of Transport. Their primary responsibility was accidents at sea involving British vessels. 'The coast-guard have no reports of a drifting boat. I think we have to conclude Tony Carlin didn't get to Kilcatrin by sea.

But I agree, sir. We should complete the investigation as quickly as possible.'

Robinson looked at her, a little startled.

'I'm sure the family would appreciate swift answers,' she said. 'And I appreciate there's political pressure.' He'd have heard Nicola Baird's soundbite. It was really his job to deal with the flak and she wouldn't be guilt-tripped.

It was one of the reasons she didn't want the DCI's job. Robinson was the expansion bolt between the operational and political side of the job. She might think differently a few years down the line but now the prospect of perpetual squeezing and stretching didn't appeal.

The muscle in Robinson's jaw twitched. 'Your DS has brought me up to speed. I want daily updates. And Inspector Wallace will be sitting in all your briefings.'

Shona stiffened. 'I don't see that's necessary.'

Robinson took a step towards the door but turned and pointed a finger at her. 'Remember, this is the MoD's mess and they can clear it up. I'm aware you knew the victim, but you can get off your white horse, Shona. I don't want you tying up officers and resources on some personal vengeance mission. Understand?'

Murdo saw her thunderous expression when she came into the CID office. 'Robocop's just left. Did he catch you?'

'He did. Face like he'd chewed a wasp. He give you much stick?'

'I've worked for you for two years. Not much I cannae handle.' Murdo smiled. 'Will he give the MoD the lead on this?'

Shona felt her spirits lift a little. It was true. There wasn't much Murdo couldn't handle, although modesty usually prevented him acknowledging it. He'd keep the team at it with diligence and compassion until every ounce of evidence surfaced.

'I think Robinson's torn between getting shot of this unholy mess and a desire to see it all blow up in my face,' Shona said. 'He blames me for Gavin Baird's death. No one likes to have their heroes unmasked. And he's only acting DCI, remember?'

'And he'll know you turned down the job,' Murdo said. 'You've seen the news?'

'Oh yes. Nicola Baird standing up like some kind of TV Jesus telling everyone the police are incompetent isn't going to help.' Shona waved her hand at Murdo, batting the thought away. She couldn't afford to get distracted. 'Get Ravi and Kate in and let's get on with business.'

When everyone was seated, Shona said, 'We need to proceed on the basis that Tony Carlin arrived at the scene in a vehicle, so finding it is a priority. It's not turned up on the roads around Kilcatrin. D'you think it could be hidden on the ranges somewhere?'

'I've checked what Fergus told us,' Murdo said. 'The family did own the farm at Kilcatrin. James Carlin senior was born there in 1946. Moved out ten years later. Security is tight, but Tony might know his way about the place.'

'Good point, Murdo. Ravi? What have you got from the house search?'

'No mobile, but we found a bag of red bills hidden. Maxed out credit cards. Got Vinny Visuals working on a laptop we recovered.'

'Laura doesn't know the password,' Kate added. 'And the boys don't have laptops or phones, just old games consoles.'

'Okay, Fergus told us his brother wanted to "turn back time" so perhaps the lack of a mobile fits. I'll check with Tommy if that's why he stood down from the lifeboat crew. I know money was tight for the family,' Shona said. There had been an argument with Jamie over a school trip and she couldn't recall the last time they'd been on holiday. 'But I wonder if Laura knows the full extent of their financial difficulties. Kate, has she mentioned anything to you?'

'No, boss,' Kate replied. 'She was a bit worried about her job at the doctor's surgery but they've given her compassionate leave for as long as she needs it. She thought Tony's pickup was at a mate's garage getting repaired. He'd borrowed her car a few times in the past, but it's parked at home.'

'Okay,' Shona nodded. 'Check Tony hasn't sold his pickup recently via local adverts or online. The DVLA might not have info on a new owner yet. How's CCTV going?'

'Working through, boss. But there's plenty of small roads not covered.'

'There's something else, boss.' Ravi said. 'We found some payslips. It seems Tony had a second job.'

'We know. He worked as a hand on the scallop boats. Campbell Shellfish, isn't it? They own most of the local dredgers.' Shona had heard the owner Michael Campbell had a reputation for ruthlessly eliminating business rivals.

'Well, a third job then,' Ravi corrected himself. 'He was working for a commercial cleaning company, Solway Spotless.'

'Okay.' It was news to Shona, but she could understand why a proud man like Tony might have kept it quiet. 'See if there're any workmates we can talk to.'

'Will do.'

'Our main focus now is recovering a vehicle,' Shona said. 'Fergus is bitter, resentful and grieving, but let's just say his theory about his brother going out there haaf-netting is right. You fish on an incoming tide, so that will give us an estimated time of arrival.' She frowned. 'Laura said Tony had mentioned "greenwashing" in connection with the MoD and Kilcatrin. Is that a commonly used term, would you say?' She looked enquiringly at her team.

'Mibbae,' said Murdo. 'The haaf-netters I talked to say it's a sustainable fishing practice going back a thousand years. They want the Scottish government to legally protect it as a cultural and historic part of the Solway, with a small quota of fish from Marine Scotland to keep the practice alive.'

'So Tony might be familiar with that term through their campaign?' Shona said. 'I can see that. But, Ravi, Kate, let's check if Tony had any links to the Kilcatrin protestors.'

'How does it tie into the idea the brothers were recovering arms?' Ravi said.

'I don't know that it does. I'll update Inspector Wallace on the results of our search, but we're missing something here and if our victim is linked to either terrorism or some environmental protest, I'd like to know about it sooner rather than later.'

–

Rob was taking a golden-crusted creation out of the oven when Shona arrived. She inhaled the warm and comforting aroma of home. The table was set. Becca's music, early Bowie by the sound of it, drifted down from the floor above.

'God, I hope that's for us. I'm so hungry I could eat a scabby dog.'

'Sorry, you'll have to make do with a salmon pie.' He grinned and leaned over to kiss her. 'And it is for us.' He picked up his phone and tapped the screen. 'I'll just text Becca.'

'Isn't she upstairs?'

'Aye, she is.' Rob looked at her blankly and, not for the first time, Shona felt she had no idea how her home actually operated on a day-to-day basis.

Becca appeared, her long dark hair tied up in a scarf that reminded Shona somehow of the Sixties. Another fashion comes around again.

'Hi Mum, what you doing back?'

'I live here.'

'I know.' Becca ducked her head to peer at the kitchen window. 'But it's still light outside.'

'Very funny.' Shona smiled. 'How's your studying going?'

'Slowly,' Becca said. 'Is it all right if I take my dinner back upstairs?'

'Yes, but don't be working too late tonight.'

'I could tell you the same thing,' Becca replied.

'I've got the evening off. We can watch a movie if you like?' There wasn't anything more Shona could do until after the PM tomorrow.

'Maybe.' Becca took her plate and cutlery from her father and headed back upstairs.

'That's the last we'll see of her,' he said. 'Face it, Shona. We're old fogies now.'

'Speak for yourself. I know all about the interweb. I've a netflicker account.'

'Well, we can't all be down with the kids like you.' Rob took a wine bottle from the fridge, checked the label and poured her a glass.

'I saw Laura today.' Shona pulled out her chair and sat down. 'She looks wrung out.'

Rob's face clouded. 'Do you think Tony Carlin knew what was happening on that beach?'

Shona took a sip of her drink. 'Nerve toxins act quickly, I doubt it.'

Rob shook his head sadly. 'No one deserves to die alone like that. I don't know what I'd do if it was you or Becca in that situation. The military has a lot to answer for. What if it had been the whole lifeboat crew?'

'Don't worry, we'll get to the bottom of it.'

'I love you, Shona,' he said, his face suddenly serious.

'I love you too, especially when you cook pie.' She grinned at him and took another mouthful of salmon. A thought occurred to her. 'You ever been offered local salmon or trout?'

'You mean back-door fish? Used to be a big thing in my mother's day when she ran the kitchen at Palnackie House Hotel. There was a bit of a competition between the men to see who could bring her the best fish.'

'What about now?'

'Can't see the harm in it, not really,' Rob said. 'I mean the land owners upstream can charge £500 a day for salmon fishing.'

'It's illegal.' Shona put down her fork and looked at her plate. 'This isn't…'

'No.' He gave her a wicked grin. 'But would I tell you if it was?' He saw the horrified look and took pity on her. 'Fishmonger's van came this morning.'

'Seriously. What if a guest gets ill, food poisoning? A DI complicit in poaching would be the last straw.'

'It's the way it's always been around here. You'll not stop it.'

'Did you ever get fish from Tony Carlin?'

Rob crossed his arms and leaned on the table in thought.

'I was expecting a quick "no, of course not" to that question,' Shona said, frowning.

'No, of course not,' he said dutifully. 'But I think his dad was one of the lads vying to impress Mum.'

Shona chewed thoughtfully. 'Is there much of this pie left over?'

'Yeah, why?'

Shona put her plate in the sink. 'I'll be back a moment.'

In the upstairs lounge, the sun cast long beams through the floor-to-ceiling windows. Soon it would sink behind the green flanked hills on the far side of the estuary. Shona lifted a framed photograph from the wall. Rob's mother, Isobel, with her blue eyes so like Rob's, stared back at her. His father was a respected auctioneer, a man who could be relied upon to put a fair price on everything from land to livestock, but it was Isobel who was most fondly remembered around the village. As a tireless and capable community stalwart, she'd run campaigns in the Seventies and Eighties to keep the village school open. The school was gone, but Isobel Oliver was commemorated in a library van that still bore her name and visited surrounding villages to this day.

Rob had wrapped the pie in foil. 'Where are we off to?' he said as Shona walked back into the kitchen.

She held up the framed picture of his mother. 'We're taking Isobel to see an old friend.'

Laura and Karen were watching *Eastenders*. Shona saw that same fearful look as when she'd turned up at the hospital and reassured Laura that this was a social call. Karen reminded Rob how he'd hung out with her big brother school holidays, and soon the three of them were reminiscing about old times.

'Dad's watching some old football thing with Jack next door,' Laura said. 'I'll need to get them both to bed in a minute.'

'I'll just pop through for a bit while you lot chat,' Shona said.

Laura looked puzzled when she saw the picture. 'Is that Mrs Oliver?'

'Rob and I were talking tonight about how she and Tony's dad were friends. I never knew her that well. I thought he might have some stories.'

'He might,' Laura said with a sigh. 'It's the past he remembers best. I don't think he's taken in what's happened.'

'I won't upset him, I promise,' Shona replied, squeezing her friend's hand.

James Carlin smiled at Shona when she came in to his neat living room. He sat in his leather recliner by the window, Jack at his feet, brandishing the remote.

'What's this?' Shona said, pulling up a footstool.

'1969. Scottish Cup Final,' James Carlin said. 'Celtic beat Rangers three–nil. Grand game.'

'Did you get to many games?' Shona said.

He shook his head. 'Not many cup games. But I was a regular at the Doonhamers.'

Shona was familiar with the nickname for the Dumfries football team, Queen of the South, and had visited Palmerston Park as part of her familiarisation when she first arrived.

'That was before the bairns came along,' Carlin said, ruffling Jack's hair. It wasn't clear if he'd confused Jack for Tony.

Shona held the picture on her knee.

'Ah now, there's a beauty.' He glanced up at Shona, scrutinising her face. 'You one of Isobel's friends, then?' He took the picture from her and smiled. 'She's a bonnie lass. D'you work at the hotel too?'

'I heard you take her the odd fish.'

'How d'you ken that?' James Carlin tapped the side of his nose. 'That's our little secret. Nae harm in it. What the bailiff doesnae know…'

'She said you used to have a farm out at Kilcatrin.' Shona smiled, but the old man's expression quickly clouded. 'Must have been fun growing up there,' she hurried on.

'Aye, it was,' he conceded. 'It was hard work, but I had my big brothers. I had a knack with sheep too.'

They talked on, Jack's attention gradually drawn from the football to his grandfather's stories of escaped rams chasing the local minister, of practical jokes played by the brothers and nights spent out under the stars. Eventually, the old man leaned back in his chair and Shona could see a weariness creep over him.

'Do you ever visit it?' Shona asked as she took back the photograph of Isobel from his failing grip.

'I still see it in my dreams. My mother in her apron feeding the hens. They say we Carlin men are cursed, but we were blessed to live there.' He closed his eyes. 'I'd know my way around the place in the dark. Every inch of it.' He lifted his hand and pointed to the wall above Shona's head. 'That's it there.'

High on the wall in a deep mahogany frame was an old map. She stood and peered at the faded outline of fields around a cluster of buildings. Running out from it were tracks and pathways. Shona orientated the farm with the river flowing to the coast, the causeway and the island.

Shona took out her phone. 'D'you mind if I take a picture?'

James Carlin shrugged. 'It's just an old map.'

Shona thanked him just as Laura came through the door announcing bedtime. Jack kissed his grandfather goodnight. Laura told Shona she could manage her father-in-law by herself and thanked her for cheering him up. As Shona stood outside, she saw Rob talking with Karen in the brightly lit living room. Shona took out her phone and pulled up the picture of the map. James Carlin saw Kilcatrin farm every day. His son Tony, growing up with the map on his wall, did too. There was every chance he knew his way about.

She texted the picture to Wallace. *Have you searched Kilcatrin Farmhouse?*

Tony was on the beach that night haaf-netting for fish as was his hereditary right. Whether that was poaching was another question. She had the reason he was there. Now it was Wallace's job to find the car so she could finish the investigation and let the family begin to heal, for however long that would take.

# Chapter 13

Shona arrived at the three-storey sandstone townhouse off Glasgow's Blythswood Square. For the past six months, she'd chosen to make the regular ninety-minute drive up from Dumfries hoping the distance would give her a little anonymity.

Should she be doing this during a live investigation? She checked her phone again and reminded herself Murdo would keep things on track. The post-mortem was this afternoon, and nothing else could be actioned until then. No one – at work or home – would be able to accuse her of skipping therapy. She took a deep breath, pressed the bell and the door buzzed open.

With the financial investigation surrounding Rob and his departure from Milton McConnell, she was aware how it might look. Were her allegations that she was drugged and sexually assaulted by her corrupt former DCI Harry Delfont merely an attempt to smear a senior officer with a #metoo moment? Were they a way to divert attention from her own and her husband's wrongdoing? A defence barrister wouldn't miss the opportunity to plant doubt in the jury's mind that this was a falling out of thieves, and she knew that sometimes that was all it took for a not guilty verdict. As she climbed the stairs, she considered for the hundredth time what would she do if Delfont walked away from court a free man. Officers leading the case, now named Operation Vita, had assured her Delfont would go down. There were allegations from at least two other women, neither of whom Shona knew so there could be no question of collusion. But the doubt was still there and Shona knew one thing for sure. Rapists never pleaded guilty.

The quiet pastel room was at the back of the building. Her counsellor, Vanda, was a slight, quietly spoken Glaswegian in her fifties with whom Shona had felt an immediate connection. Both had seen the worst of human nature. In other times they might trade war stories over drinks in a noisy bar, but here Vanda's role was to help Shona unpick the fallout from Delfont's criminal actions against her and prepare her for what lay ahead.

'The court process can be a means of taking back control,' Vanda said when they were both settled on matching sofas. 'It's an opportunity to seek justice and prevent the perpetrator from attacking others. It's your choice to go to court and there is no shame in not seeing it through. Your wellbeing and emotional protection are vital. You can testify by TV link or we can screen you from the accused. Forgive me, you know all this but it can be different seeing the process from the survivor's perspective.'

Survivor. It was a term Shona appreciated. In law and police procedure, she was a victim. I'm not a victim, Shona wanted to scream. I am someone who has had a crime committed against their person, who has been betrayed on every level by a senior police officer, a man sworn to uphold the law. She'd searched for another word but couldn't locate it. Until she did, survivor would do.

She was proud of how her team reacted to the news once the shock and anger wore off. She took two weeks leave to make sure Becca was okay but refused to go on the sick. God knows, the stress of the last few months would justify it.

Her colleagues' support was unwavering and Shona was surprised to find it had strengthened their bonds. In the back of her mind she'd wondered if other officers would view her as a failure, unable to protect herself so how can she protect others? But the reverse had happened. Murdo was even more of a stalwart. Ravi deployed his irrepressible cheek with even greater empathy. Kate's precise caution, combined with ambition, seemed more finely honed. Pat yourself on the back, she told herself, you've built a great team.

'It's not what happened that's really troubling me,' Shona said. She knew she'd coped better than many and part of her felt a fraud for even being there. 'It's what might happen if I can't remember.'

'That's understandable. It's common to feel all control has been taken from you. Being unable to fully remember is part of that loss.'

'I'm worried it'll make me appear a terrible witness.' She'd seen far clearer evidence than her own demolished by a half-competent barrister.

'That's something you can discuss with the legal team. They'll help prepare you,' Vanda said firmly. 'Do you want to talk about anything else around the case? The video or image evidence that the jury will see?'

Delfont had filmed the assaults for his own gratification and as a method of blackmail. It would be the final nail in his coffin, she hoped. Shona had identified herself from still images the officers had shown her. The video was harder to watch, but it didn't seem like her. She was so sedated, she looked dead.

'It's just,' Shona began. 'It's not like a normal case, is it? I can't remember the assault.' She was convinced her drink contained GHB, a clear, tasteless liquid that acts within fifteen minutes and leaves the bloodstream within eight hours, but there was no way to prove it.

'The jury will be taken out and shown the videos in a side room,' Vanda said. 'It won't be seen in open court.'

'I know,' Shona said with more force than she intended.

'Sorry. Of course you do,' Vanda said.

'I understand this has to happen. That the jury has to see what Delfont did, carry it in their heads. It makes me so angry. I mean, here in Scotland there's a dedicated jury counselling service, but in England and Wales, there's nothing.'

'Shona, let's just focus on your needs for the present. Fixing the world can wait for a bit.' Vanda gave her a knowing smile. 'But anger can be a positive emotion. It motivates us to find courage, to survive. Just don't bottle it up. Physical exercise or even throwing stones into the sea can help.'

Shona smiled ruefully. It was good advice. But a sliver of her attention was already on her phone and the coming post-mortem. She forced her attention back to her therapist.

'It can help to consider two lists,' Vanda continued. 'One containing the activities that nourish you, the other with those activities that deplete your reserves. And forgive yourself for any coping methods you feel unhappy about. Drinking to excess or self-harming in other ways.'

'Yes, I try to keep a healthy balance.' On the plus side, she had Rob and Becca. She had her team, and it was always a result when they locked the bad guys up. And she had the lifeboat. It was tough, but it nourished her.

After a shout, Tommy would often say *that was a life saved* and there was no greater buzz. She had a lot to be grateful for.

'What about your relationship with your husband? It might be useful to think about some couple counselling.'

Shona gave an inward sigh. Rob was already getting help for his gambling and attended a support group. She had these monthly sessions. Becca had seen someone during her recovery from the accident last year. Literally, how much support could one family deal with? Rob had a B&B to run. She had a suspicious death and major environmental incident keeping her busy. The Milton McConnell investigation was hanging over them all. She let the sigh escape. 'Maybe. I'll think about it. When things are more settled.'

For a while, the physical side of their marriage had suffered. It was difficult for Rob. I can't help thinking about what that bastard did to you, he'd said. Shona had decided she didn't want to discuss it in the house, so they'd gone out and found a quiet part of the shore. There was a difference, she explained. Sexual assault was a violent act about fear and control, and they'd gone on to talk about what consent meant. But Shona knew the difficulties in their marriage went beyond the assault.

Shona glanced at the clock. Their time was almost up. 'Thanks, Vanda.'

Outside, the May air promised warmth to come. The trees opposite in Blythswood Square shimmered with birdsong above the low hum of the M8 motorway that bisected this part of the city. She had a missed call from Simon Wallace.

'Your hunch was right,' he said when she called back. 'We found the pickup concealed in a barn. He's bloody lucky we didn't target it on exercise.'

Shona didn't think Tony Carlin could ever be described as 'bloody lucky'.

'I'll send forensics down,' she said, looking at her watch. 'It'll be a couple of hours.'

'I've had a look,' Wallace replied.

Shona bit her tongue. He might be a forensically aware police inspector, but he was MoD, an organisation that could ultimately be implicated in Tony Carlin's death. 'Best you leave that to us,' she said smoothly. She visualised Wallace tied to a stone and lobbed into the sea. Yes, she could tell Vanda. It helped a bit.

'I thought you'd like to know immediately.' He brushed aside her concern. 'There's no phone, but there's a cool box and nets. Poaching might explain Carlin's unauthorised presence in a restricted area, but as a commercial fisherman it wouldn't be out of keeping for him to have that equipment in the vehicle.'

Shona could tell he was reluctant to give up his theories of a terrorist motive, but she wasn't about to commit either way before she had the full facts in front of her.

'Let's see what forensics say. We'll talk later.' She ended the call.

As she crossed the road to where the Audi was parked, she felt a vibration in her pocket. She thought it might be Wallace again but Tommy McCall's name flashed up on her phone. For a second her hand went automatically back to her pocket for the lifeboat pager, but she only carried it in the village and never when she was at work.

'I thought you'd like to know,' Tommy said. 'We're getting a temporary replacement for the lifeboat.' She could hear the despondency in his voice.

'It's not the same, is it?'

'No,' said Tommy. 'I just hope you get to the bottom of what happened to Tony and make sure those responsible are held to account.' Shona knew he was thinking of his fellow crewman, but also of the *Margaret Wilson*. The attachment sailors and fishermen felt for their vessels was hard to explain. She wondered again about the financial hole the Carlin brothers found themselves in. A bit of poaching wasn't going to fix that. What lengths might they have gone to keep *Arcturus*? Perhaps Professor Kitchen could give her some answers.

# Chapter 14

Professor Kitchen was already dressed in green scrubs when Shona arrived at the Queen Elizabeth University Hospital mortuary.

'How are you, Shona?' she said with genuine warmth. 'How's the family? Becca still planning to grace us with her presence in a year or two?'

Professor Kitchen coached the fencing team at Glasgow University. Becca, with her father's height and broad shoulders, was already in the frame as a potential recruit.

'Would you consider taking her off my hands now?' Shona said with a sigh.

'No chance, kiddo.' Sue laughed. 'It's why I chose tutorials and not bairns. You can hand them back at the end of the day.'

'She's fine, really. Just stressed about exams.' Shona took a bagged set of cotton scrubs from Sue. 'A few unsuitable friends, but that's teenagers for you.'

'How unsuitable?' Sue said as she pushed open the changing room door.

Shona thought for a minute. 'I picked her up from the demo at Kilcatrin. Tell the truth, she looked scared to death. There was a girl with her, from an alternative community we've on our doorstep.'

'Activism's a good thing for the young. Just needs pointing in the right direction and I'm sure you're up to the job.' Sue nodded at the bag in Shona's hand. 'Get changed. There's more where that came from.'

Shona felt clumsy in her extra layers of protective clothing. The respirator was claustrophobic and pinched the skin around her face. Elbow-length, rubber over-gloves restricted her grip and dexterity. How Professor Kitchen and her mortuary assistant coped with long hours and handling sharp objects she couldn't imagine. Shona supposed practise and necessity extended your tolerance. Clipped to the suit was a radioactive dosimeter. No one was taking any chances with this autopsy.

'Every body has a story to tell,' Slasher Sue began.

Shona felt like she'd joined a lecture. She didn't mind. Knowledge, facts, was what she needed right now.

'To understand that story, we need to ask the right questions, and this case raises more questions than usual.' Sue unzipped the body bag that lay on the dissection table. Inside was another protective layer, which she also unfastened. With the help of her assistant, they manoeuvred the naked corpse on the grey metal surface.

'Clothes have gone up to forensics at Gartcosh, but I doubt you'll get anything significant from them. I mentioned in my initial report that we'd confirmed the presence of phosphorous. We've also detected…' She stopped and looked at Shona. 'I thought you were looking a bit pale when you arrived. You were exposed. Any lingering symptoms?'

'Nope,' Shona replied. She decided not to mention the dull, near constant buzzing and thickness in her head since the incident as she'd chalked that up to general stress and screen time.

'Good.' Sue nodded emphatically. 'Probably no need to worry. Your exposure was short, but you'll need monitoring. I recommend blood tests for decreased triglycerides and elevated white cell counts. There's a risk of anxiety, depression, neural cell death and epileptic seizures.'

'Okay. That's reassuring,' Shona said.

'This is probably the point where you wish you'd pursued an alternative career path. Accountancy? Banking?' She stopped and Shona knew she must have remembered that Rob was under threat of prosecution. 'Possibly not.'

'Definitely not,' Shona replied in an attempt to lighten the conversation. 'Honestly, it's fine Sue. I will follow up the monitoring.'

'Our first assessment detailed extensive damage to the skin on both the front and back of the body,' Sue continued. 'That indicates he was probably mobile at the time and not lying in contact with the ground. Less damage to the hands raises the possibility of gloves.'

She looked at Shona, who shook her head. 'None recovered from the scene.'

'The key questions are, how did this person die and what, if anything, contributed to their death.' She pressed around the abdomen and nodded. 'Liver's enlarged. I'd say the victim had been a heavy drinker for some time.'

'Did that contribute to his death? Would a healthy liver have helped him to survive the toxicity of the chemicals?' Shona was thinking of how the factors in the post-mortem report could be spun to absolve the MoD of liability.

'The healthiest of livers wouldn't have saved him. Toxicology will confirm if he'd alcohol in his system. I'd normally note a smell when we open him up, but that's not going to be possible today.' Sue tapped the front of her respirator. Shona was glad that for once she'd be spared the odours of the pathology room.

Professor Kitchen strode around the table with her customary speed and purpose. In twenty minutes, the body was opened and the major organs removed.

'Okay, I'll give you the headlines,' Sue began, pointing to one of the larger organ dishes. 'Lungs are not shiny, wet and pink but hardened and dark, indicating inhalation, and there's evidence of blood and dried frothing in the bronchia.'

'Is this the cause of death?' Shona said.

'A contributor. The skin is the largest organ in the body and in other circumstances I'd conclude the toxic shock, in conjunction with the inhalation, would be fatal.'

'In other circumstances?'

Slasher Sue's green eyes glittered behind her mask. Shona thought this must be the last thing one of Professor Kitchen's fencing opponents would see before she delivered a match-winning *coup de grâce*.

'So the cause of death is?' Shona prompted.

'Sharp force trauma.' Professor stepped up to the table, her feint and parry complete.

'He was stabbed?' Whatever Shona expected, it wasn't this.

'Here.' Professor Kitchen indicated a narrow red mark with one gloved finger. 'Single wound to the chest. Penetrated the heart.' She took up a probe and measured.

'The wound is fifteen centimetres deep.' Professor Kitchen stretched out the finger and thumb of her gloved hand to their full extent. 'About this long. A thin, ultra-sharp blade.'

'He was dead when I arrived at the beach,' Shona said, puzzled. 'But I didn't notice much blood.'

'You wouldn't. Bled mostly into the chest cavity.'

'Could this be accidental?'

Professor Kitchen's head bobbed from side to side for a moment. 'Unlikely. Given the state of the body I can't be sure, but I'd have expected other wounds or abrasions if he'd, for example, fallen on the object.'

'Could he have done it to himself?' Shona thought of the agony Tony Carlin must have suffered from the chemicals burning through his skin, his mental state confused by the possible inhalation of nerve gas.

'Put himself out of his misery? That's harder to say. Most people have a rough idea that the heart is on the left side. If he was right-handed, the wound here is consistent with self-administration.' Professor Kitchen demonstrated, sweeping her clenched fist up to her chest and mimicking a stabbing action. 'Possible, if he was alone at the time of death. Was he alone?' Her piercing gaze studied Shona through the respirator.

No, thought Shona. He wasn't. 'So, suicide or murder?'

'Ah, that's something I can't help you with. You'll have to work that out for yourself.'

# Chapter 15

'Right, listen up.' Shona strode into the CID room at Cornwall Mount. 'We have a revised cause of death and Tony's vehicle.' Robocop had told her to include Wallace in her briefings, but she wasn't about to hold things up. The MDP officer would have to make do with a phone call when she'd appraised the new evidence.

Kate and Ravi ended calls and picked up their notebooks. Murdo beckoned the support staff forward and they gathered around the whiteboard, a few perching on desks, others standing behind.

'Reset. Back to basics,' Shona said. 'Let's start with a revised timeline.' Shona swept the board clean and uncorked a marker pen. 'Ravi, you can do the honours.'

'Last confirmed sighting of Tony Carlin was…?'

'Laura,' Kate said. 'He left their home for work with Solway Spotless at eight a.m. on Friday.'

'And we're sure he turned up at his job?'

'Yes, boss,' Ravi said over his shoulder as he wrote on the board.

'So someone else may have seen him. Go down to Solway Spotless and talk to any witnesses who had contact with Tony that afternoon. What was his mood? Did he mention plans for the weekend? Kate, didn't Tony come home that evening?'

'Laura thought he'd come home and gone out again, but she was at work at the doctor's surgery that afternoon and didn't actually see him.'

'Anyone else at the house?'

Kate shook her head. 'The carer came in for James Carlin senior in the afternoon but didn't see Tony. Laura picked Jack up from an afterschool club. She mentioned Jamie was late home from school. They had words. Her first thought when she found his bed empty was that he'd run off.'

Shona remembered Laura's calls at the lifeboat station on the morning of Tony's death, how she'd asked if she should call the police and report Jamie missing. 'I know there was some tension at home with Jamie. Had he gone off before?'

'Once or twice,' Kate replied. 'But never overnight.'

'Ravi, you're friendly with the school support officers, aren't you?' Shona had previously sent her gay, Scots-Asian detective constable on a round of diversity talks for the Specials and suspected he'd followed them up in his own time, keen to make a difference in the area which scored low on ethnic diversity and LGBTQ awareness. 'Laura mentioned Jamie had been in trouble at school, check what that might be.'

Ravi nodded.

'And no one saw Tony Carlin after that until the mayday call?' Shona said.

A wave on headshakes and *no, boss* circled the room.

'Jamie's bike is still in the garage, so either they met somewhere, or Tony came home later and picked him up. We know he got to Kilcatrin in his pickup, so concentrate on tracing a route between his cleaning job, his home and Kilcatrin.'

'Forensics are with the vehicle now, boss,' Murdo said. 'Nothing to indicate he was stabbed in or near the vehicle and no sign of any phosphorous contamination.'

'Murder weapon?' Shona said.

Murdo shook his head.

'In that case we need to widen the search area around the farmhouse. Get someone to check if there's a dog available.'

'Will do,' Murdo replied. 'Does Slasher Sue think the body can tell us anything else?'

'She's taken some nail scrapings in case Tony had contact with whoever stabbed him, but all the forensic material is contaminated. It'll take twice as long to process and may be, in her word "banjaxed" anyway. I think that's a scientific term for don't hold your breath.'

'Should we be looking at any of the Kilcatrin personnel?' Ravi said.

'Inspector Wallace says there was no firing on the range that weekend and only a small security staff.' Shona mentally counted the personnel she'd encountered. No more than a dozen. 'I think that's something the MoD don't want widely known, given the protests.' The lack of CCTV of Tony's pickup also raised questions in Shona's mind about the shoestring security. 'He says everyone is alibied and there are no reported injuries. Apart from the six sentries on duty, the others were all together at birthday drinks in the mess and watching DVDs. So I think at present, unless we find a connection to Tony Carlin, we can exclude the base personnel. Kate, what's the latest from the hospital on Jamie?'

'Still unconscious. He'll stay that way until they decide he doesn't need help breathing and they can remove the tube from his throat.'

'Remind me what the doctors said about his pattern of injuries?'

Kate fished a paper from her folder. 'Damage to his lungs... chemical burns to his face, hands and inner arms and upper front torso.'

'If he had close contact with his father, it might explain the pattern of his injuries.' Shona stretched out her arms. 'But was he embracing or attacking him?'

'You think he may be the killer?'

'At present he's the only other person we know was on the beach, so we have to eliminate him.'

Everyone sat in silence as they processed the implications of pursuing a critically injured twelve-year-old boy for the murder of his father.

'I want to know everything there is to know about Tony Carlin,' Shona said. 'Currently we have two lines of enquiry. Firstly, did Jamie Carlin kill his father? Secondly, did a person or persons unknown kill him, potentially as part of a terrorism plot? There's no firm evidence to support this, but we have to consider it. It's possible that anyone else on the beach might also be injured by the phosphorous grenades, so can someone check that?'

'I'll get someone to chase it up, boss,' confirmed Murdo.

'There is a third option. Suicide. Professor Kitchen thought it possible but unlikely. Given the financial pressures, we need a clearer picture of Tony's state of mind before we can rule it out completely. So, what's his routine? Who are his friends? His daily contacts? Kate, Ravi, I need you two to work closely on this. Double check everything.'

They nodded, faces solemn.

'The rest of you,' Shona said, taking back the white-board marker from Ravi, 'Murdo will allocate tasks.' She tapped the pen on the board. 'Fill that timeline.'

'You know the family,' Murdo said. 'What's your feeling on this? Any thoughts?'

Shona let out a long breath. It was a natural response from her sergeant and she'd been preparing for this question all the way back from the post-mortem in Glasgow.

'Honest. Community-focused. A hard-working family. That's how I'd describe them.'

When she thought of the time she'd spent with Laura on nights out or running, it was often Shona who talked about her problems. She felt a twinge of guilt that perhaps she should have been listening more but balanced that against her copper's nose for trouble. If Tony had been up to anything beyond a bit of poaching, a whisper would have reached her through lifeboat helm Tommy McCall or Rob, whose status as a local boy kept him in the gossip loop.

'The fatal wound wasn't delivered with particular force, so we can't rule out that Jamie did it. We need a clearer picture of him.'

'Does this mean we've seen the back of our MDP friend?' Murdo said.

'I'd like to think so,' Shona replied. 'But if it wasn't Jamie, then I'd say this makes his theory of a terrorist link more likely.'

Murdo nodded solemnly. 'Only one way to find out.' He clapped his hands together and got to his feet. 'Right folks, see me for your homework.'

A hum of activity returned to the CID room as the support staff set about their tasks, Murdo moving from desk to desk issuing instructions and checking progress.

A short while later, Ravi came in to Shona's office to say he'd found a dog for the search tomorrow.

'While you're here,' Shona said, typing the final line of an email and hitting send. 'Any background come up on Tony Carlin re the protestors at Kilcatrin?'

'Sorry, boss, meant to update you.' Ravi closed the office door. 'Nothing on our records to link Tony Carlin with any protest group. The girl you asked me about is called Willow Moon. She's twenty-three and we do know her. Only address we have is the Gaia Collective at Bankend, which is not that far from the Carlins' place.'

Shona looked up. She'd been so concerned about Becca that it hadn't occurred to her. 'Think they knew each other?'

'Can't see an obvious connection, but Tony Carlin was a haaf-netter, involved in traditional, low impact fishing practice, right, and Willow Moon is an environmental activist, it's possible their areas of interest overlap. Not enough to bring her in for a chat, though, is it?' Ravi smiled. 'Anyway, she's got multiple arrests for public order at Faslane and a few roads protests. She was involved in the Stop the Pylons campaign over in Galloway.'

'Okay, thanks.' It wasn't welcome news but it was hardly unexpected. All the same, she needed to have a chat with Rob about it when she got home so they could agree a joint strategy on Becca's friendships.

Ravi's hand rested on the door but he didn't move.

'Anything else?' Shona looked up from her laptop screen.

'A potential connection to Tony Carlin isn't the only reason you're looking at Willow Moon, is it? I had a scan of the surveillance pictures from the protest. I couldn't help notice Becca was there. Hope you don't mind me asking, is everything all right?'

Ravi, like many of Shona's fellow Glaswegians, was ever happy to venture an opinion. Mention a thorny personal issue on any bus in the city and you'd have a full range of advice and opinions before you reached your stop. Therapy by public transport. But Ravi's heart was in the right place and Shona knew he recognised Becca as a fellow rebel and had a soft spot for her.

'She's decided to save the world.' Shona sighed. 'I'm concerned about the collateral damage she might inflict on herself in the process.'

Ravi nodded, considering. 'Peaceful protest over green issues is good. She's exploring ideas of moral and ethical judgement in a practical way.'

'I know, I'd just rather that exploration doesn't lead to the inside of a custody suite.'

'A lot of stuff I do with the schools is about helping kids make better choices through critical thinking. Observe the issue, analyse the data, draw your conclusions. When they realise there's a process for making choices, it can help them feel they have more control over their lives. D'you want me to have a chat with her?'

Ravi was closer to Becca's age and Shona knew she'd listen to him. But there was also the chance it might backfire.

'Thanks, Ravi. I'll talk to her myself,' Shona said.

'Okay. I'm still working on the other thing you mentioned, Emma Johnstone the blogger. Mate of mine's getting back to me tomorrow.'

'Thanks, Ravi.'

'And you're sure you don't need me with you at Kilca-trin?' he said. 'The search dogs sometimes wear those little boots. They're so cool.'

'I need you here working your schools contacts.' Shona knew Ravi had a new partner, Martin, who worked in addict rehab. 'You getting broody for a fur baby?'

'Man, that would be great. But it's not really fair on a wee pupster with me and Martin both full time. But who knows, things might change.' He smiled. 'Becca never tap you for a dog, then?'

'Her father's against it. He claims allergies and the B&B guests,' Shona replied. 'But he really thinks he'll end up walking it and he's probably right.'

'Hey, maybe she'd do doggie-daycare for me.'

'She's doing exams. No distractions. And that goes for you too, pal.' Shona pointed her pen at the door. 'If you're a good boy, I'll send you a picture of the dog in his wee shoes.'

'Belter.' Ravi loped away, clicking his long fingers and earning a reproachful glare from Kate as he returned to his desk.

Shona finished her paperwork and pulled on her jacket.

'Kate,' Shona called. 'Let's have chat with Laura. She may have remembered something more and I'd rather answer any post-mortem questions in person. D'you know where she is?'

'At home,' Kate replied. 'She just texted to say victim support had called. Said they were really helpful.'

Shona looked up at the clock. It was after five. 'Jack will be there and she's probably busy with her father-in-law, but I don't think we can wait.'

'Might it be easier to get childcare and bring her into the station?' Kate said.

'I don't think that's necessary, at this point. We need to find out if Tony was depressed. The PM results are going to come as a massive shock. We'll go gently and it'll be best if we do it at home.'

# Chapter 16

As Kate drove them out to the Carlins' home, Shona decided they could afford a quick detour via Kirkness. Her energy levels had dipped. She'd barely stopped to eat since setting off for Glasgow early this morning.

'Did you have lunch?' Shona asked Kate. When she shook her head, Shona texted ahead and asked Rob to do them both a sandwich. She felt she owed it to Laura that they had some reserves available, physically and emotionally, to make the interview as supportive as possible.

As they headed along the seafront, Shona saw the lifeboat station doors were open. Tommy McCall climbed onto the tractor and backed the temporary replacement for the *Margaret Wilson* into the boat bay.

'Pull up for a minute,' Shona instructed Kate, who brought the car to a halt in the empty tourist parking by the waterside.

'Tommy,' Shona called, as she walked across the road. The evening was calm and bright but there were fewer people around than normal. The tables outside The Crown, usually full of early evening drinkers, lay empty. Further along on the corner, the semi-retired couple who owned the cafe and gift shop had pulled down the shutters, abandoning their usual practice of staying open until dusk to serve ice creams and coffee to the families of sunset walkers.

'This the new boat?' Shona said. One of the shore crew, Andy Graham, who worked in the garage up the road, stood nearby in jeans, RNLI top and yellow wellies. He nodded hello. Tommy hopped down from the tractor.

'She'll do the job,' Tommy said reluctantly.

'She got a name?' Shona asked, assessing the D-class rib in its cradle.

'Nope, just a number,' Tommy said glumly.

The boat was identical to the *Margaret Wilson*, equipped like the 110 other craft of her type in stations around the UK, but Shona knew many of the crew would feel the same as Tommy.

While Andy finished stowing away, Shona took Tommy's arm and drew him aside.

'Tony stopped carrying his mobile phone. Is that why he wasn't boat crew?'

Tommy shook his head. 'He still had his pager and turned up. I think he was struggling with things at home and keeping the business afloat. To be honest, I wasn't unhappy when he opted for shore crew. He was drinking more than was good for him. I'd concerns about his reliability on shouts.'

When she told him Tony's cause of death and Wallace's theory of a terrorist link, the eyebrows on Tommy McCall's lined face shot up.

'This is just between you and me,' she said.

'Aye, of course,' he replied, thoughtfully. 'I cannae believe it.'

'Tommy, have you heard anything? Anything at all.'

He pressed his lips together and shook his head. 'I doubt he even took a single salmon on the quiet, although plenty might think it. He loved the *Arcturus*. It belonged to Old Jimmy, his father. Did you know that?'

'I didn't,' Shona admitted. 'What's this story about a curse on the Carlin brothers?'

'Jimmy's the youngest. There were a couple of older boys.'

'What happened to them?'

'Drowned. They were crew on the *Juliet*. Trawler. Went down off the Isle of Man in the late Fifties. Never recovered. Jimmy lost a couple of uncles, too. There's always been talk of a curse on the Carlin men, but it's a load of rubbish. They're not the only family round here to lose men that way over the generations. The *Arcturus* meant a lot to Tony. He must have been desperate at the thought he'd lose her.'

'Desperate enough to try recovering material from Beaufort's Dyke?' Shona saw a look pass across Tommy's face. 'What?'

'Tony Carlin was boat crew for fifteen years. I was just thinking, all that training we do, and you couldnae find a more experienced fisherman. Knew the waters inside out.' He gave Shona a shrewd glance. 'What is it your lot say? Means, motive, opportunity? You could say he had all three.'

And suddenly Shona could see it, too. The proximity of Beaufort's Dyke meant they'd trained to deal with armaments at sea. Tony fished the North Channel and had every right to be there. His motive? Money, driven by the fear and shame of losing his boat. What was the going rate for dirty bomb material? Recovering armaments was a huge gamble, but people had gambled for less.

'Thanks, Tommy,' Shona said.

'Go careful, lass,' he replied. 'I'll listen out for anything.'

Shona started back over the road to Kate's car. She didn't relish the tough questions she now had for her friend Laura. Halfway across, she heard shouts from the cafe and turned to see Jean Robb, the owner, taking to task a woman in a flowing, flowery dress and matching coat. An angry finger jabbed in the tourist's face. The woman replied, something Shona couldn't hear, and Jean let fly. She pushed the tourist back towards the quayside where the girl stumbled and fell, almost toppling into the water.

Shona set off at a run along the quayside. Kate was busy on her phone, but Andy Graham had also seen the exchange. As Shona got closer, she saw with a shock that the woman on the ground was Emma Johnstone, the blogger staying at High Pines.

'Jean, step back now,' Shona said to the cafe owner, placing herself between the furious woman and her victim.

Andy went straight into casualty mode, checking Emma over before helping her to her feet.

'That bitch, publishing her lies,' Jean spat. She was in her sixties but fit, and Shona didn't relish the thought of publicly restraining the older woman in full view of the village. 'She's staying at yours, isn't she?' Jean rounded on her. 'You should be ashamed. Send her packing. Stirring up nonsense, she is. Ruining people's businesses and waltzing off back to Glasgow.'

Andy was walking Emma back to the lifeboat station.

'You've seen the stuff her and her like are saying, haven't you?' Jean went on. 'The Toxic Coast. Deadly Tides. Who's gonna come here for their holidays now?'

'I agree it's not helpful,' Shona said, deescalating the situation. 'You can't blame one individual for the conduct of the media in general.'

'Why is she asking all these questions then? Lookin' down her nose at us.'

Shona didn't use the cafe much but she couldn't remember oat milk lattes being a strong suit. Perhaps, given the uncertainty on how long the beaches would be closed and businesses affected, a simple expression of disapproval of the lack of a hipster menu was all it took. She glanced over her shoulder. Kate was standing by the driver's door, shading her eyes and wondering what the delay was.

'Look, Jean,' Shona began. 'What you did was an assault. D'you understand how serious this is?'

'She stumbled.'

'I saw you push her.' Shona pointed to the security cameras on the front of the lifeboat station and the half-a-dozen people who'd gathered to watch the exchange. 'Plenty of witnesses.'

'You gonna arrest me then?' Jean's voice climbed a notch, but the defiance had drained from her features.

'I suggest you apologise now. If Emma doesn't make a complaint, it'll go no further.'

Twenty minute later, Shona, Kate and Emma John-stone came through the front door at High Pines.

'Sure you're okay?' Shona said.

Emma held up her hands, showing skinned palms. 'Bruised my backside probably, and my pride. But the old dear apologised and I'm not out to make enemies.'

Rob came down the stairs. 'Thought I heard you arrive. Hi Kate, looking good as usual. Hi Emma.' He gave them the particularly charming smile he reserved for guests.

Emma grinned back, but Kate blushed and studied the parquet floor in the hall.

'Too posh for the back door now?' He kissed Shona.

'Shona was good enough to rescue me,' Emma said.

Shona bristled a little at the familiar use of her first name but she decided to let it pass.

'Aye, she's famous for it. You don't look like you've been plucked from the sea.'

'Near enough,' Emma said, giving Rob a dazzling smile and recounting the incident at the cafe.

'Sure you're okay?' Rob said, his face full of concern. 'Can I get you a brandy or something?'

'It's fine, but I might take you up on that another time.'

'Good,' said Shona. 'You must excuse us.' She held out her hand to the guest suites and Emma took the hint.

'Oh my God, I will kill Jean,' Rob said when they got to the kitchen and he'd placed plates of ham sandwiches down on the table for Kate and Shona.

'I'm sure it won't affect your write-up,' Shona said dryly. 'A brandy? What are you? A St Bernard?'

'It might harm the review. Being knocked on your arse by the local cafe owner tends to put a dampener on a weekend break. Listen, can't you do Emma a wee favour and give her the heads-up on what's happening with Tony's death?'

'No. I can't.' Shona glared at him. 'Thought she was a lifestyle blogger? Is she asking you about the case?'

'She writes other stuff, too,' Rob said. 'The case is all anyone's asking about.'

'Well, you keep quiet. She'll need to go through the Division press office like everyone else. I mean it, Rob.'

'Suppose. What you doing home anyway?'

'Kate and I are going over to see Laura.'

'Any nearer winding this up?' Rob said, pouring two mugs of coffee.

Shona and Kate exchanged a look. 'It just got a bit more complicated,' Shona said. She finished her sandwich and kissed him. 'Thank you, you're a star. I'll be back later.'

Kate put her plate on the worktop. 'Thanks, Rob,' she said.

'What, no kiss?' he said, smirking, as Kate fled from the kitchen.

'Stop it, Rob. You're embarrassing her. Leave the lassie alone or I'll do you for harassment.'

'Only if you promise to bring the handcuffs.'

'God, that joke never gets old, does it.' She kissed him again and smiled. 'I might be back late. Make sure Becca gets to bed at a decent time. Love you.'

'Love you too, darlin'.'

–

At the Carlins', the curtains were drawn and Old Jimmy's next door was in darkness.

'I put Dad to bed. He was exhausted,' said Laura, who Shona thought looked tired herself. 'Jack's over at Karen's. I just popped home for a bit. I'm back at the hospital later.'

'We'll not keep you long. How's Jamie?' Shona said, sitting down next to Laura on the sofa. Kate took the chair opposite.

'He's stable. That's all we can hope for at the minute the doctors have said.'

'Okay, that's good,' Shona replied. For the briefest moment they sat there and it felt like they should be opening a bottle of wine and getting out a DVD for a girl's night in.

When Shona revealed the cause of death, Laura looked at her as if she was mad.

'What? No! That's a mistake. The phosphorous grenades killed him. The MoD did this to get themselves off the hook. His body was out at Kilcatrin. They must have done this to him then.'

'Laura, Professor Kitchen is an independent pathologist and one of the best. I trust her judgement entirely.'

'I can ask for another post-mortem, can't I?'

'The result would be the same,' Shona said gently.

'I don't believe it.' Laura sat back, crossing her arms. She shook her head and repeated herself until Shona leaned in and touched her arm.

'Laura, I'm really sorry but I have some questions. Do you feel up to answering them?'

Laura looked at her friend for a moment and then gave the barest of nods.

'Can you think of anyone who would harm Tony?'

'No, of course not,' she replied.

'Did he owe money to anyone he was frightened of?'

This time, the answer took longer. Laura rubbed her hand across her forehead. 'We were in debt, but I don't think he went to a loan shark, if that's what you mean.'

'What about colleagues at work? Did he get on with them?'

'Yes,' she said with a hint of exasperation. 'Shona, this is Tony we're talking about. You knew him. He was with the lifeboat. A fisherman. A haaf-netter. His family have lived here for years. He got on with everyone. Ask Tommy McColl, he'll tell you.'

'Okay,' Shona soothed. 'You understand this is just procedure and we're following a number of lines of enquiry.' Shona stopped. She'd said it a dozen times to bereaved families but now it sounded like a platitude trotted out to stop people asking questions in return.

'I didn't know Tony as well as I should have,' Shona continued. 'But I know you, Laura. Tony met his death through violence and I will do everything I can to get the answers you need.'

Laura blinked back the tears and flapped her hand in front of her face. 'I know, I'm sorry. I just can't take it in.'

Kate passed her the box of tissues from the coffee table.

'I've a couple of tough questions for you,' Shona pressed on. 'It's important you understand we're not accusing Tony or Jamie of anything, just trying to build a picture.'

'Okay. What is it you need to know?' Laura said, her eyes suspicious but her breath coming more evenly.

'How was Jamie getting on at school?' Shona said.

Laura blinked at her as if she couldn't understand the question. 'Fine. Well, not fine, actually,' she corrected herself. 'He hasn't settled at high school and he's skipped off a few times. I think he was getting bullied on the bus.'

'How did he get on with his dad?' Shona said carefully.

If Laura thought Shona suspected her son of murdering his father, she gave no sign of it.

'Good,' she said. 'I mean Tony's drinking upset him and he was the oldest, so he got shouted at, but they got on fine.'

'Okay,' Shona smiled. 'We know Tony had a connection with Kilcatrin through the farm. Was he in touch with any of the protestors?'

'The hippies?' Laura looked confused. 'No, why would you ask that?'

'We're just eliminating things that have come up,' Shona replied. 'Was he in touch with any campaigning or political groups?'

'Nor unless you think the haaf-netter association counts.'

'So he wasn't involved with anything like the Stop the Pylons campaign? No one you didn't know ever visited the house or came asking for Tony?'

She shook her head.

'One last thing. Can you tell me how Tony was in himself? Was he ever depressed?'

Laura sighed. 'I suppose he was. It was why he was drinking. I should have done something earlier, but I was just so embarrassed, and I had to keep going for the boys, for Dad. I should have got him more help. He wouldn't go to the doctors. You're lucky Shona, Rob listened to you.' She stopped. Her eyes went to Kate, then back to Shona. 'Oh, I'm sorry, I didn't mean…' and then the tears overwhelmed her.

'It's okay, Laura.' Shona moved closer and hugged her friend and took a moment to regain her own composure. Her friend had been suffering and she was too wrapped up in her own problems to see it. 'That's all for now. Look, are you going to be all right here?'

'It's okay.' Laura wiped her eyes on her sleeve. 'Fergus is coming over to stay with Dad. I'm going back to the hospital. They've got a fold-up bed they say I can have. I just want to be near my boy, for as long as I have him.'

## Chapter 17

Any sense of a rural idyll had fled Kilcatrin farm years ago. In that sense, it matched the purpose it had been put to, the rehearsal of war. The windows in the single-storey stone house were partly boarded and the roof almost gone. Two low barns that met it at right angles had fared better, acting as storage dumps in the past. They retained their slates and it was in one of these that Tony's pickup had been found. By the corner of the farmhouse ruins, Shona saw a flash of blood red against the grey. A clump of tulips, perhaps planted by Tony's mother, fragile escapees of a garden obliterated by high explosives.

Shona zipped up her fleece like she was donning armour as Simon Wallace strode towards her across the rutted and overgrown farmyard. His face was so devoid of expression that if he hadn't been moving, she could easily have mistaken him for a waxwork mannequin.

'Expected a heads-up on this, DI Oliver,' Wallace said formally. 'I thought forensic examination concluded yesterday.'

'Consider this an update.'

A white van and a dog handler were parked up next to a military escort vehicle. The forensic technician, a young woman who Shona thought didn't look much older than Becca, donned a white paper suit over green wellies. That must be how police officers knew they were ageing, when the forensic staff looked like bairns. Forty this year, Shona reflected. Quite a milestone. The dog handler was from a subcontracted private company and she could hear Robocop clearing his throat at the bill, but if there was any evidence still on the ground at Kilcatrin, then time was of the essence. A dog could search in three dimensions, didn't require luminol to detect blood or body fluids, and could quickly cover an area it would take trained officers days to fingertip search.

The handler introduced himself and his dog as Brian and Bram from Yorkshire, and asked Shona to confirm the search area. She consulted the photo she had of Old Jimmy's map on her phone, then traced the probable route from the farmhouse to Kilcatrin Island causeway with her finger on the handler's updated Ordnance Survey version.

'We think he came in here.' Shona showed him a second track marked on the old map which ran from the farm back to an unclassified road on the Kilcatrin Range's perimeter. 'I'll need you to search that area first as it's less likely to have been disturbed.'

'Will do, lass,' Brian said, screwing up his weather-lined face and calculating. 'First sweep'll take an hour. Bram's trained on cadavers, blood and semen so let's hope them squaddies haven't been up to owt int bushes.' He indicated the forensics technician. 'Suzanne'll walk wi' me. But all them other buggers stay here.'

'Of course.' Shona didn't want the military escort trampling any evidence either. 'You've been warned about live rounds.'

'Aye,' said Brian flatly. 'I were ten year in Royal Engineers as a lad. I know a firework when I see it.'

'Murder weapon is still outstanding,' Shona said.

'If there's owt there, he'll find it.' He gave Bram an affectionate pat, pulling on the dog's velvet ears. The black Labrador looked up at him and whined, anxious to be off. With the clock ticking, he wasn't the only one.

Shona had left the Audi at the gate so she sought shelter from the wind in the passenger seat of the forensics van. Wallace sat in one of the Land Rovers, his eyes fixed on the horizon. All he needed was one of those quartered circles on his forehead, Shona thought, to pass as a crash test dummy. She ignored him and worked her way through her calls.

She was just starting to wonder if there was any coffee in the van when she spotted Suzanne's white suit returning up the lane. Brian and Bram followed.

'Nothing, ma'am,' the young woman said, pulling her beany hat more firmly over her cropped hair. 'Do you want us to action the second search area?'

The forensics team had swept the beach less than forty-eight hours ago and was still processing material recovered. Just as Shona was about to answer, her phone rang. Robocop's name lit up the screen. Your move, Shona.

'Morning, sir. I was just about to call you.'

'You've got a firm suspect?'

'Not yet, sir.' Shona dug her nails into the palm of her hand. Jamie was still the only person confirmed on the beach and he was in no state to be interviewed.

'You're five days into this investigation. You seem to be playing catch up with this.'

'To be fair, sir, the post-mortem results did change things.'

'All this stuff in the press is concerning and not at all helpful.' he said. 'We need to shut it down with results.' Now that the first wave of outrage at a man's death had subsided, calls for the killer to be found and beach re-openings had increased to a clamour with politicians like Nicola Baird having a field day and conspiracy theories feeding press speculation.

'I agree, sir. I'm at Kilcatrin now, liaising with Inspector Wallace.'

'Thought you'd finished at Kilcatrin. Wrap it up, now. The forensics bill is sky high already. And what's the MDP's continuing interest? Is someone at Kilcatrin a suspect?'

DCI Robinson, it seemed, wasn't entirely in the loop about a potential terrorist threat. From the corner of her eye she saw Wallace had got out of the Land Rover and stood watching her.

'Just protocol, sir.'

'Well, you've got until Friday, then I'm calling in DI McLellan from Ayr for a case review.' He ended the call.

Shona felt the urge to hurl the phone across the yard. Instead, she took a couple of deep breaths. She was conscious of multiple pairs of eyes on her. The tide times app showed an hour-long window before the causeway would become inaccessible.

Shona turned to Suzanne. 'Search the beach.'

The convoy of forensics van, dog wagon and military Land Rover made its way across the mile of the ranges to the shore. Shona and Brian consulted his map. Wallace insisted the two squaddies cross with them in the Land Rover and position themselves to watch the tide. Shona set the timer on her phone, just in case. Her forensics bill would be truly astronomical if the search team were trapped on Kilcatrin Island with the clock still running.

Shona watched the Land Rover diminish against the brighter green of the island. When she returned to the forensics van, a flask and two mugs sat on the bonnet. Wallace picked one up and held it out to Shona. Whether it was a peace offering or not, it had been a long morning and she wasn't about to refuse.

'How did the Carlin brothers first show up on your radar?' Shona said, when she'd taken the mug. Behind them the land rose up from the wide bay and she could just see the farmhouse perched behind the trees. It must have been a glorious place to live.

'Anonymous tip off.'

'What was the tip off, exactly?'

'That the brothers had links with terrorism and were recovering ordnance from the sea for sale.'

'And that was enough to set your entire operation in motion.' She sipped her coffee. It was surprisingly good.

'The threat level is under constant review. It's the ones we miss we're remembered for,' he said.

'So, were you running surveillance on Fergus and Tony?'

Wallace's head tipped a little as he considered. 'We were monitoring their movements via the coastguard and operating digital surveillance until Tony ditched his phone.'

'I know the *Arcturus* was disappearing off radar. And you didn't think to share that with me?'

'There was nothing relevant to your enquiry.'

'So you don't know where Tony was in the hours before his death either?'

'Like I said, he ditched his phone.'

'There's a certain irony, isn't there?' Shona said. 'You couldn't find him, yet here he was on an MoD property.'

Wallace continued to look out at the island and said nothing, but there was the ghost of a frown on his smooth features.

'This tip off,' Shona said. 'Not much to go on.'

'It was a trusted source. It's come good before. A shipment of arms to Belfast.'

'Were the Carlin brothers involved in that?'

'There's nothing to link them at this stage,' Wallace replied.

'Is there likely to be?'

'It's a lucrative trade. They were short of money.'

Shona stared at him.

'And the business is,' he paused, 'diversifying. In the 1960s, the IRA was badly equipped, old World War Two kit. When Gaddafi took over in Libya in 1969, he saw them as brothers-in-arms against British imperialism and was responsible for much of the updated weaponry shipped in via the Irish Sea.'

'I'm aware of the history and potential for trafficking in my area,' Shona said.

Dumfries and Galloway was a crossing place. It sat on the borders of England, Scotland and Northern Ireland and the A75 Euro-route ran through it on its way to Stranraer. No one knew what the road would be called post-Brexit but Shona had no doubt the challenges, by land or sea, would be the same. Drugs. Trafficked individuals. Weapons. Those sorts of connections were worldwide.

'Terrorism is always evolving,' he said. 'It's not just Islamic groups, we've got everything from far-right supporters targeting public figures to Incel groups planning their attacks online. The market had expanded and it's not all about politics, mostly it's just crime. Bad men doing bad things. Criminal gangs spotting an opportunity.'

'I agree,' Shona said. 'But it's important we keep an open mind. A case like this sends shock waves through a community. You can toddle back to wherever it is you came from. No matter what the outcome, we still have to police it afterwards.'

'I'm not unsympathetic to your position,' he said. 'But if Tony Carlin was not killed by his own hand, or by his son, you must accept the possibility that he met a contact on the beach that night and the deal went wrong. And yes, I'm aware of the irony of that too. Right under our noses.'

They talked on until Shona's phone alarm bleeped. She looked up at the causeway, shading her eyes, and was relieved to see the Land Rover making its way back. It stopped when it reached the end and the search team got out.

'Ma'am!' The shout came from Suzanne, the forensics technician, who hurried up from the shore. She held two plastic evidence bags. Next to her, Bram was chasing a ball repeatedly thrown by Yorkshire Brian. Shona's heart quickened. The dog had obviously earned his reward.

'What have you got?' Shona hurried over, Wallace close behind her.

'A knife, ma'am. It's about fifteen centimetres.' She held up the bag. Inside was a thin blade with a red plastic handle, the sort of thing that might be used for fish gutting. 'Bram found it in the bushes on the middle of the island, and this too.' The second evidence bag contained a pale shape. 'It's a latex glove with some sort of stamp on it.'

Shona peered at plastic inside plastic but could make nothing of it. She showed it to Wallace, who shook his head. Then she remembered Professor Kitchen's comment about the comparative lack of damage to Tony Carlin's hands.

'It looks like the knife was cleaned but there's a blood trace around the blade where it joins the handle,' Suzanne said.

'Can you get that back to Gartcosh and push it through straight away for me?'

'Yes, ma'am.'

Wallace looked at her, and for once, she knew what he was thinking. She had the same questions. It could just be another piece of flotsam, washed up on Deadman's Point, but if this was the knife that killed Tony Carlin, whose traces might they find on it? It would lead them to one of two places: a hospital bed in Dumfries, or out into a shadowy world of terrorism.

## Chapter 18

The news of the find at Kilcatrin gave everyone at Dumfries CID a boost. When Shona got back to the office, Ravi had pinned images of the knife and glove to the whiteboard. He'd also printed out a picture she'd sent him of Bram and stuck it next to the exhibits under the commendation Constable of the Week.

'Some of you already know Inspector Wallace from the Ministry of Defence Police,' Shona said to the assembled team. Murdo leaned in and shook Wallace's hand. Ravi gave him a nod. 'He'll be with us for a couple of days, so feel free to pass him queries via Murdo.'

It hadn't been an easy decision, but she had no choice if she was going to clear this up by Friday. What is it they say? Keep your friends close and your enemies closer. Wallace wasn't an enemy as such, although she certainly didn't trust him. But standing on Kilcatrin shore, the knife lying in its evidence bag, something unspoken had passed between them. A truce of sorts. One thing was certain, they both needed a result.

'Murdo,' Shona began. 'Where are we on the appeal for witnesses?'

'No one's come forward with anything useful,' Murdo replied. 'No reports of anyone needing treatment for burns either.'

'What about his haaf-netter friends? Did he mention Kilcatrin to them?'

'He talked a bit about how he wasn't happy with the MoD contamination, but neither were they. No one's quite sure why salmon numbers are falling and there are various theories, from local pollution to global warming. The boys I spoke to seemed to think his connection to the place was purely historic, though. He never mentioned fishing there.'

'Okay.' Shona scanned the room for Vincent Greig, her visual investigation officer, without success. 'Is Vinny Visuals is still working on the laptop?'

'Aye,' Murdo said. 'He thinks it hasn't been used much, but he's checking for any hidden files.'

Wallace raised a finger and Shona nodded.

'It may be useful to copy me in on any files he finds,' the MDP officer said.

'Agreed,' Shona replied. 'Who went out to Solway Spotless?'

'Me, ma'am,' Special Constable Rhys Marshall said, getting up from his chair. They regularly used the Specials for door-to-door enquiries and Shona had agreed with Murdo's suggestion to send the lad.

'Go on,' she said.

'Tony Carlin didn't come in to the office that day but went straight to the job in Annan. The boss,' Marshall looked down at his notebook, 'Dylan Brown, talked to him on the phone. They were cleaning out a warehouse.'

'They?'

'Yes, ma'am.' Marshall looked momentarily as if he didn't understand the question. 'Tony Carlin and his brother, Fergus Carlin.'

'Ravi, when you interviewed Fergus, did he mention that?'

'Nope.' Ravi tapped the desk with his pen. 'Said he hadn't seen him for a couple of days.'

'Okay, well, that needs chasing up. Good work, Rhys.'

'Ma'am.' Special Constable Marshall sat back down with a look that was a mixture of relief and pleasure on his face.

'What about CCTV from this job in Annan?' Shona said.

Chloe, one of the young data analysts, cleared her throat. 'We've found him arriving and leaving the warehouse in the pickup, and along the A75. Last sighting was at New Abbey. There're no cameras near his home, but he was heading in that direction.'

'Good. What about the route to Kilcatrin?'

Chloe shook her head. 'No sign of him, but it's possible to reach the locus on back roads.'

'Okay, let's do a sweep of properties and businesses along potential routes. It was probably dark when he went out there, but we might get lucky. Also, Laura said he sometimes used her car.' Shona glanced at Wallace, who was leaning against a desk, his arms folded. 'Check if his wife's vehicle comes up anywhere in the two weeks leading up to his death.'

Chloe made a note as Ravi held his notebook out with the registration details of Laura's red Renault Clio.

Shona took a deep breath. 'Ravi? What did the school have to say regarding Jamie?'

'They confirmed Laura Carlin's view about him not settling. He's been in a bit of trouble.'

'Laura said she thought he was being bullied.'

'They were reluctant to say much, given the state he's in, but they think it was Jamie doing the bullying.'

Shona pictured the pint-sized Jamie and wondered if offence was his best defence. 'Could it be he's just standing up for himself?' Becca had run into similar problems when she defended another pupil and found herself accused of being the bully.

'Maybe, but it seems there was an escalation.' Ravi shifted in his seat. 'About a month ago, Jamie took a craft knife from an art lesson and threatened another pupil. He said it was a mistake. He didn't realise he'd put it in his pocket, but the school excluded him for the rest of the week.'

There was a pause while everyone took in the implications of Ravi's words.

'Is Kate at the hospital with Laura?' Shona directed the question to Murdo, who nodded. 'Any update?' He shook his head. 'Okay, everyone, well done and keep at it. We should get any forensics back on the knife tomorrow so let's tie up any outstanding actions by then.'

–

When Shona got back to High Pines, there was little sign of activity in the kitchen. Murdo had suggested they take Inspector Wallace for a meal, but the MDP officer decided he'd go back to his accommodation at Kilcatrin, leaving Shona free to go home.

'Rob?' she called out. The guest suites on the ground floor looked empty too.

When there was no answer, she followed the sound of the TV up to the lounge on the top floor and found Becca sprawled on the sofa.

'Where's Dad?'

'Dunno.' Becca shrugged. 'He's showing that blogger the sights.'

Shona tried Rob's phone. Straight to voicemail.

'How's my best girl?' Shona reached out and smoothed her daughter's long curly hair. 'What's this about?' She indicated the screen filled with dolphins.

'David Attenborough. *Our Planet*. You should watch it. You might learn something.'

'Okay, I will. Just let me get a cup of tea.'

Becca looked at her with surprise and paused the TV. 'Sure it's your thing?'

'Why wouldn't it be? I'm interested in the natural world,' Shona said. 'You know, every time a ship is wrecked, a huge amount of diesel and cargo comes ashore. A big part of the lifeboat isn't just about saving lives, we want to protect the environment too.'

'So how come you and the other Frans aren't nailing the MoD over Kilcatrin?'

'Frans?'

'It's what Willow calls the police.' Becca grinned. 'You know? Pigs. Bacon. Francis.'

'Willow needs to mind her manners. She wasn't so picky when she needed a lift home.'

'Willow's cool. You'd like her if you knew her better.'

'I asked you to stay away from Bankend,' Shona said, frowning.

'I have. But you didn't say I couldn't see Willow, did you?'

It was true, Shona hadn't, even if that had been the gist of her instruction. She slid into the seat next to Becca. 'Why would I like her?'

Becca studied her mother. 'Is that your listening face? Am I under caution?'

'Stop it.' Shona grabbed her daughter and gave her a playful tickle. 'Go on, tell me. You obviously think she's great.'

'It's just, she's not on the treadmill,' Becca said. 'You know, school, job, mortgage. She sees a bigger world.'

'Has Willow always lived at the Gaia Collective?'

'Since she was fourteen. Her mum moved to Spain and left Willow her van, so she's had her own place for ages. She's been all over. Portugal. Copenhagen. All the big protests.'

So far, everything tallied with what Ravi told her. She could see how Becca would admire this picture of globe-trotting activism, but Shona suspected the true picture was less rosy. It sounded as if Willow had fended for herself from a young age. Shona grew up with her grandmother on a housing scheme on the outskirts of Glasgow, her own mother and absent father claimed by drugs. She got out, many didn't, and she knew the toll early independence could take.

'She sounds like she's had an interesting life,' Shona said. 'So what's your plan?'

'How d'you mean?'

'From your unique perspective,' Shona said. 'How would you like to make a difference?'

'Wow, Mum. Counselling's really rubbing off on you, isn't it?' Becca said. Then her face fell. 'Oh God, I'm sorry. I didn't mean that.' Becca threw herself at her mother and hugged her tight.

'It's all right, sweetheart.' Shona squeezed her back. 'Don't worry. It's just Ravi said something today about having goals beyond school and career.'

'Ravi's pure brilliant, ain't he?' Becca said, and it was evident that her London accent was slowly being replaced by Scottish phrases. 'What's his non-career goal then?'

'Getting a dog, I think,' Shona replied, and saw Becca's eyes light up. 'Before you ask, the answer's no. Your father put his foot down on that.'

'Ravi's loved up with his bae. He keeps posting about it on Insta.'

'I think he's got a point about non-career goals,' Shona said.

'So, I can ditch my exams?' Becca replied, with a mischievous look.

'You know what I mean. You're nearly sixteen. I'm just asking what's important to you beyond university and getting away from Kirkness to the bright lights of Glasgow.'

Becca considered. 'I don't know yet. Does that sound dumb?'

'No, it sounds honest. I couldn't have answered that at your age.'

'I just see all this stuff that's wrong with the world. People getting away with shit they shouldn't. Killing people cos they're gay, or black. Destroying the environment to make money. It so unfair. I just want to do what I can to stop them.'

Shona heard the distant echo of her own reasons for joining the police, but she wanted Becca's route to be different. 'University is a good place to get into activism. As long as you don't get arrested.'

'Yeah, maybe. If I go.'

'Changed your mind about archaeology?'

'No. It just seems a bit… remote. If things need changing, why not just get out and change things. Like that girl

149

Greta and her school strike. What's the point in education if there's no future?'

Shona wasn't sure she could answer that, not on an empty stomach at least.

'Shall I make dinner?'

Becca pulled a face. 'No offence, Mum, but do you have to? Couldn't we just get a takeaway?'

Shona phoned for a pizza. They watched a couple of natural history documentaries and discussed them. Shona felt her daughter slipping away from her into the uncertainties of the adult world. Becca was smart and resourceful, but also impatient and had a temper to match Shona's own. As a small child she'd had a remarkably sunny disposition, but now all Shona could see were storms ahead, and no amount of reassurance on her part that things would work out, or an unpicking of the issues, seemed to offer any solutions. Faced with so much uncertainty, Becca's mood had plummeted.

'You got any studying to do?' Shona said.

'A bit.'

'I've got some paperwork. Shall we rendezvous for hot chocolate in an hour? I don't want you up too late.'

'Okay.'

Shona couldn't bear to see her daughter so down and she searched for something to cheer her up.

'Oh, I meant to ask, is Ellie coming over for your birthday? What's the plan? You'll want to go out, get yourself pierced,' Shona said archly. 'But we should do a family thing too.'

'Do we have to?'

'Compulsory, until you're eighteen. It's the law. What d'you fancy? Bowling? Meal out? Or what about something here?'

'You're not planning a surprise birthday tea or anything?' Becca looked at her mother with suspicion.

'No way.' Shona reflected her daughter's horrified expression. 'You lot high on fizzy juice and me cleaning jelly off the carpet. Think we're past all that. What about a barbecue?'

'Bit boring.'

'Well…' Shona said. 'What about a barbecue on Ross Island? The owner has just installed a new solar and wind system and lives sustainably. There's only him and his wife so he's mad to talk about it. He says you can swim and play your music as loud as you like.'

'Seriously?' Becca said, her eyes widened. 'There's Bronze Age cup-and-ring marks on a site there.'

'He owes the lifeboat a favour. He broke down a couple of months back in rough weather and we towed him in,' Shona said. 'Tommy will take us on the *Silver Crest*.' The lifeboat skipper's pride and joy was the thirty-foot vintage fishing vessel built in larch over an oak frame by his father. The hold had been replaced with a comfortable seven-berth cabin, a small kitchen and steps up to the wheelhouse.

'Also, sixty years ago there was a grisly murder.' Shona rubbed her hands together. 'One of the lighthouse keepers was found dead, and the other sentenced to hang for it.'

'Great,' said Becca, grinning at her mother. 'Something for everyone.'

Shona wrestled with a team performance matrix until the figures swam before her. An action list for tomorrow sat completed on her screen and she decided both she and Becca had done enough.

She tried Rob's phone again without success. Where on earth could he be? Her limbs felt heavy and her head ached. Time to sleep. Becca didn't protest and was soon tucked up in bed.

Shona had just dropped off when she heard Rob on the stairs. She turned on the light.

'Where have you been. I've been ringing you.'

'Shit, sorry. My battery died. I drove Emma around for a bit, then popped in to the Royal for a quick drink,' Rob said. He leaned down to kiss her and she could smell the booze on him. More than one drink and, judging by the clock, not that quick.

'Why is she still here?' Shona said. 'How long does it take to write a review of a B&B?'

'We talked about the background stuff,' Rob said, struggling to get out of his jeans.

'What stuff?' Shona sat up, suddenly awake.

Rob waved his hand vaguely. 'Why we opened High Pines. Our experience and ethos.'

What exactly was Emma Johnstone after? Police had already charged Harry Delfont with three counts of sexual assault. It was sub-judice until the trial, so there was nothing for Emma there. Reports of the Milton McConnell fraud investigation had made the newspapers, but no charges yet. Could Emma have made the link with Rob? Or was it Rob's gambling? Becca's role as a witness in Gavin Baird's death was covered by reporting restrictions on under-eighteens but she could have picked up on either of these around the village.

'Don't worry, it's fine, Shona. It's all under control.' He leaned over to kiss her goodnight. 'Anyway, she'll be gone after the weekend.'

'Is that a promise?' Shona muttered, but judging by the snores, Rob was already asleep.

## Chapter 19

Shona arrived at Cornwall Mount just after seven a.m. Murdo had beaten her to it, as usual. He stood by the kettle, eyes on his phone. When Shona pushed through the door, laptop case in hand, he lifted her mug from the cupboard. It also surprised her to see Special Constable Rhys Marshall sat at a computer screen in the far corner.

'Lovely morning, boss,' Murdo said.

It was. The half-hour drive east from Kirkness across the low rolling hills had promised a fine day, but Shona caught that morning's shipping forecast on Radio 4. *There are warnings of gales later in Lundy, Fastnet, Irish Sea, Malin.* They should enjoy it while it lasted.

'Morning, Murdo. Hope that's not coming out of my overtime budget?' She indicated the Special.

'He's watching some training video. Strictly on his own time, boss. He's keen. Don't you go scaring him off.'

'Wouldn't dream of it,' Shona grinned. 'Any updates?'

'Everything's under control. Oh, I had a call from one of the haaf-netters last night.' Murdo picked up both mugs and followed Shona into her office. 'He remembered, about a month ago, Tony Carlin got in a rammy with another fisherman. Came to blows, apparently. He didnae witness it himself, and couldnae say who this fisherman was, or what it was about. Ravi's gone to have a word with Fergus Carlin. I've asked him to see if he knows.'

'Did the harbour master mention anything about that when you spoke to him?' Shona asked. She unzipped her bag, slid her laptop onto the desk and switched it on.

'No,' Murdo replied. 'So I'm thinking it wasn't with one of the crew off the scallop boats, but I'll give him a call anyway.'

'Anything else?' Shona took a sip of her coffee.

'Still working through the CCTV and I'll chase Vinny Visuals.'

'Good. Check he's got what he needs. He does my nut in at times, but we don't want to lose him. I think his time on secondment to Op Fortress turned his head. If he's pining for pastures new, I don't want our MDP friend Inspector Wallace pinching him.'

'Righto.'

As the CID office filled up, Shona worked her way through her emails. A report on workforce wellbeing, performance and professional standards needed a response. Then she reviewed the tasking and priorities, matching them against resources. She called the super with the lead on the beach clean-up and checked in with her fellow DI based over in Galloway. Phosphorous grenades were still coming in, but the flow had reduced and the public were heeding the message not to touch anything they found but to call it in.

Shona leaned back and stretched the muscles in her neck. The headache was back, sitting like a weight around her eyes. She got up from her desk and looked through the glass panel of her office. The whiteboard was an unaccustomed blur. She blinked at a bright fuchsia blob that could only be Ravi's cashmere sweater and tapped the glass for him to come in.

'What's the score with Fergus Carlin?' she said and sat back down behind her desk.

'Said he didn't mention the cleaning job because he didn't think it was relevant to Tony's death,' Ravi replied. 'Not sure if I believe that, but it could be a pride thing. He's not keen on people knowing what they were doing to make ends meet.'

'Did he say anything about Tony's fight with another fisherman?'

'Claimed he didn't know but pointed out Tony was drinking a lot.'

'So it might have happened in a pub? See if uniform can shed any light on it.'

'Sure, boss.' Ravi got up. 'One other thing. Fergus mentioned he asked if Tony wanted to get some fish and chips after the job, but Tony said he couldn't because Laura had the dinner on.'

'Laura told us she didn't see him come home' Shona nodded. 'D'you think it's possible he let them both think he was with the other because he was meeting with someone else? Get Kate to double check that with Laura.'

'Okay. Any news on the knife?'

'Still waiting.'

'I'm just going out for a sandwich,' Ravi said. 'Want me to get you one?'

Shona took a ten-pound note from her purse. 'Anything but egg would be great.'

'I'm off to that wee place that does the Punjabi samosas.' Ravi raised an eyebrow in enquiry.

'As if you have to ask.' Shona smiled.

The email from forensics at Gartcosh dropped just as Shona had finished the fragrant potato and pea samosas and was about to bite into her sandwich. She scanned through the abstract and skipped straight to the conclusions. The blood on the knife was Tony's. No fingerprints or DNA. It had been wiped clean. Shona cursed. The glove was more interesting. It contained the DNA profile of the victim and two others, neither of whom were currently on the Police Scotland DNA Database.

'Murdo,' Shona shouted as she crossed to the whiteboard. In the CID room, faces turned, calls were quickly finished as people got up from the desks to hear the news. Shona relayed them the headlines.

Special Rhys Marshall raised his hand and pointed to a picture on the board. 'I thought I recognised the glove, ma'am. It's the same brand that Solway Spotless use.'

'Good work, Rhys. That's our connection. The DNA is from the inside, so two other people wore this glove at some point and either or both were potentially on the beach with Tony. We need to exclude his workmates. Murdo, how many staff have they got?'

'Around fifty, all on zero-hours contracts.'

Shona winced inwardly. That would put another hole in her budget. 'Have we got enough DNA3 pink kits?'

'I'll check, but I think so,' Murdo replied. 'I'll tell the owner, Dylan Brown, to get his staff in.'

'Do that, and I want everyone who's trained to take swabs down there. We can't wait for a forensics team, and it's within our remit, so let's get on with it.'

–

Shona arrived first at the industrial unit which housed Solway Spotless and could tell immediately it wouldn't be as straightforward as she'd hoped. A man in his forties wearing an ill-fitting grey suit, who Shona assumed was the boss, was remonstrating with a group of around twenty men in jeans and overalls. She got out of the car.

'Mr Brown,' she called, and showed her warrant card.

'I'm no' having this.' A man in a blue polo top with the company logo on it stormed off.

'Sir, if you could just wait a moment.'

He ignored Shona's attempts to call him back, got into his car, and sat glaring at her through the windscreen.

'It's not compulsory this, is it?' Dylan Brown said. 'I cannae make them do it.'

'Sir, if you can just get everyone together, I'll explain why we need your help.'

Complaints came from the crowd. *No way. You're bang out of order, lassie. This a police state?*

A few of the other men went to push past her but she stood her ground. She held out her arms. 'Please, just hear me out. Mr Brown is right, this is voluntary. All I want is ten minutes of your time. You're free to go at any point but I really believe you can help me resolve this case and bring closure for Tony Carlin's family.'

When reinforcements had arrived and Brown had gathered the staff he could into the loading bay, Shona looked at the rank of hostile faces in front of her. Murdo and Ravi smiled reassuringly at the men while covering the exits. A couple of Specials and two trained civilian workers waited in the wings.

'Thank you for all staying,' she said. 'The Criminal Justice Act, 2003, allows me to ask for voluntary DNA samples. These will be used for the specific purpose of eliminating you from our enquiry into the murder of Tony Carlin. They will be held for a defined period of time and searched only in relation to this crime.'

'Why d'you need it?' an older man in overalls challenged. He had a fighter's face, the bridge of his nose flat and wide. He stood with his feet planted apart, hands in pockets, his jaw set firm.

'It relates to a piece of evidence recovered from the crime scene,' Shona replied. 'We are anxious to exclude people from our search. This will enable us to do it quickly. You will appreciate how this is affecting the family. I know a few of you are fellow fisherman. Tony had two young sons, one of them critically injured. I'm sure you understand the pressure they face having lost their breadwinner.'

There were a few nods and murmurs among the men.

'In a minute, I'll ask you to allow one of my officers to take a mouth swab. I'll need your written consent which you can withdraw at any time. Please, I would be really grateful for your help.'

After a brief pause, the man with the boxer face nodded and stepped forward. There were the standard jokes about paternity claims and the presence of animals in the family tree, but Shona sensed the tide had turned. There was also the question of the thirty or so other staff not present who'd have to be traced. Shona asked Dylan Brown to make out a list.

'I know you,' the man said to Shona after he'd given his sample. She couldn't place him but didn't think the last time she'd seen him was inside a cell or across Dumfries Sheriff Court. 'Lifeboat, right?' he said. 'You came out to the *Kitty Mac* about a year back. Scallop boat.'

Shona smiled. 'We don't get calls from fishing boats that often.' She thought for a moment. 'Ah, the *Katherine M*?'

'Aye, well, only the coastguard calls her that.' He grinned and offered his hand. 'Donald Finlay. Thanks for what you did.'

'No problem. Happy to help,' Shona said. 'Did you know Tony?' When he nodded, she drew him away from the others lined up, and lowered her voice. 'So why are you working here, if you don't mind me asking?'

'I was on the boats twenty years.' He shrugged. 'Fishing's no' the industry it was. The boats go, and it's like a rocket's hit the place. Businesses close, shops shut. The Isle of Man scallop fields have these restrictive new licences, harming Scottish boats. There's talk of lads takin' matters into their own hands.'

'Tony had a fight with a fisherman. Is that what happened? Did someone decide to take matters into their own hands?'

'Tony could start a fight in an empty hoose.' Donald Finlay shook his head. 'It's no' just the scallop boats. I used to work the cockle fisheries, till the government closed the beds. You know, Solway cockles fetch two thousand pounds a ton in Spain? You want to help fishermen, then the police should be stoppin' English pirates sneaking over from Cumbria. No wonder cockle numbers arenae recovering. How are wee lads like Tony's bairns gonnae have a future in the industry?'

'Mr Finlay, I promise if you bring me evidence of a crime of that sort I will look into it, but at present what I really need is anything you can tell me about why Tony Carlin may have been murdered. Did someone make threats?'

Donald Finlay thought for a moment, then shook his head. 'The way Tony was going wi' the drinking, I don't think anyone would bother threatening to kill him. He was doing a good enough job by himself.'

–

When Shona got home, she found Rob and Becca planting out herbs in the steep terraced garden that surrounded High Pines. She kissed them both and said she'd take a walk down to the bay, just to clear her head before dinner.

A sunset song of birds followed Shona along the shoreline. Gulls, oyster catchers, and the strange whistling calls of curlews by the water matched the blackbirds and thrushes to landward.

The lifeboat station and Tommy's yard next door were locked tight. The wind was getting up, herald of the storm forecast out in the Atlantic. Later, it would make itself felt even in the shelter of the estuary.

Shona stood on the quayside, her back to the Royal Arms, looking out at the far bank where the trees were thickening with green. She replayed what she'd learned today, turning the pieces in her mind like a jigsaw but failing to make them fit.

A figure came up on her shoulder. Shona caught a whiff of perfume, heavy and sweet.

'I hope you'll let me buy you a drink to thank you for your hospitality,' Emma Johnstone said. 'Rob's told me all about your work with the lifeboat. It sounds fascinating.' She paused.

Shona stood impassive looking out over the water.

'And, of course, your B&B is in the perfect spot.' Emma continued. 'It really is the most beautiful location. Must be quite a change from... Camden, wasn't it?'

'What is it you want, Emma? Because fabulous as this view is, I don't believe it's what's keeping you in Kirkness.'

The young woman smiled as if Shona had offered her a compliment.

'Okay,' Emma said slowly. 'Why did you search Tony Carlin's house?'

Shona was tempted to trot out the line that it was routine, but she didn't think that would satisfy Emma.

'It was with the family's permission,' Shona said. 'Mr Carlin's mobile is unaccounted for, but he may not have been carrying one.' She hoped that was both specific and vague enough to satisfy the journalist.

Emma nodded. 'I'd like a chat with Tony Carlin's widow, and I hope you can help me with that. It would be a really sympathetic article. I hear you're close to her.'

'Did you also hear I'm a detective inspector?'

'It really would be much better if you were friendly with the press,' Emma said.

Inside, Shona stiffened, but she was careful not to show it. 'Is that some sort of threat?' She gave the woman a questioning smile.

'I just mean we could help each other,' Emma said soothingly. 'An exclusive interview with Laura Carlin is all I want, then I'll be quite happy to leave you in peace.'

'How can you help me? If you know something about Tony Carlin or his death, I strongly suggest you tell me, because if I find out you've withheld information, I'll arrest you for attempting to defeat the ends of justice.'

'Wow! No. Nothing like that.' Emma blinked in wide-eyed shock, but Shona wasn't fooled. 'I just mean,' she persisted, 'Laura Carlin and her family will need help to get over this. I'm sure I can get one of the nationals to offer a good fee. We can help set up a fund for donations. A Just

Giving page? The public can be very generous when they understand the full impact of a loved one's tragic death. I mean, does she plan to sue the Ministry of Defence for example?'

'Look, Emma. I suggest you make your request to the press office and join the queue.' She didn't have time for the woman and her petty ambitions. 'Now if you'll excuse me.' Shona walked off back up the hill to her home and her family.

## Chapter 20

The pager sounded just as they finished dinner. Coat, shoes, keys. Rob shot her a look.

'See you later.' Shona kissed Becca. See you later, never goodbye.

'Stay safe, Mum.'

'You're not going, are you?' Rob said as she reached up to kiss him. 'Let someone else take it for a change.'

'Doesn't work like that,' Shona said. 'Don't worry. If Tommy decides he doesn't need me, I'll call you. But I'll stay at the station till we're stood down.'

It was still light and a few sightseers gathered as the station alarm sounded. Two of the shore crew prepared to clear a path to the quayside once launch was confirmed. Tommy stood at the door in his immersion suit and lifejacket.

'What's the shout?' Shona said.

'Fire on a fishing boat,' Tommy said. 'Coastguard helicopter is on its way and Workington are tasked.'

Workington's all-weather Shannon lifeboat, the littlest of the big boats, was stationed across the Solway on the Cumbria coast and had the power and range to take the lead on jobs out into the Irish Sea.

'Coastguard asked us to stand by,' he continued. 'The fishing boats generally help each other out, so if they've called in, it's likely serious.'

Shona knew there were limited options for a fire at sea; fight it safely or abandon ship. More often, abandoning ship was the way to go, but that could be deadly in itself. A life raft in these seas might be difficult to spot in the peaks and troughs of the waves.

'And it depends where the fire is,' Tommy said. 'Most of the firefighting kit is stored at the bottom of the hold ladder. A fishing vessel carries a lot of fuel because they're out at sea for a long time. It's basically a floating bomb.'

Shona changed into her kit along with the others and came back into the boat hall. Tommy was on the phone. She looked out at the waves stumbling up the estuary from the firth, their tips an angry white. Either they'd be stood down before they even got out there or they were in for a very rough shout indeed.

Tommy ended the call. 'We're on.'

In the heavy swell, it was hard to see the waves coming. Shona's grip tightened on the anchor points as they crested each peak and slammed down the other side, the impact travelling up through her knees to her back. Callum had gone on a trip with his girlfriend to Spain, so Shona was joined by local plumber Dave Thomson.

After twenty minutes, they spotted the twelve-metre-long *Harvester* and Shona radioed the coastguard for an update. A pile of oil-soaked rags had ignited on the deck. A crew man who tackled it successfully extinguished the blaze but had severe burns. Workington lifeboat was still some way off. The coastguard helicopter hovered a hundred metres away. It would soon be dark.

Shona relayed the report to Tommy. 'You've the most casualty experience,' he shouted to Shona over the roar of the wind. 'If his injuries are severe, there's a chance we can airlift him before the light goes.'

As they closed on the small, three-berth wooden trawler with its metal deck gantry, Shona was even more conscious of how everything moved, all the time. The lifeboat, the kit, the target vessel. The trawler had heaved to, but two vessels alongside each other were a truckload of interaction that might crush her. Far out, over the Irish Sea, the sun dipped below the clouds, sending a sheen of fiery light over the waves.

The two uninjured fishermen aboard the trawler stood by the rail. As they got closer, Shona prepared to jump across. At the last moment, with Dave steadying her, she reached up both arms. The fishermen's hands shot out. The trawler rolled and lifeboat disappeared from under her. For a moment, she was suspended above the waves. She dipped her chin as her helmet hit the side of the boat. But then she was over the rail and stood on the *Harvester*'s deck, blinking under the arc lights at the skipper and crewman.

'Thank you,' she said. 'I'm Shona.'

'I'm glad you're no' one of yon big fellas,' the skipper said, clapping her on the shoulder. 'You might have got a dookin'. C'mon, Billy's below. He's my brother's lad, so I don't want owt happening to him.'

The injured crewman was a bear of a man wearing only a pair of grey cotton tracksuit bottoms and work boots. His crewmates had doused him down and applied a few inadequate low-adherent burns dressings to his hands and wrapped him in a foil survival blanket. An expanse of white back contrasted with the skin on his arms and chest, which was pink and raw.

'I need to have a quick look under those dressings,' she said, rubbing her own hands with an anti-bac wipe. She took a sharp inward breath at what she saw. The skin was already peeling from his fingers, and she was immediately reminded of Tony Carlin's injuries.

She looked carefully at his face but saw no signs of chemical contamination, rather the tell-tale banding around the eyes and scorched eyebrows of flash burns where he'd screwed up his face in a reflex action.

'Billy, you must have been very close when the rags went up,' Shona said. 'You're sure that's what it was? You didn't pull anything aboard?'

'We weren't trawling at the time,' his skipper said quickly.

'You know there's a marine notice in force for ordinance from Beaufort's Dyke?'

She saw the glance that passed between all three of the crew.

'Aye, of course I do.' The skipper did his best to look offended. 'Look, this was a simple accident.'

In the confines of the cabin, the smell of burning clung to her nostrils, but below it there was another, more pungent smell. It wasn't just the fustiness generated by three fishermen in an enclosed space. She picked up the fisherman's damaged jacket. There were scorch marks, and the fabric had melted.

'We need to get you to hospital,' Shona said to the casualty. 'You've areas of third-degree burns on your hands. They need proper medical attention within three hours for a positive outcome.' It was already more than ninety minutes since the incident. There was also the danger, as the adrenaline dropped, he'd go into shock.

Shona radioed the coastguard. The casualty couldn't be winched safely from the deck of the fishing boat due to the overhead gear. Shona's heart sank. They'd have to transfer him onto the lifeboat.

On deck, under the illumination of the arc lights, and despite the spray from the waves, Shona could see rainbow patterns of diesel or petrol on the deck around the area of scorching. Whatever had caused the fire, they were lucky the whole boat hadn't gone up. She searched around for any sign of ordinance from Beaufort's Dyke but could see nothing.

Despite his size and injuries, Billy proved surprisingly nimble, hopping into the lifeboat in a single confident bound. Shona followed.

Tommy McCall was one of the best helmsmen on the Solway, but it took all of his skills to match the helicopter's speed and heading as the winchman prepared to transfer into the D-class's tiny space travelling at speed across the rolling sea. You need to move a lot of air to keep eight tons of metal in a hover. Shona felt the hot blast from the engine buffet her face as the aircraft steadied above them. The winchman sent down a line to help guide him in. Dave grabbed it and a moment later, the paramedic dropped like an ungainly seabird into the rib. He confirmed Shona's assessment and a minute later both winchman and casualty were yanked upwards. Fifteen minutes more, and the casualty would be in hospital and hopefully retain the full use of his hands.

The *Harvester* turned for her home in Maryport, Cumbria, one soul lighter but thankfully in one piece. Tommy gave her and Dave a thumbs up and they responded in kind. Job done.

Tommy leaned across to her and grinned. 'You did a well there. But next time, dinnae head-butt the fishing boat. We don't want skipper complaining you've dunted their vessel.'

They got back to the station just before midnight, surfing in with the wind and tide. After the debrief, Shona left the shore crew and Tommy clearing up and resetting for the next shout. Every bit of her ached, her legs and back from the battering of the waves, shoulders and arms from being yanked aboard the *Harvester*. But it was worth it. Billy's hands and probably his livelihood had been saved. The skipper was cagey with her, and she felt they weren't telling the whole truth, but he probably didn't want the Marine Accident Investigation Branch crawling all over his boat. There'd be questions from his insurers and the coastguard would probably want a word.

She decided to leave the Audi at the lifeboat station and walk the short distance up the hill to High Pines, easing out her tight muscles and buzzing mind as she went. The wind had dropped. Above, stars came out, and she caught the garden scents of damp earth and the azaleas and rhododendrons which cloaked the steep gardens, thriving in the mild climate that earned the area its nickname, the Solway Riviera.

Rather than walk around to the drive, she unlatched the gate and took the steps up through High Pines's terraces that wound between the rock outcrops that gave the house its enviable position and panoramic view. Halfway up, her muscles protested but a hot shower would fix things. She'd sleep like a log tonight. As she reached the top, she caught the scent of the Scots Pines and was reminded again of the unidentifiable smell she'd noticed on the fishing boat. It wasn't the garlic and rubber tones she'd experienced on Kilcatrin beach. She was exhausted and probably worrying about nothing.

Along a terrace off to her right, a candle in a glass lantern flickered. It was in a sheltered spot where Rob had set a bench and table and sometime retreated away from guests and family to read his cookery books. He must have waited up for her. She knew he worried. His earlier annoyance had gone. Rob's emotions were like passing squalls. The sun always came out quickly with him.

Shona walked quietly along the paved path between the rosemary and sage bushes. There was another scent, sweet and heavy and a moment later a low laugh. Shona's heart thumped as she stepped closer. Through a gap in the rhododendrons, she saw them. Rob and Emma Johnstone. Wine glasses on the table. He was laughing at something and then Emma leaned in and kissed him.

Shona stepped forward into the circle of light, her face white with rage. 'Pack your bags,' she said in a low growl.

For a moment, they just stared at her as if neither was sure that the order was directed at them. Then the spell was broken. Rob jumped up.

'Shona, it's not what you think. *She* kissed *me*. I couldn't stop her.' He reached out but Shona shrugged him off.

She jabbed a finger at Emma. 'You. Out now.' Was that a calculating smirk on the woman's face or a trick of the candlelight? 'Move!' Shona barked.

Emma jumped up and set off along the path back to the house. Shona followed. Rob stared after them, frozen in shock.

Shona didn't trust herself to get too close to the woman. It was dark, the garden steps were steep. One hard shove and Emma might find herself at the bottom and Shona would have a lot of explaining to do. This pathetic, manipulative would-be hack just wasn't worth it. Sleekit bitch.

She stood over the woman as she packed and escorted her to her car.

'Wait, Shona. Please. This is all a misunderstanding,' Rob said. 'It's after midnight. Where's she gonna go?'

'She's a big girl and I don't care.' Shona gave him a look that stopped him in his tracks. 'And neither, if you've any sense, should you.'

## Chapter 21

Shona arrived red–eyed but composed the next morning. Ravi brought her coffee, a sheaf of files under his other arm. She took off the jacket of her navy suit and hung it over her chair. This morning she'd showered, straightened her hair into a dark bob and put on her favourite purple silk blouse. Anyone who looked at her would see she was professional, polished and in control.

'Still having problems with your eyes? Should get them checked, boss.'

'I wasn't aware you had a medical degree, DC Sarwar,' Shona snapped.

The slight raise of Ravi's eyebrows was his only reaction. He put the Charles Rennie Mackintosh mug on the desk, adjusting the coaster so it sat square.

'I've got a wee update on the blogger Emma Johnstone,' Ravi said.

Shona kept her gaze on the laptop in front of her. For one awful moment, she thought Emma might have called in a complaint about being booted out of her accommodation late at night. Well, that was tough and she could leave all the critical reviews she liked on TripAdvisor.

'The problem with Ms Johnstone has resolved itself,' she said, tapping the keys.

'Aye, let's hope so,' Ravi replied. 'Because it seems she has a pen name, The Insider. She wrote a whole serious of articles connected to the Faslane Camp and how Scotland is the becoming Europe's dumpsite for arms and contaminated waste. She's close to a group that tried to take the Scottish government to court. Questions at Holyrood, the works.'

Shona felt a stab of ice in her heart. So that's what she was after, not just a heart-rending exclusive from Shona's friend, but an inside track on the Beaufort's Dyke story too, and she was prepared to use Rob to get it. Shona should have gone with her gut and got rid of her quicker.

Murdo tapped her door.

'Thanks, Ravi,' Shona said evenly. 'Like I said, she's moved on.'

'Boss, something's come in on the overnights,' Murdo began. 'Thought you'd like to know. A fisherman's been found dead in his car.'

'What's his name?' Surely Billy off the *Harvester* hadn't discharged himself from Dumfries Royal Infirmary? With injuries like that, he'd be there a few days. Tommy and Dave would take it hard if their work had ultimately been in vain.

Murdo consulted a call sheet. 'Name's Ben MacNeill, aged fifty-six, address in Auchencairn. Neighbours found him this morning in his garage with the engine running and a hosepipe from the exhaust.'

So not their rescued trawlerman. 'Any indication we should be looking for anyone else?'

'Paramedics think he's been there all night. Laura Carlin's got a friend with her, and there's no change at the hospital, so I've sent Kate to check it out.'

'Okay, good.'

'Seems a straightforward suicide. Thing is, he's on our list from Solway Spotless to chase up for a DNA sample.

The neighbours said it was sad, but not completely unexpected, however, they told uniform they'd heard raised voices and a scuffle a couple of weeks back.'

'Domestic?'

'No, he lives alone. This was in the street with another fisherman, apparently.'

'Could it be Tony Carlin?' Shona's interest jumped a notch.

'Aye, that was my thought too. Neighbours didn't know. It was dark. I've asked Kate to get statements.'

'Thanks, Murdo.'

Shona's phone buzzed. Murdo and Ravi left her to answer it. Robocop. That was all she needed. The threatened case review hung over her but she thought she'd at least get to the end of the day.

'Sir, I've just had an update,' she said before he delivered his verdict. She relayed the circumstances of Ben MacNeill's death and his possible connection to Tony Carlin.

'You think he might have killed Tony Carlin and done away with himself?' Robinson said.

Shona thought it was too early to say, but if it kept Robocop off her tail, then she was happy to let him think it. 'We were due at his place this morning to request a DNA sample.'

She held out the prospect of a tidy conclusion and he grabbed it.

'Fine,' he said. 'Let me know when you've finished on this.'

Of course, it was a legitimate line of enquiry but it also begged the question, if Ben MacNeill *did* kill Tony Carlin, then *why*? Beyond both working for Solway Spotless, there seemed no other connection.

Shona sat for a moment, her head resting in her hands. She pulled open the desk drawer, took out two painkillers and a vitamin pill, and washed them down with coffee, then picked up her phone. Simon Wallace answered his mobile after the first ring. 'Ben MacNeill, fisherman,' she said. 'Does the name mean anything to you?'

'No,' Wallace replied. 'Why?'

She told him her theory and the potential connection with Tony Carlin.

'I agree. It's worth pursuing. I'll check our system.'

'Are you still at Kilcatrin?'

'Yes.'

'My DC, Kate Irving, will be back in the office later and Vinny is finished with Tony's laptop. Why don't you come over?'

There was a brief pause and Shona thought the line had been cut.

'Thanks, DI Oliver, I will.'

'I think you should probably call me Shona now.'

'Okay, Shona. I'll see you later.'

Shona worked through her to-do list until just before noon when Kate arrived back, her cheeks flushed.

'The neighbour's description matches Tony Carlin,' she said. 'And they saw a silver pickup parked in the street. Forensics are at the scene. Uniform are doing a door-to-door. There's a late-stop shop in the village with CCTV.' She held up a memory card. 'It looks like Tony Carlin's Nissan.'

'Good work, Kate,' Shona said. 'Make sure forensics are aware of a potential link to chemical weapons and get that card to Vinny and see if he can work his magic. I want it confirmed that's Tony Carlin's vehicle and if anyone's with him. Get it on the timeline and run Ben MacNeill's name past Laura. There might be some trivial incident she's forgotten about that gives us a lead.'

Shona looked up as the CID door opened. Ravi had collected Wallace from the front desk. As the MDP inspector came across to shake her hand, she was aware once more of his assessing look. He had on a dark Barbour jacket over a sweater and jeans, black brogues polished to a shine. Shona thought this was possibly as casual as he got but he still managed to make it look like official dress.

'Simon, come this way,' she said. 'Kate, can you send Vinny in to me with the verdict on Tony Carlin's laptop when you see him. Murdo?' She beckoned her DS to join them.

Wallace followed her into her office.

'Any luck with Ben MacNeill?' She pointed to the chair opposite her desk and he sat down.

'He is someone we looked at,' Wallace began. 'But just in the general sweep. He made regular trips across to Northern Ireland in the past, but he has family connections there and nothing in his file set alarm bells ringing.'

Murdo came through the door and closed it behind him.

'Got a bit of background on MacNeill,' he said, joining Wallace as Shona perched on the desk.

'Last year, he was given a Sheriff's warning over a road rage incident,' Murdo said. 'Seems he was a bit of a face in his youth. Drugs, fights, you name it, but nothing that ever got him locked up. He calmed down a bit when he got married. Two kids. Worked the scallop boats here and on the Isle of Man.'

Wallace nodded. 'His daughter lives over in Ardglass now, married to a pot fisherman. That's our Ulster connection. So MacNeill knows his way around the Irish Sea.'

'About ten year ago his marriage broke up,' Murdo continued. 'That seems to have sent him into a downward spiral.'

'So that's his connection with Tony? The scallop boats?'

'Mibbae, but I talked to the haaf-netters. Seems Ben MacNeill also held a licence until a couple of years ago, when he didn't bother reapplying.'

'That could put him on the beach with Tony.' Wallace nodded.

'Did MacNeill have a boat?' Shona said.

Murdo shook his head. 'Nothing registered. But he obviously knew how to handle one and may have had access to someone else's.'

'So what are we thinking?' Shona went back to her seat and pulled up Professor Kitchen's post-mortem report. She tapped the screen. 'Sue said Tony was a drinker, and we've confirmed that from multiple sources. Blood alcohol levels from the PM are elevated but inconclusive due to the necessary delay.' Shona spared them the details on effect of decomposition, contamination and putrid fermentation which Slasher Sue had added as bedtime reading. 'So, a covert fishing trip with a mate? A few drinks and tempers flare? MacNeill stabs him and escapes by boat, leaving Tony and Jamie to their fate?'

'When you put it like that,' Murdo said, 'it's plenty of grounds for suicide. If he felt no remorse over killing Tony, what happened to Jamie must have been on his conscience. And he probably heard from his workmates we'd be there today for a DNA sample.'

'And if the target of their fishing expedition was beyond the usual poaching, they'd have every reason to keep it quiet,' Wallace said. If their positions were reversed, Shona had to admit, she'd have said the same thing. Despite that lack of any evidence beyond the manner of his death and an anonymous source, they couldn't entirely rule out Tony Carlin's involvement with a terrorist plot just yet.

'I keep coming back to Jamie.' Shona rested her chin on both her palms and stared at the screen as she tried to reposition the facts into a cohesive whole. 'Tony Carlin was a lifeboat man, and a good one according to Tommy McCall, before the drink took him. Make your assessment, weigh the risks. He must have known how dangerous it was, so why would Tony Carlin have taken his son with him?'

'By all accounts, their relationship wasnae that good at the moment,' Murdo said. 'Jamie resented his father's behaviour and was in trouble at school, which would have elevated family tensions.'

Shona shifted uncomfortably. She knew Laura was under pressure but she hadn't recognised the multiple sources. She'd been wrapped up in her own problems and thought it was just family life.

'The incident at school with the knife isnae in Jamie's favour either, is it?' Murdo continued.

'Perhaps the fishing was an attempt at re-bonding with his son,' Wallace said.

There was something in his tone that made Shona look up. Though she had the sense he knew plenty about her, beyond Simon Wallace's inspector's rank and his Teflon exterior, she knew nothing about him. Was he speaking from experience? He didn't wear a wedding ring, but that didn't mean there wasn't a family somewhere. Long periods on secondment around the country's far-flung MoD sights would have an effect.

'If Tony wanted to bond with Jamie, a trip to the multiplex might have been more effective.' She sighed. 'We'll know more when we get MacNeill's DNA back. If it's a match for the glove, it'll put him in the frame, but let's not forget they worked together. It's an alternative vector for DNA and the fiscal will want more than that to build a case on.'

'I'll see if the door-to-door or CCTV throws up Ben MacNeill's movements on the night Tony died.' Murdo jotted himself a note.

Ravi tapped Shona's door. In his left hand, he cradled Tony's laptop. Vinny, in his black skinny jeans and skater hoodie, followed close on his heels, looking apprehensive. Wee Shona was known to draw blood if she considered anyone had left a job half-done. 'Boss?' he said.

'Come in,' Shona said. They'd reached a natural end to their picking at the tangled threads of Tony and Ben MacNeill's deaths.

'What am I lookin' at?' Shona said as Ravi put the computer on the end of her desk and they all gathered round.

'Bank records,' said Ravi. 'See these? They're cash deposits. Regular amounts about every fortnight.'

'Do we know where they came from? Anything else in the files that gives us a clue?'

Vinny swept back his long fringe and shook his head. 'He only used the laptop for his accounts and a bit of browsing. He tried to delete his history but there's only a bit of moderate porn in there.'

'Any evidence he accessed the dark web?' Wallace said.

'None,' said Vinny with a snort, which earned him a warning look from Shona.

'Kate's just asked Laura Carlin about the deposits,' Ravi said. 'She said they're cash-in-hand payments for cleaning jobs. I've just rung Solway Spotless and they categorically deny they've ever paid their workers in cash. Here's the interesting bit. I wasnae too happy with Fergus Carlin's jinking about over the statements he gave us around Tony's movements, so I had a look at his bank record too. Matching cash sums. Usually £200 to £500 a time.'

'So where did the money come from? Are we talking drugs? Chemical weapons?' Shona shot a look at Wallace.

'Well Tony can't tell us,' Ravi said. 'D'you want me to have another go at our friend Fergus?'

Shona's jaw set firm. 'It's time we put the wind up Fergus Carlin. He's playing silly buggers with us and it needs to stop. I think Inspector Wallace and I will pay him a visit. What d'you say, Simon?'

Simon Wallace nodded slowly. 'I'd be very interested to hear what Fergus Carlin has to say for himself.'

# Chapter 22

'We'll take my car, if you like,' Simon Wallace said as they reached the bottom of the stairs. 'I can drop you back.'

Shona pushed the exit button and held the door for him.

He must have seen her expression, 'It's okay, it's not the Land Rover.'

In a visitor's bay sat a shiny black top-of-the-range Mercedes SUV. Normally, Shona wouldn't be parted from the Audi, but the prospect of being driven in comfort after the night she'd had was appealing. There would be time to order her tired thoughts and work through a strategic approach to Fergus Carlin. No way was he wriggling off the hook this time.

'Okay,' she said. 'That would be great.'

They took the bypass and headed west. Wallace was a skilful driver and Shona enjoyed the unfamiliar sensation of not having to keep her attention on the road all the time.

'How did you come to join the Ministry of Defence Police?' she said as they left the town behind. The hills ranged around her like the rim of some great green bowl, cows scattered like black-and-white jigsaw pieces across the springy turf.

'I was a with the military police, an army redcap,' Wallace replied. 'You could say I joined the MDP for a quiet life.'

'The Force Intelligence Bureau isn't exactly risk free.'

He smiled but didn't deny it. There was something about Simon Wallace that Shona recognised as not just a regular Ministry CID but as a Crime Intelligence officer, and she wondered what else was keeping him on her patch beyond this case. The opportunity to scrutinise the Kilcatrin protestors and woo, cajole or intimidate potential intelligence sources from among them would be top of her list.

'How does your family feel about your work?' she said.

It wasn't the most subtle way to enquire about his home life but he if he was offended he didn't show it.

'I'm divorced, one son.' He delivered the facts bluntly and without any emotional inflection. 'Sean's at Glasgow University studying medicine. We both have flats in the city, close enough to each other, but not too close.'

He came up behind a tractor and pulled out to overtake and slotted them back smoothly into their own lane. Shona waited to see if he would add any more.

After a pause, he continued in a more reflective tone. 'There was a point when I thought we'd lose touch. But now, every Sunday morning, when we're both in town, we meet in a bar off Byres Road for lunch. I read the newspapers, he scrolls through his phone. Sometimes we talk. It's all very civilised.'

'You sound as if you're not quite sure how that happened,' Shona said.

'I'm not. He lived in the US with his mother for most of his teens. Perhaps that avoided the worst of it.'

Shona thought of the storms she'd endured with her *I'm nearly sixteen and an adult* daughter, Becca. 'I think you may be right.' She smiled.

They pulled into the square behind the harbour, mercifully free of stilt walkers and bank holiday crowds.

'That's his place over there.' Shona pointed to Fergus Carlin's flat, the converted upper floor of a rundown Victorian terraced house. At the end of the row was a pub, The Masonic Arms. In the harbour, the line of scallop boats rode at anchor and to Shona it looked as if they hadn't moved since her last visit.

'Let's see if he's in,' Wallace said and got out of the car.

They skirted past the scallop boats to check *Arcturus* was still on its mooring and locked up tight, then crossed to the flat. They tried the bell and hammered on the door without success. Shona stepped back into the street and shaded her eyes to look up at the windows. The curtains were open but there was no other sign of life.

She glanced along the pavement towards the pub. Two lads in their twenties were having a smoke and watching her with keen interest. One of them flicked away his cigarette butt and re-entered the pub.

'Come on,' she said to Wallace, and she set off at speed along the pavement and almost collided with Fergus Carlin as he tried to leave the pub.

'Fergus, that's lucky,' Shona said. 'We were just coming to see you. Shall we go upstairs?'

'Can't we do it here?'

'Oh Fergus,' Shona said, dropping her voice. 'I've got a few things to say to you that you'll not want your pals to overhear.' She took his arm and, with Wallace on the other side of him, marched him back to his flat.

It was just as Ravi said. A TV you could almost step into, speakers stacked on each side. A games console, complete with headphones and a DJ mike for the full experience. The rest of the flat was fairly clean and presentable, and Shona wondered if there was a woman in Fergus's life to complete the picture.

'Why did you tell us you hadn't seen Tony for days?' she began when they were all seated.

'He died out at Kilcatrin. I didn't think it mattered about the cleaning job. I told your guy that,' Fergus said, a hard edge to his voice.

'It did matter and I think you knew that very well, Fergus,' Shona replied. 'Now we can have a chat here, or I can call for a uniform car, caution you, take you back to Dumfries and hold you in a cell for twelve hours till I get the truth out of you.' Shona indicated Wallace sitting beside her, impassive on the sofa. 'And then when I'm finished, Inspector Wallace here of the Ministry of Defence Police can have you, and believe me, he's not nearly as friendly as he looks. He can hold you for twenty-eight days under anti-terrorism measures.'

Fergus Carlin shifted in his seat, his brow furrowed.

'And if you survive that, I'll have HM Revenue and Customs go over your flat and boat with a fine-tooth comb, so I hope you've got a receipt for everything you've bought from a toothbrush upwards for the last seven years, because they're gonna want to see them.'

'Terrorism?' Fergus said. 'You joking? My brother was killed by the MoD. And now you want to fit me up.'

'No one's fitting anyone up, Fergus. We're just here for a chat, but I want the truth from you.'

'You should listen to her,' Wallace said. 'If it was up to me, you'd be in custody already.'

'What for?' His voice rose and Shona thought he might at last be spooked enough to give some honest answers.

Wallace took the roll of printed sheets from his wax-cotton jacket. 'These payments.' He ran a finger down the cash sums listed on the bank statement.

'They're cash-in-hand jobs,' Fergus said. 'Industrial cleaning. Dylan pays us off the books and takes a cut.'

'That's not what Dylan says,' Shona shot back.

'He's no' gonnae admit to it, is he?' Fergus shoved his hands in his hoodie pockets and slumped back on the sofa in an unconvincing show of bravado.

'You're earning this from cleaning?' Wallace said.

'Full industrial cleans cost thousands, look it up.' Fergus shrugged, regaining some of his swagger. 'It's companies that don't want to pay the going rate. Dirty jobs like flushing oil tanks or refrigeration deep cleansing.'

'Did you ever go to Kilcatrin with Tony?' Shona said.

For a moment, Fergus looked confused. 'To the farm? No. What would I go there for? I know Tony thought he'd somehow been cheated out of his rights, his inheritance, but I felt no connection to the place. I grew up in the house he and Laura are living in, and I've never been interested in farming.'

'If there's something else you'd like to tell me, Fergus, about your relationship with your brother or what he might have been up to, now would be the time,' Shona said. 'Because the next time we speak it'll be in an interview suite at Dumfries.' She tipped her head at Wallace. 'That's if you're lucky.'

Fergus looked from Shona to Wallace and back again. Then he shook his head.

Shona got to her feet. 'We'll be checking out what you've told us with Dylan. You should have been straight with us from the start.'

Shona and Wallace returned to the car. They sat for a moment, each contemplating what they'd heard.

'Think he's telling the truth?' Wallace said.

'Nope,' said Shona.

'Me neither,' Wallace replied. 'Now we just have to prove it.'

# Chapter 23

As Wallace drove Shona back to Dumfries, they talked over the case and explored lines of enquiry they might pursue. Each avenue led back to the same point. Jamie Carlin, their key witness, still hadn't been interviewed. Why were they on the beach that night? Did he see an argument between his father and Ben MacNeill? Or was it Jamie Carlin who wielded the knife? Shona told Simon she'd update him as soon as news came from the hospital. Meanwhile, he would review the intelligence they had for anything that might have been missed.

Kate met her on the stairs.

'Vinny's cleaned up the image from the shop CCTV. It's definitely Tony Carlin, but it's impossible to tell if anyone was with him.'

She took in Kate's raincoat and bag. 'Okay. Where are you off to now?'

'I thought I'd catch Laura. She couldn't place Ben MacNeill so I'll show her a picture.'

'Any news on Jamie?' The longer he was on a ventilator in an induced coma, the less likely he was to recover.

'They're reassessing on Monday,' Kate replied. 'There's a specialist coming from Glasgow. She worked with Kurdish children who survived chemical weapons attacks.' Kate swallowed. 'I still can't take it in. This, here in Dumfries. It shouldn't have happened.'

Shona touched her elbow. 'No, you're right. It shouldn't. And whatever the outcome of this case, you can be sure I'll be pursuing the MoD, the Scottish government and whoever else I can get my hands on to make sure it doesn't happen again.'

Kate nodded. 'Let me know if I can help.'

Shona updated Murdo and Ravi on Fergus Carlin's explanation for the funds in his account. Tomorrow, they'd both pay Dylan Brown a visit.

'If Solway Spotless have been cutting corners on industrial cleaning, there's an environmental issue there too,' Ravi said. 'What were they doing with the waste and run-off? You can't just put that in your wheelie bin?'

'That's your leverage with Brown,' Shona said. 'He'll know he's up for a fine. But if he won't corroborate Fergus's story, get a warrant to seize his books and search his premises and home and mention he'll be looking at a prison sentence.'

There was nothing else that could be progressed until the forensics from Ben MacNeill's garage came back. She'd asked for the DNA to be prioritised. If it matched the glove, he'd become their prime suspect. Door-to-door reports were still being done on those households where everyone had been out at work all day. She drank another coffee and flicked through her notes. There was a message to herself to contact DC Dan Ridley over in Cumbria. He'd sent her a number of texts, apologising for his lack of progress tracing the Beaufort's Dyke dumping crews from the 1970s. The case of the disappearing tractors had kept him in court longer than expected.

It wasn't urgent, but a loose end worth tying up. She meant what she'd said to Kate. The beach clean-up was nearing its end. Wallace would pursue the terrorist aspect, but if she could put some background and recommendations about Beaufort's Dyke into her report, it might stop a tragedy like this happening again on her patch. She texted Dan. *Progress on BD dumping?*

The office was emptying. Murdo came in to check if there was anything else she wanted before he went home himself. He and Joan had promised to set up tables that evening for a church fayre the next day, but he'd keep his phone on.

'It's fine, Murdo,' Shona said. 'Off you go.'

She couldn't put off her own return home any longer. Rob had apologised profusely. He'd been trying to the perfect host, get them a good review. That was all. In her heart she believed him but she felt drained by the whole episode.

On the bypass, the rain had started. Shona pulled the Audi into the garage to fill up. The one disadvantage of Kirkness was its lack of a nearby petrol station. When they'd moved from London, it was one of the major adjustments she'd had to make. Keep your tank topped up. It was Becca's birthday weekend. Rob and Tommy were in charge of most of the barbecue arrangements but some last-minute dashes to the supermarket were not out of the question.

She lifted the nozzle and watched the dials tick up. Something tripped in her mind. She was back standing on the deck of the *Harvester*. She glanced down at the rainbow patterns of fuel splashes across the wet forecourt and felt something click into place. The phone in her pocket buzzed. She resisted the temptation to check it until she'd paid the cashier and was back in the driver's seat.

*Maryport tomorrow. Will update.* She stared at Dan's text, then replied.

*Fancy some company?*

Dan came back immediately with a venue and a time. Simon Wallace may have his intelligence network but Shona had one of her own. Lifeboat crews. Port pilots. Time to call in the marine mafia.

–

Rob had made an effort. He wore jeans but with a willow-pattern blue and white shirt which brought out the colour of his eyes. Shona liked it, and Rob knew Shona liked it. There was her favourite food, a salt-baked cod. Good wine. Candles. Rob was so very sorry.

To Shona's knowledge, Rob had never strayed. He was a flirt and made an effort to be charming to both sexes. If she pictured him, it was always like this. Clothes that flattered his height and colouring. He would smile as he poured you a glass of wine. The sun came out when Rob smiled and the dark corners grew a little lighter.

What had she really seen on the terrace? A manipulative woman out to spite Shona for her lack of assistance and have herself a little fun into the bargain? Rob was foolish. He'd let his desire to rescue the business from the verge of collapse get the better of him and, not unwillingly, to be flattered in the process. She was prepared to forgive him only because she felt she shouldered part of the blame. Rob had never strayed. His vices lay in another direction and yet here they were, once more, in a storm largely of his making. For the first time, Shona wondered if they weren't getting a little too old for this.

'I'm sorry. I was stupid. I'd didn't see it coming,' Rob said, moving Shona's empty plate as he took her hand.

'Throwing her out at midnight, though? You could have had a more moderate response.'

This wasn't something you said to a woman who was firearms trained and had access to a boat.

'That was the moderate response. She was after a Beaufort's Dyke story as well as Laura. Honestly, Rob. We both had a lucky escape.'

'Listen, I was thinking. Maybe I can help you with Tony Carlin's murder,' he said, and she sensed he was desperate to make amends any way he could.

'How?'

'If Tony and this other fella were poaching, they'd have to sell the stuff around here.'

'Not on the internet?' Shona asked.

Rob took a sip of wine and shook his head. 'How would you get it there? Couriering chilled foodstuffs is expensive. Can't really stick a salmon in the post.' He ventured his charming smile. But like the fish, she wasn't biting. 'And you wouldn't want to leave an electronic trail.'

She thought of the way drug dealers used social media, but had to admit, although the business had a Facebook page, Tony's technophobic qualities didn't fit the picture, although Fergus was another matter.

'Who would you ask?' she said cautiously.

'Other B&B association members for a start. They might deny it to you, but they'd give me the nod. And I'm a local lad, remember. I might hear something in the pub. That would help, wouldn't it?'

She had to admit, eliminating the idea it was poaching that led Tony to Kilcatrin might take them one step closer to finding the real reason.

'It would be handy to know if he was close to any of the other fishermen. I don't think he'd have gone haaf-netting at night on his own. He was a good lifeboat man. He wouldn't have put himself or Jamie at risk.'

'Was he still turning up at the lifeboat station?' Rob said and poured her a mug of coffee.

Shona shook her head. She could only remember him on the edge of things, never at the centre. Laura was always the more outgoing of the two. She'd organised the live 'Where's Wally?' fundraiser that had seen Shona and many of the crew and their partners dressed in a stripy tops and glasses, hiding themselves around Kirkness and giving stickers to the kids who spotted them. On nights out, Shona and Laura had often found themselves drawn together and sharing a cab home, a chance to lament their busy lives and fantasise about a girls' holiday somewhere hot without partners and kids.

The front door bell rang. Becca was upstairs in her room, *giving her parents some space*. Shona knew she'd guessed something was wrong, but neither of them were keen to enlighten her. Rob put down his glass. 'Probably the guests. They'll have forgotten their key.'

One of the ground floor suites had been taken that morning by an older couple, down for a wedding, who'd phoned on the off chance after their original accommodation was flooded by a burst pipe.

Shona wrapped her hands around her mug and wondered if the solution to Tony Carlin's murder lay in an overheard pub conversation. She didn't want to share the terrorist angle with Rob. Tommy McColl hadn't found even a whisper. It had been kept quiet and the last thing she wanted was a renewed storm in the press.

She had her back to the kitchen door but could hear a young woman's voice in the hall. Surely Emma Johnstone didn't have the bare-faced cheek to turn up here again? Shona got up. Footsteps approached.

Rob came through the door, a look of apprehension on his face, followed by a tearful Laura Carlin.

'I didn't know where else to go.'

Shona grasped her friend's elbow as she stumbled forward and felt her shaking. 'Laura, you really shouldn't be here.'

'Your officer, Kate? She's not telling me anything,' Laura said. 'I'm his wife. I have a right to know.' Laura took a huge gulping sob. 'Please, I'm asking you as a friend, as a wife and mother. I need to understand what happened to my boy, to my husband.'

'We're still looking for evidence.' Shona guided Laura to a chair.

'Did this guy Ben MacNeill do it?'

'We'll know more tomorrow when some forensic results come back.'

'Because if he didn't,' Laura continued, 'you're gonna think my boy Jamie did this to his father. Aren't you?'

It was exactly what they thought, but Shona saw no sense in confirming this to his mother while he lay unconscious in hospital and before they'd even interviewed the boy.

'We're following leads to establish if someone else was on the beach,' she said evenly. 'That's all I can tell you.'

Rob took out another wine glass and offered Laura a drink.

'I don't think that's wise,' Shona muttered to him. 'Can you get some tissues?'

Shona reached out and switched on the kettle. 'Have you got someone staying with you? Is Karen there?'

'Last thing I need is her sobbing all over the place.' Laura swept her hair back from her forehead. 'I'm sorry, that sounds so ungrateful. Jack's gone over to her house. He's friends with her Connor. It's just, Karen's taken it hard. She and Tony were at school together and I think she had a bit of a crush on him. Look, I'm sorry for barging in like this.'

'It's okay,' Shona reassured her. It was an opportunity to see if Laura was coping or if Shona needed to have another word with Kate about bolstering support services. 'How's Tony's father doing?'

'I'm not sure he understands.' Laura sniffed. 'Fergus is keeping an eye on him when he can.'

'There's an empty room here,' Rob offered. 'You'd be welcome to stay.'

Shona stared at him with a slight shake of her head. They might be friends, but Shona was the SIO on the case, and she was sure having the victim's widow in her spare room breached any number of protocols. 'It would be better if you were at home, Laura. The forensics will be back tomorrow and they may tell us what happened.'

'Will they tell us *why*, though? *Why* did this happen, Shona?' Laura gave her a pleading look. 'One minute I had a family, now it's just...' She threw out her hands and made a sound like an explosion.

'I don't have an answer for you yet, but there will be one,' Shona reassured her. 'I know it seems slow but when the breakthrough comes, we'll have the answers you need.'

Shona made her a coffee and walked her to her car. 'You all right to drive? I've only had one drink. I can drive you home and you can leave your car here. Collect it tomorrow.'

'Maybe you're right. Don't want you having to arrest me. I've got to get back for Jack. Sorry, again.'

'It's fine, Laura. I can't imagine how difficult this must be.' Shona picked up her keys and put her arm around her.

'I'm not even thinking about the future. Just a day at a time.'

'I think that's best.'

Shona drove her home. As they arrived, Fergus was by the door. When he saw it was Shona behind the wheel, he turned and went back inside.

'Everything all right with you and Rob?' Laura said.

What could Shona say? That she caught him kissing another woman, drunk or not? That he might be having an affair right under her nose? She dismissed the thought, but in that second, she knew Laura had seen her hesitation.

'It's fine,' Shona said. 'We're all finding things hard at the moment.'

'I'm sorry,' Laura said.

Shona smiled at her friend and hugged her. 'One day, we'll have a drink and I'll tell you the whole story. And we'll laugh about it.'

'Promise?' Laura said. She squeezed her friend's hand.

'Promise,' Shona said.

## Chapter 24

Shona saw the fish van pull up close to the lifeboat station. She'd just had a quick word with Tommy to confirm everything was okay for Becca's boat trip and barbecue out on Ross Island. Fish vans, butchers' vans, bread vans, there was an entire gyratory system of vans in constant orbit around the villages. The weather was fine and a queue was already forming, a mixture of locals and tourists.

Shona nodded to the fishmonger. 'Morning, Freddie. All looks good.'

She wondered if she should ask him about the issue of back-door fish. But perhaps Rob was right. He'd be more likely to talk to Rob and she wouldn't make herself popular quizzing a well-regarded local about the legality of his stock in front of a queue of customers.

'Aye, this is how a fish van should be dressed.' He stood back proudly as the first customer stepped forward and enquired about the best mix for a fish pie.

From the corner of her eye, Shona saw a familiar figure approach, braided hair swinging behind her. Willow stopped and folded her arms. Weight on one hip, she considered the van.

'Is the fish locally caught?' she said.

'The scallops are local,' Freddie replied, and handed the first customer her change.

'Not the fish?'

'There's no fishing here now.'

Shona saw Willow stiffen.

'You should be ashamed.' Her voice rose. 'Lying to your customers. You're a fake. The tourists think they're getting something local, something special and are happy to pay over the odds for it. You're no different from a supermarket. People like you are destroying the seas.' She turned on the queue, who shifted uneasily and glanced at each other.

'D'you know what scallop dredgers do?' she said to them. 'They scour the seabed with huge metal raking plates, killing everything in their path. It's the most environmentally damaging fishing practice in the UK. A hundred per cent mortality to the species that live there, and to the seabed habitat.'

'Now just a minute, miss,' Freddie began, his face puce with embarrassment and anger. 'These are sustainably fished.'

Willow glared back at him. 'No. Such. Thing.'

She folded her arms again and regarded the queue, some of whom turned and walked away muttering.

Shona stepped forward just as Freddie opened his mouth to protest.

'It's okay, Freddie,' Shona said with a reassuring smile to both him and the customers. 'Willow, I think you've made your point.'

To her surprise, Willow allowed Shona to take her arm and lead her away.

When they'd gone a little distance, Willow pulled free.

'Got educate them, haven't you?' she said and smiled.

'I'm not sure that's the way to do it,' Shona said severely.

'Well, everyone in that queue will remember it and hopefully they'll make better choices in the future.'

The pomposity of youth, Shona thought. She wasn't sure Freddie would see an attack on his business in terms of consumer choice. 'What are you doing in Kirkness anyway?'

Willow gave her a challenging look. 'I'm here to pick up Becca.'

'Oh, where are you off to?' Shona kept her voice light.

'Thought we might tar and feather the local MP,' Willow said, and grinned. Shona's look wiped some of the smile off her face. 'We're actually off to a tree planting, if that's okay with you?'

'Sounds good,' Shona said. The girl set her teeth on edge, but she didn't want to give her the satisfaction of knowing it. She unlocked the Audi. 'Try to stay out of trouble. I don't fancy a detour to Dumfries police office to ferry you home again.'

—

Shona set off for the south, across the border to Cumbria. Just over an hour later, at Carlisle, she turned west and crossed the more ancient line of Hadrian's Wall. This was the Solway from the other side. The local accent changed from Scots-infused English to Cumbrian English and the legal system, government and school system changed with it. But they also had much in common beyond shared elements of language. The social pressures of towns and villages where the old industries of fishing and mining had gone. The lack of work. Second-homers who'd sent the price of local houses skyrocketing. Young people gone to the cities. Here they shared something else too. There was no desire for Scottish independence and the further entrenchment of a geographical line that many of them crossed, on a daily basis, for work, healthcare and education.

The satnav brought Shona between the Georgian terraces of Maryport to the working harbour and the Lifeboat Inn on the quayside. Dan was waiting outside, a denim jacket over his hoodie, his fair hair trimmed short. In a suit, he tended to look like an awkward schoolboy. He was nearly a decade her junior but in casual clothes he looked more mature. Next to him, in her jeans and RNLI fleece, they might have passed as a tourist couple.

'Thought you might appreciate the location,' he said with a nod to the pub. The first time they'd met was nearly a year ago when Shona had come ashore in Cumbria in the Kirkness lifeboat with a body on board. It was a case that pushed them both to the limit and forged their friendship, and she probably owed him her life.

'Dan, how are you?' She shook his hand. It felt weird, but this was technically business and a hug would have been weirder. 'What have you got?'

Before he could answer, Shona's phone went. She looked at the screen. 'It's Murdo, I'm just going to take this.'

'Quick update, boss,' Murdo said. 'Seems Ben MacNeill is alibied for the night of Tony Carlin's death. House-to-house discovered he got himself barred from the local pub.'

Shona's heart sank. 'They're sure it was that night?'

'Yep. There was a quiz on and he started an argument over it. It's still possible he could have gone out with Tony but we can't pick his car up on any traffic cameras.'

'Okay, thanks, Murdo. Let me know if the DNA comes back.' Shona ended the call and made a face. She updated Dan. 'I may have just lost my preferred suspect.'

'Who else is in the frame?' Dan said.

'The boy we picked up at Kilcatrin. The victim's son.'

'Ah,' Dan replied.

'DNA results on the glove found on the beach should clarify things. Anyway, what have you got for me?' She shivered and dug her hands into her pockets. After the heat of the car journey, she felt the chill. 'This Cumbrian air is fresh, isn't it? Come on, let's walk.'

They set off along the broad harbour wall. Despite the loss of her suspect and the raw weather she felt her heart lighten and her shoulders relax. It was good to be away from her desk and in Dan's company. As a copper he lacked experience but his instincts were good. Murdo was solid, Kate and Ravi had their respective strengths, but it was Dan who was truly on her wavelength. He was adept at hooking out those things that were bugging Shona on cases. He wore his accomplishments lightly and every encounter seemed to deepen the bond between them.

'I contacted a friend of my father's. He worked with him on the arms dumping ships.'

'What did he say?'

'He was cagey. He did tell me that after 1945, over a hundred thousand tons a year were going into Beaufort's Dyke but by the time he and my dad were going out in the 1970s, it was more like three thousand tons. Regular money and quick trips, not like the fishing when you were gone for weeks on end.'

'So what can I do for you?'

'I think he might talk to you.'

'We could give it a try,' Shona said. 'Where is he now?'

'He's at the Lord Nelson. I said I'd meet him for a drink.'

'Okay.' Shona smiled. 'There's a couple of things you can do for me?'

'Fine. What?' Dan stopped.

They'd walked to the end of the harbour wall. Below a line of small trawlers, the last remnants of the once prosperous fishing port's Irish Sea fleet rocked gently in the swell.

'You ever hear anything about cockle rustling?' Shona said.

Dan laughed. 'You what? How is possible to rustle a cockle?'

'They're worth a packet,' she replied. 'Two thousand pounds a ton on the Spanish market, I'm told. The cockle beds on the Scottish shore are shut. I checked with Marine Scotland. They're monitoring the population, but, for whatever reason, the numbers are static or falling. Someone told me that's because the Cumbrian boats are coming across at night to boost their catches.'

'Shit. Cockle wars?' He grinned but Shona could tell he was taking her seriously.

'Exactly. I don't want that hitting the press after the last week. I'll ring around Silloth and Workington lifeboat stations. Get them to talk to the harbour pilots. You ask around your PCSOs and local uniform. Has anybody heard anything?'

'Okay, I will. That it?'

'No, there's something potentially more explosive. Pun intended.' Shona leaned back against the coarse, rock-faced blocks of the breakwater and told him about Simon Wallace, the MDP officer, and the possibility that Tony Carlin's death was terrorist related.

Dan was quiet for a moment. 'Shit, that's really not funny. There's not a whisper here of anything like that.'

'Well let's keep it that way until we've something firm. Thing is,' Shona continued, 'I was called to a Maryport boat on fire the other night. Rag pot, spontaneous combustion. It's poor practice, but it happens. A crewman, Billy Kennedy, had severe burns. We extracted him via a coastguard helicopter.'

'I think I heard about that. Which fishing boat was it?'

'The *Harvester*,' Shona said. 'In fact, that *Harvester* there.' She pointed to the wooden trawler tied up at the end berth. A van was parked on the harbour wall beside it and voices came from below. 'I'm not convinced the source of the fire was correctly declared,' she said. 'The Carlins' boat *Arcturus* also had a fire recently. I've got forensics on that, but I'd like you to back me up as local CID in a little cross-border co-operation, if it's needed, while we have a chat with *Harvester*.'

'Two boats, two fires. You think this is linked to the MDP's line about recovering phosphorus grenades for sale?'

'That's my concern. The skipper was quick to deny they'd hauled anything aboard.'

'If it was grenades, couldn't they just have claimed it had been caught in their nets accidentally?'

'Yes. So why lie?' Shona said. 'Thing is, when I filled up the Audi yesterday, I realised what I smelt aboard. It was petrol. I saw a slick on the deck close to where the fire started. Fishing boats run on marine diesel. Whatever they were up to, they weren't telling the truth.'

'Okay,' said Dan, his face solemn.

Shona led the way to the *Harvester*. From the quayside, she could see the tell-tale mark from the fire had already been sanded away. A two-metre-wide area stood out pale against the blue painted deck where a fresh coat of primer had been applied to the wooden deck. The skipper came out from the cabin and stared at her.

'Mr Kennedy. Hello,' Shona said. 'I just came to see if you're all okay.'

Kennedy's eyes narrowed. 'What you after? A donation?'

'I'm sure Workington lifeboat would be glad to have your support.'

'How much?'

'I'm sorry?' Shona said.

'How much to leave us be?'

'Mr Kennedy, I'm DC Ridley from Cumbria CID.' Dan stepped up and showed his warrant card.

'She put you up to this?' The skipper jabbed a finger in Shona's direction.

'I'd be interested to know how the fire started on your boat?' Dan said.

'Ask the coastguard. It's int' report. I'm not bothering the insurers and Billy will be looked after. So there's nowt more to be said.' Kennedy looked at Shona and something like guilt passed across his face. 'Thanks for coming out,' he added quickly, then turned and stomped off to the other end of the deck, where, with his back to them, he began clearing his tools.

Dan looked at Shona, who shrugged. He took a quick picture of the van. Running the plate might give him a reason to rattle Kennedy's cage in revenge for his ingratitude to Shona.

## Chapter 25

'Well, that was interesting,' Shona said, as they walked back along the breakwater. 'I usually get at least a cup of tea and a biscuit. Where's this pub?'

'Not far. It's down one of the backstreets.' Dan got out his phone and checked the directions. 'This way,' he said. 'Mr Kennedy was obviously not pleased to see you. Did any of the other lifeboat crew witness the fire?'

'No, only I went aboard. Looks like they've already fixed the damage. Marine inspectors are good at spotting insurance jobs, but if he's not claiming anything and the coastguard is happy it was an accident, I'm not sure where we go from here.'

The Lord Nelson was far less grand than its namesake. The streaked, grey render was cracked and missing in places, black paint peeling from around the window frames. In a Highland holiday setting, the building might be deemed quaint, the low ceiling beams hung with tankards. Shona and Dan pushed open the door. Here, they had to make do with cobwebs and a level of nicotine staining many years in creation.

The pause in conversation was so tiny and so fleeting that most people would have missed it. The same fishermen and boat owners who in other circumstances would cross the street to buttonhole her or Dan about police inaction over outboard motor thefts or casual vandalism, now seemed absorbed in earnest discussions with their neighbours or studying the bubble rising in their pints with intense interest. Eyes were anywhere but on Shona and Dan, although she guessed their every move would later be analysed and a topic for discussion. Now, everyone avoided them. No one wanted others to get the idea that they were colluding with the police.

It wasn't the first time she'd experienced a frosty reception. In some London pubs, the temperature plummeted so far when she walked through the door that she needed crampons and an ice axe to make it to the bar.

But in a place like this somebody always knew something. What happened to a community when people chose to turn a blind eye? Could you still call it a community? Individuals had their own priorities, driven by greed, lust, fear and revenge. As they made their way to the bar, Shona wondered which one of those sins proved deadly for Tony Carlin?

Shona insisted on buying the drinks and sent Dan across to break the ice with his father's friend. Harry Jackson looked at them with watery blue eyes and Shona was reminded of another seafarer, Old Jimmy Carlin. Harry's tweed jacket looked worn, but he had on a clean shirt and tie. A flat cap lay on the table beside his empty pint glass.

'Tha' Eddie's boy then?' he said to Dan. Looking him up and down without much enthusiasm. 'You must take after tha mother.'

Shona joined them with the drinks, the landlord reluctantly divulging the old man's regular tipple, a pint of Jennings bitter.

'This your lass?' he asked.

'Not quite,' Dan said, a blush creeping up his cheeks. 'This is my friend and colleague, Shona. She's with the lifeboat over in Dumfries.'

A twinkle of amusement bloomed in the old man's face. 'Are you the lass that went oot t' *Harvester*?'

Shona nodded. 'That's right.'

'Nearly got yerself a dookin' I heard.' The old man wheezed a laugh. The story of Shona's near miss crossing from the lifeboat was obviously doing the rounds.

She grinned. 'That's right too.'

'Ah, proper brewer you are, int ye?' He gave her a shred look. 'But Billy still has all his fingers thanks to you.'

'I'm glad he's doing okay.' She took a sip of her tonic water. 'Dan said you sailed with his father. That must have been a tough job?'

'That were a long time ago.' Harry Jackson eyed her again for a moment. 'This about that little lad and his old fella who died? The phossy grenades on the beaches?'

'I'm interested in anything you can tell me about what went out on the ships,' she said quietly. Around her, the background noise of conversations seemed to have died away. 'The official records are poor.'

The old man took a pull of his pint and licked the foam from his lips. 'It din't seem to matter at the time. We were all doin' it. It was regular work, but a pittance. Skippers din't want to risk their vessels. Loads that should have been disarmed went off all the time. Truth is, lass,' he leaned towards Shona, his elbow planted on the table, 'when weather were poor, we never bothered goin' all that way out to the Dyke. There were times we just discharged the cargo a few hundred yards off the shore and got 'ome as quick as we could.'

'So some of the armaments never went into Beaufort's Dyke in the first place?'

'Nay, nay. They were chucked any old place.'

'The cable company denied they were working near the Dyke, didn't they?' Shona said to Dan. He nodded.

'If Dan came back and showed you a chart, d'you think you could pinpoint where the dumping went on?' Shona said, quietly. 'Jamie Carlin is not the first child to be injured from ordinance coming up on the beach, but I'd like him to be the last and you can help make that happen, Harry. I'm not looking to blame or prosecute anyone, but as a senior police officer, I can make recommendations on clean-up in my report. I just need to know where to look.'

Harry Jackson's gaze dropped to the table and Shona thought she'd lost him. Conversations in the pub sprang up. But then he took out an iPhone from his jacket pocket and tapped the Marine Traffic app on the screen and slid it across the table to Shona. 'You should get yourself one of these,' he said, his twinkle returned. 'Have a gander. Where were them cablers working?'

Could this be the answer to the deadly tide? That the armaments weren't just in Beaufort's Dyke but scattered over a wide area for any subsea operation to disturb? Much more action would be needed to clean up the seabed and make it safe. Shona studied the chart on the screen where brightly coloured arrows indicated the current position of ships in the Solway. Harry, it seemed, hadn't entirely given up his interest in the sea. She indicated a section of the North Channel, a dozen miles south from Beaufort's Dyke, between the Rhins of Galloway and the Northern Irish Coast. 'They were cable laying here.'

'Aye,' said Harry. 'That'll be reet.'

# Chapter 26

On the way back north across the border, Shona's phone rang. It was Murdo.

'Not good news, boss. Ben MacNeill's DNA sample doesnae match the glove and there are no other hits so far from Solway Spotless.'

'Okay, that's disappointing,' Shona said. 'I think we need to rule him out as the second person on the beach, unless you've anything that contradicts that?'

'No, nothing. We'll keep on chasing the other Solway Spotless staff, but that's gonnae take time,' Murdo said. 'We've got exclusion samples from Laura, Jamie and Jack and, after a bit of resistance, Fergus. I've asked them to prioritise those in case it's contamination from the family home but I've the sense we're wearing out our welcome with forensics at the minute.'

'Well, give him your best patter because I've got another job for them.'

'Oh aye? What's that?'

'The Carlins' boat, *Arcturus*?' Shona said. 'I want that burn examined. Specifically, was it electrical or phosphorous or a fluid accelerant like petrol? If you get stuck, I can ask Simon Wallace to progress it but I'd rather we kept it in the family.'

'So we're not counting Wallace as family just yet, then?' Murdo said.

'Not just yet,' Shona replied, evenly. 'How did you get on with Dylan Brown?'

'Categorically denies he was paying the Carlins off the books, although he wondered if they could have been undercutting him or stealing business through contacts they have in the fishing trade.'

'Didn't Fergus say they looked at recycling shells? I suppose that counts as commercial waste. Maybe that was their plan B if the fishing dried up completely?'

'Aye, that's a thought. D'you think Laura Carlin can tell us anything?'

'I'm beginning to think Laura didn't have much idea how bad things were,' Shona replied. 'It's like Ravi said, a pride thing. From what she told me, I'm not sure Tony or Fergus confided much about the business to her beyond getting her to do the Facebook page.'

'You heading home now, boss?'

'Yes, unless you need me, Murdo?'

'No, it's all under control here. It's your lassie's birthday tomorrow, isn't it?'

'Yes, sixteen. How did that happen?' Shona said.

'Well, give her all the best from us.'

'Thanks, Murdo. Call me if you need to.'

'Away you go and enjoy yourself. Rome won't fall if you're not in the office for one day.'

'Thanks again. Oh, how did the church fayre go?'

'Went fine. Joan's still counting up but it'll be a few hundred notes for the new kitchen and the food bank.'

'Well done, Murdo.'

'Aye well, if it gives even a few families a helping hand, it'll be worth it. Can't help thinking, if we did more to support folk there'd be less business for us down the line.'

They ended the call and Shona passed the point where the M6 crossed the border to become the A74(M). She took the first exit, turning west into the lowering sun. In forty minutes, she'd be home. Her last evening as a mother of a child. Tomorrow, Becca would be technically, if not functionally, an adult.

At High Pines, Rob was unpacking the freezer in the utility room. 'Half this is vegetarian.' He nodded to a stack of boxes on the worktop. 'Doesn't seem right to call it a barbecue. I've to bring two grills apparently, so there's no contamination.'

Shona went for a shower and returned to find Rob finishing his preparations. He'd ordered items from a list provided by Becca and was packing them by the back door, ready for transfer into Tommy's boat, the *Silver Crest*, in the morning. 'No balloons, no Chinese lanterns.'

'Thank God,' Shona said. 'I'd hate anyone calling the coastguard thinking they were distress signals.'

'Yeah, it'd be fun if they sent a lifeboat and found you and Tommy flipping burgers.'

'We'll be doing the eating; you'll be doing the flipping.'

Shona's phone rang. It was Murdo. She frowned.

'Sorry to call you, boss, but I think you'll want to see this,' Murdo said. 'Vinny has been following up an earlier request to look at Laura's car to see if Tony was using it. This came from a camera in a pub car park. I'll send it over.'

A few seconds later, a video clip dropped on Shona's phone. She opened it to find Laura's red Clio. Laura was standing by the driver's door. There was no sign of Tony. A second later, a man stepped into the frame. He embraced Laura and pushed her up against the car. Her arms went around his neck as his hands roamed over her in a way that left no doubt they were having a full-on affair. A minute later, Laura Carlin's secret lover stepped away. As he did so, he turned towards the camera.

There was no doubt. Shona recognised him immediately. Fergus Carlin.

## Chapter 27

They assembled on the dockside at six a.m. to catch the tide. Shona greeted the half-a-dozen hyper teenagers. One of them gave Becca a pink birthday T-shirt with the legend, *Don't grow up, it's a trap!* She wore it over her jeans-shorts and wetsuit. Her old school friend Ellie and a girl, Hannah, from Becca's online study group were with her. There were also two lads from the village who Shona thought were probably a couple. Becca had hooked up with them last summer, paddle-boarding around the waterside at Kirkness.

Shona wasn't completely surprised to see Willow at the rear of the group. The girl hung back from the others and stared out towards the woods of the far shore, looking vaguely bored. Shona didn't remember seeing her name on the guest list and thought, beyond Becca's newfound environmental consciousness, she wouldn't have much in common with teenagers seven years her junior.

'I wanted Willow to come. Not a problem, is it, Mum?' Becca said.

Shona handed Willow a lifejacket. 'Course not.'

The girl gave her a smile that said they both knew otherwise.

When everyone was aboard the *Silver Crest*, Tommy took them out across the flat, May calm. Becca and her friends crowded the foredeck and side rails with their legs dangling over the glassy water, on the lookout for grey seals and bottlenose dolphins. Shona sat with Rob on the cushions by the stern rail, Rob's arm around her shoulder, and tried to put work out of her mind for a few hours.

Murdo and Kate were interviewing Laura Carlin over the CCTV of her kiss with Fergus. Shona had proposed to do it herself. The boat trip could go ahead without her. Murdo tactfully disagreed, pointing out it would be good practice to let him put the allegation of an affair to her friend. He was right. Shona unpicked how she felt about this. There was a sense of betrayal and she was a little hurt that someone she was so close to hadn't confided in her. Tony was with the lifeboat and Laura knew that the crew often forged strong bonds. Perhaps she thought Shona's loyalties would be split. But this was a murder enquiry and Laura should have told her sooner about the true nature of her relationship with her brother-in-law.

The green knoll of Ross Island appeared like the rounded back of some sea serpent above the fine sea mist. The lighthouse stood on the far point. At the opposite end was the owners' cottage. On the island's western flank lay a wide, sheltered bay with a long shingle strand. Tommy put down the anchor. They got the dinghy and paddle boards down from the cabin roof and Shona rowed back and forward until the food, barbecue grills and charcoal, and the dry clothes were transferred to the beach. All of Becca's friends, except Willow, opted to swim the short distance ashore with the boards and emerged chattering and laughing at the chilly water.

The owners, William and Lyndsay Rivers, came to meet them. While Tommy, Rob and Shona set up the barbecue, the Rivers took Becca and her friends on a tour of the island, its ultra-modern power system of solar panels and wind turbine in stark contrast to the Neolithic carved stone monuments. Shona hoped the owners were ready for questions from Becca, and probably Willow, but since they didn't get many visitors, perhaps their tolerance was higher than most.

When the party returned an hour later, the cooking was underway, and they decided to head into the water. Shona issued stark warnings about wearing floatation vests and not going too far out of the bay where the Solway's contrary winds and tides might take them. She also had on her wetsuit and, after some cajoling from the youngsters, swam out and was applauded for her rudimentary paddleboarding skills. Rob refused to go in, declaring the only good thing about water was that you could freeze it into ice for your whisky, but he and Tommy looked happy enough overseeing the burgers and stuffed vegetables on the twin grills and judging by the music playing they'd won temporary control of the day's soundtrack.

Rob had made a three-layer chocolate cake which had, more or less, survived the crossing. The sixteen candles needed sheltering from the wind, but they finally succeeded in singing happy birthday and Becca blew out the tiny flames before the wind battered them flat again.

After they'd eaten, Shona left everyone relaxing on the springy turf by the beach and walked up behind the bay.

'It's beautiful, isn't it?' Shona said to Tommy as he came up behind her. 'Thanks so much for doing this. Becca's made up.'

'Aye, it's fine. I'm enjoying giving the boat a run out.'

'She looks a picture.' Shona smiled. The blue and white fishing boat sat serenely in the perfect curve of the bay. How lucky they all were to have this on their doorstep. 'It's so quiet here.'

'It'd be too quiet for me,' Tommy said.

'No pubs.' Shona grinned.

'Aye.' He cleared his throat. 'Shona, I hope you don't mind me saying this, but it's all over Kirkness that Rob's been cavorting wi' that blogger lassie?'

Shona was aware that Rob's standing with Tommy had dipped in the past. In his view, Rob had the benefit of education and good family and didn't take his responsibilities as seriously as he should. Rob's mother's saintly standing didn't help. It was a lot to live up to.

'It's fine, Tommy,' Shona said, irritated that he'd mentioned it on this perfect day.

'No it's not. Bringing her into the Royal Arms. Sunset walks on the beach. He should have more respect.'

This was uncomfortable news to Shona. If Rob's association with Emma Johnstone was the talk of the village, then the kiss in the garden seemed like less of an isolated incident.

'She was after a story about Tony's death and MoD negligence over the beaches,' Shona said. 'Rob just got caught in the crossfire.'

'Is that what you'd call it?' Tommy gave her a sceptical look. 'I'm just saying watch yersel. I know things haven't been easy but letting anyone pull the wool over your eyes isnae going to make things better.'

'Tommy, it's Becca's birthday.'

'I know, and it's you and her I'm thinking of.'

'Look.' Shona rounded on him. 'I know you mean well, but it's really not your business.' Then she turned and headed back down the slope, furious with Tommy, furious with Rob, but even more furious with herself that she hadn't seen this coming.

When she got back to the camp, Becca told her Rob had gone off to see the lighthouse then plunged happily back into the sea. Maybe it was just as well. She needed to calm down and think this through before she said anything.

Everyone but Willow had wetsuits. Lyndsay had offered to dig one out for her, but she'd refused. While the others practised paddle-boarding and rowed the dinghy around, Willow sat on the shoreline.

Shona offered a can of a fizzy elderflower drink that Becca liked.

'No booze?' Willow said.

Rob had wanted to pack wine and beers, but Shona pointed out the potential for disaster mixing teenagers, deep water and alcohol, and Tommy had agreed.

'Just soft drinks, I'm afraid,' Shona replied. She sat down beside her. 'Don't you like the water?' Willow shook her head and Shona wondered why she'd bothered to come out with them.

'Been back out to Kilcatrin much?' Shona said, recalling their first encounter.

'Not much. Have you?'

Shona turned to look at her. The girl reclined on the grass on one elbow, studying a tiny clump of wild violets that pushed their way up between the green blades.

'Willow, I'd like you to be careful with Becca. She's been through a lot in the last year.'

'I know. She told me,' Willow replied.

Shona could see how her daughter might confide in the older girl and hoped she hadn't inadvertently given Willow ammunition that might ultimately rebound on her.

'Feelings are running high about Tony Carlin's death,' Shona said. 'It's hit everyone hard. I'm sure a tragedy at Gaia Collective would be felt in the same way.'

Willow conceded Shona's point with the barest of nods.

'I appreciate you hold strong environmental views, but you'll only put people's backs up by causing a scene like you did the other day at the fish van.'

'The man who died was a fisherman, wasn't he?' Willow said, eyeing Shona.

Please don't say all meat is murder, Shona thought. Instead she remembered the conversation with Ravi where she'd pondered how Willow might fit into the picture.

'Did you know Tony Carlin?' Shona said.

Willow shook her head, the shells of her braids clacking.

'Then you might be interested to learn he was an advocate for haaf-netting, an ancient sustainable fishing practice, and the group were lobbying the government for marine habitat restoration. He wanted greater protection for Kilcatrin, too. Sure you never met him? At a protest maybe?'

'I'm sure,' Willow replied. 'And just because he does a few good things, doesn't excuse his other crimes.'

'What crimes?'

Willow shrugged. 'Working the scallop boats for a start.'

'How d'you know he worked there?' Shona said, and the young woman's closed expression gave her the idea that Willow knew more about Tony Carlin's death than she was letting on.

'I read the papers. I go online. I educate myself.' Willow got up and dusted down her jeans. 'And if you want to ask me any more questions, I suggest you interview me formally.'

Shona watched her go. Was it a desire to protect her daughter that made Shona suspicious of everyone who came close? Ravi had scoped Willow out and found nothing. Shona sighed. So much for a day away from the office.

Becca stood on the shingle, a towel round her shoulders, the wetsuit slick from the sea. Her friends whooped and splashed out in the shelter of the bay. Becca laughed as she watched them. Shona went forward and put out her arm and to her surprise, Becca didn't resist but stepped into the space as Shona pulled her close.

'Oh, you're soaking,' she said, laughing, as Becca shook her wet hair at her mother. 'Sixteen, eh? Look at my wee baby girl all grown up.'

'Thanks, Mum.' Becca hugged her mother. 'And thanks for today. It's been brilliant. William and Lyndsay said I could come back anytime. I might use their power set-up for a case study, and the cup-and-ring marks are amazing.'

Shona smiled at her shining daughter. Becca was tougher than she looked. She'd proved it before. Shona should stop worrying.

'You know I'm proud of you,' she said.

'Proud of you too, Mum.'

The day was over too soon. Tommy wanted to bring the *Silver Crest* to her mooring before the tide fell. They packed up and headed back. An impromptu karaoke started among the teenagers at the bow of the boat and even Willow joined in. Shona and Rob returned to the seat at the stern.

'Everything okay between you and Tommy?' Rob said.

'Yes. Why?' Shona decided to give Tommy's news further thought before she said anything to Rob.

'You've hardly said a word to him. I thought you were taking the helm for a bit on the way back.' He looked at her serious face. 'What is it? He sacked you from the lifeboat? Did you not tie a knot properly or something?'

Shona sighed and told Rob the news of his *affair* was all round the village, and she was annoyed she had to defend him to Tommy, who had been a rock for the family since they'd arrived.

Rob shook his head. 'Are you still on about this?' He squared his shoulders to look at her. 'You've no idea what it's like. I'm a local lad. My family has been in this village for generations, but people have been looking at me funny when I go into the pub since we came back here and it's not because of some *affair*.'

'What d'you mean?' Shona felt a hard anger rising.

'It's because you're a cop. And that rebounds on me.' He shook his head. 'I'm trying to help you with this case, digging around for you, and you still don't trust me. How d'you think that makes me feel, Shona?' He didn't wait for her answer but got up and made his way unsteadily to where Becca was sitting and put an arm around her, his back firmly turned on his wife.

Shona swallowed hard. Then she got up and went to the wheelhouse. In London, it had been different. The cases she worked never came this close to home. In this tight-knit community, every decision had an impact she could see and feel on a daily basis, rippling out like a stone dropped in a rock pool only to reach the edges and return amplified.

'I'm sorry, Tommy,' she said. 'What I said earlier, that was rude of me.'

'Aye, well. Me and my big yap,' he said. 'You're right, it's no' really my business.'

He glanced at her as she stood beside him at the wheel, then nudged her with his shoulder. 'Pals?'

Shona smiled. 'Pals.'

'Here, I promised you a go.' He swapped places with her as Shona took the wheel and pointed the *Silver Crest* at the mouth of the wide Kirkness estuary and home.

When they got back within range, Shona's phone pinged. A message from Murdo. *LC denies affair. Claims one-off drunken incident.* So, Laura wasn't admitting to an affair, just an inappropriate alcohol-fuelled grope. Shona began to review where that left the case. She was out of time. Robocop would ring her tomorrow and announce a review and take her off the case. She had nothing left to stop him with. Perhaps he was right, she was just too close to see the true picture.

When they got back to Kirkness, Shona was surprised to see Murdo's car on the quayside. He and Ravi stepped out as the boat approached, and Shona was touched by their kindness at coming to visit Becca on her birthday. She hoped they hadn't bought her an expensive or inappropriate gift. Childless men had a habit of doing that for young folk in their orbit. But as the *Silver Crest* came alongside, she saw they stood empty handed and their faces were grim.

'Hi Murdo,' Shona said, stepping ashore. 'Everything okay?'

Becca hoped off behind her. 'Ravi, you should have come. We had the best time.'

'I know, but my wetsuit is at the dry cleaners,' he grinned. 'Happy birthday, darlin'. I'd hug you, but this is cashmere.'

Becca laughed and gave him an arms–length embrace. 'Hi Murdo.'

'Happy birthday, Rebecca. You look like you had a good time.'

'They did,' Shona said. 'You coming up to the house? There's cake.'

'Need a quick word, boss, if that's okay,' Murdo said.

'Sure,' Shona said, her smile fading. Rob and Tommy were unloading the kit and Becca's friends all seemed to have lifts. She followed Murdo and Ravi a little way down the quay.

'Thing is,' Murdo began. 'Emma Johnstone's been found dead. Single blow to the back of the skull. She was on steps down to the water by Kirkcudbright harbour. We've just come from the scene. Phone and bag missing. What isnae clear is if she fell or she was pushed.'

# Chapter 28

Shona sat in the Monday morning traffic and tapped the steering wheel of the Audi.

'C'mon, c'mon.'

The lights changed, but the queue remained stationary. Her windscreen wipers squeaked as they cleared the thin drizzle and the car rocked in the occasional powerful gust. Yesterday's carefree sunshine seamed a million miles away.

Last night, Rob had gone white when she'd relayed the news of Emma Johnstone's death to him. He'd denied any contact with her after she left, claiming she'd texted him her hotel details, but he'd blocked her. Get your phone, Shona had demanded. Show me. He'd looked ready to refuse. She pointed out his close contact with Emma less than forty-eight hours before her death, and the village rumours of their affair. If this turned into a murder hunt, he'd be required to give a statement and so would she. At that, the realisation had finally hit home. He'd unlocked his phone and held it out to her. He'd been honest about blocking her, at least.

When the traffic lights ran through their sequence again with no progress, Shona pulled the Audi into a U-turn and threaded through to the backstreets and one-way system to Cornwall Mount.

There was little else that could be done about Emma Johnstone until after the post-mortem confirmed the cause of death. Murdo had established she'd stayed in a budget hotel, checking in after midnight on the Thursday. Shona told him Emma had been questioning her about the case and generally making a nuisance of herself and she'd asked her to leave High Pines. The hotel cleaners went in on the Saturday morning and it didn't look like she'd returned to her room after that. Shona had asked her team to pull together a timeline of Emma Johnstone's movements, starting at the steps next to Kirkcudbright harbour, where her body was found, and working backwards via CCTV and vehicle pings, and checking with the town's shops and cafes for sightings and witnesses.

The CID room was busy when she arrived. 'Morning,' she called and made her way into her office through a chorus of replies.

There was a note on her desk. The pathology service had called to say Emma Johnstone's PM was scheduled for that afternoon at the Dumfries Royal Infirmary. Professor Kitchen would attend.

Murdo put his head round the door as she dumped her bag and hung her grey suit jacket and purple pashmina scarf over the back of her desk chair.

'D'you want five minutes, boss?' he said.

'No. I want the three of you in now,' Shona said. A cup of coffee was already on her desk, the coaster balanced on top to keep in the heat. She took a sip. Still warm.

All actions were still in progress on Emma Johnstone, so when Murdo, Ravi and Kate joined her she went straight to their other case, Tony Carlin's murder.

'So Laura denies the affair,' Shona said. 'Do we believe her?'

'Fergus seems to spend a lot of time at the house,' Kate ventured.

'Yes, he cares for his father, Jimmy,' Shona replied. 'You saw what the family are up against, and Laura's adamant they'll not put him in a home.'

Kate looked uncomfortable. 'I didn't want to mention it before. I know she's a friend of yours. But the other morning, I turned up to take Laura to the hospital. I swear they'd slept together.'

'Based on what?' Shona frowned. 'Fergus could have been next door with his father.'

'It was more the way they were with each other. They were...' Kate wound her hands around themselves, searching for the term. '...touchy-feely.'

Shona was about to dismiss Kate's woolly assessment but then she pictured the CCTV from the pub. There was no misinterpreting that, despite Laura's denial.

'I believe it's not beyond Fergus Carlin to exploit Laura's vulnerability,' Shona said. 'But we've no choice but to regard them both as persons of interest in Tony's stabbing.'

'Can we put either of them at the scene?' Murdo queried. 'There're no witnesses and no CCTV at the beach.'

'See if Vinny can find any more sightings of Laura's vehicle,' Shona said. 'Let's see if her story of a one-off incident stands up. What about Fergus's vehicle? Have we looked at that?'

Murdo consulted his notes. 'He has a driving licence, but no cars or vans registered.'

'Ravi, you mentioned a mountain bike?' Shona said.

'Aye,' replied Ravi. 'Technically, it's a trail bike, one of them four grand jobs. Had it parked in the hall.'

Shona scrolled through her memories of the flat and couldn't locate any bike. 'It wasn't there when Simon and

I visited. Check what happened to it.' She paused and considered. 'How long would it take to get from Fergus's flat to Kilcatrin Ranges on a bike, d'you think?'

'Forty minutes, easy,' Ravi calculated. 'He's fit.'

'So he could have gone there, met Tony on the beach and been back home within three hours?' The others nodded, Shona continued. 'We need something to back that up.'

'He's not alibied for Thursday night,' Ravi said. 'Claims he was at home all evening.'

'Okay, there's CCTV on Harbour Square. Let's see if we can pick up Fergus leaving the flat on his bike.' She paused as the others updated their action notes. Beyond the glass partition of her office, the CID room was a hive of activity, but Shona knew the clock was ticking. 'Anything else to report?'

Kate raised her pen. 'I've just heard that Jamie Carlin's specialist will begin withdrawing his intubation and they're bringing him round.'

'Okay, I want you up there in case he says anything. I'll join you after the PM on Emma Johnstone. Keep an eye on Laura, especially if it doesn't go well. The hospital will issue a statement and the press will be there, maybe some of the environmental protestors too. If he isn't going to make it, we can expect a reignition of the political issues.' For *political issues* read Nicola Baird MSP on her high horse, thought Shona. 'I'll call Kilcatrin and give them the heads-up. There may be some escalation of protests there too.' She got up from her desk. 'Murdo, get everyone's attention, will you?'

She followed the others out into the main office. Calls were finished and a hush fell.

'You should know I'm expecting DCI Robinson to call me shortly,' Shona began. 'He's likely to instigate a case review. Now, unless one of you brings me something soon, this case will go to another team.' She paused and looked around the assembled faces and was gratified to see they weren't happy at the prospect. 'Murdo is gonnae crack the whip this morning and I want you to give him your all, because I don't think there's a team out there that can do a better job than us. Is there?'

There were nods of agreement.

'Right, c'mon then.' Shona clapped her hands together. 'So let's prove it.'

Shona went through the witness statements again, Murdo at her shoulder. They combed and cross-checked for anything they'd missed. One of the civilian staff, Hannah Crawford, a fifty-something, highly efficient collator, whose soft spot for Murdo was well known around the office, tapped the door.

'I've just come across a note of a domestic incident at the Carlins two months back,' she said. 'Shall I put it on your desk, Murdo?'

'That's fine, Hannah,' Shona said. 'You can give it here.' She held out her hand as Murdo rewarded Hannah with a smile.

Shona read through the scant details. Victim unwilling to give statement. Not pursued. 'Shit,' said Shona. 'I had no idea things were this bad.'

'So did Tony know about the affair?' Murdo said. 'He had a temper and a drink problem. Did he assault Laura?'

'It's something to ask her, but let's do that later,' Shona said, mindful of the expected update on Jamie's condition and what that might bring. She glanced at the clock. 'See if anyone's come up with anything.'

She was interrupted by an incoming call. Robocop. Time's up.

'Sir,' Shona answered and then ran through the current lines of enquiry.

DCI Robinson listened, and she heard him sigh. 'I think you're too close to this but it seems you have friends in high places.'

Shona knew Detective Superintendent Munroe supported her and she was thankful for that. He was due to take his deferred retiral soon and her job might get that bit harder afterwards.

'Yes,' Robinson continued. 'You seem to have impressed the MDP. They've requested you continue and Mars Bar has rubber-stamped it.'

'It makes sense, sir,' Shona said in a consolatory tone, while mentally punching the air. 'I'm sure we're close to a breakthrough.'

'Let's hope so. Because, otherwise, this is a stay of execution, that's all,' he replied and ended the call.

She updated Murdo and his relief was visible. 'There's a ton of CCTV we still need to get through. It just pairs of eyes we're short of. I've told Vinny he should stop dabbling in crypto currencies and invent some sort of robot super-spotter to do the job for us.'

'Crypto what?' Shona said. 'Wait, don't tell me. I always have the sense with Vinny that one day I'll be chapping his door, taking him in for questioning over something, and I'll not have the first notion what it's actually about.'

At lunchtime, her phone pinged. It was a message from Becca. She opened the attached picture. It was a selfie of Becca outside a piercing and tattoo parlour in Dumfries, giving a thumbs up. Next to her was Willow. Looked like the nose piercing was on. *Sure about this?* Shona texted back. *Yes*, came the immediate reply. Another message flashed on her screen. It was from Kate to say Jamie Carlin was off the ventilator and being brought slowly round. The morning had turned full circle and now there was the possibility of a witness and time for Shona's team to interview him.

## Chapter 29

Jamie's condition made the lunchtime news. Shona watched it in silence with the others in the office, eating her sandwich stood up between the desks. Ravi was out quizzing Fergus Carlin about his bike, so she'd had to make do with a less informed choice of a cheese ploughman's and no samosas. Jamie's condition was still touch and go. There were calls for a public enquiry. When Nicola Baird appeared, Shona turned away.

Shona arrived at Dumfries Royal Infirmary. A small cluster of environmental protestors sheltered from the wind in the corner of the car park. Professor Kitchen was already in the mortuary, dressed in her scrubs and drinking a cup of coffee with the assistant.

'What have you got for me this afternoon then, DI Oliver?' Slasher Sue grinned when Shona had got changed and joined her in the post-mortem examination room. 'Something a bit less complex than our last outing?'

'I try to keep you on your toes, Professor Kitchen, and I'd hate to bore you.'

'Well, your cases are never boring, that's for sure.'

Shona's face turned serious as the cover was drawn back by the mortuary assistant. 'A twenty-eight-year-old woman, Emma Johnstone. Found dead at the bottom of Kirkcudbright harbour steps. Possible she slipped and fell backwards. There's blood traces on one of the granite setts.'

'An accident?' Sue scrutinised her. 'But you don't think so?'

'She was a journalist looking into Beaufort's Dyke, Tony Carlin's death and one or two other environmental stories.'

'So she may have made enemies?' Sue paced around the table, then lifted Emma's hair to examine the wound.

'I'd say she had the knack.'

'Want to expand on that?' Sue said as the mortuary assistant left to fetch some additional evidence bags.

Shona sighed. 'She booked in at High Pines under the guise of a travel blogger. I had to ask her to leave a few days before she died. What she really wanted was a tip on the case and she also got a bit up close and personal with Rob.'

'I can imagine the sort of tip you gave her,' Sue said, but her face was serious. 'You don't think she and Rob were...'

Shona looked away from the corpse on the table. 'No, no,' she said with a little too much vehemence. 'It's just, do you ever really know? I've met the wives of killers and rapists who were devastated. You can just tell they knew absolutely nothing.'

Sue's frown deepened.

'Oh, I don't mean that.' Shona pushed away the thought and rubbed her hands across her face. 'I can't say I liked the lassie, just the opposite in fact, but her death is a tragedy and if someone killed her, I like them even less. What I'm saying is, I want to make absolutely, one hundred per cent sure we look at everything.'

'Well,' said Sue, putting her hand on Shona's shoulder. 'You've come to the right place.'

The post-mortem proceeded at Slasher Sue's trademark pace.

'Time of death?' Shona said.

Sue consulted the notes. 'The doctor who attended recorded her temperature and the ambient air temperature, but her feet and legs were in the water for part of the time so that widens our estimate. Rigor was present so more than two hours before she was found, less than twenty-four.'

'The last sighting we have is CCTV from a pub at nine p.m. She ordered a soft drink and seemed to be on her own.'

'Could someone have followed her?'

Shona nodded. 'Her phone and bag are missing. Robbery could be a motive.'

'Well, I'd agree with the certifying doctor's time of death, between ten p.m. and four a.m.'

Sue closed the file. 'We'll look at her blood for alcohol or drugs but there's no visual indication from her organs she was a heavy user of either.'

'Any signs of sexual assault?'

'I'll take swabs, but I wouldn't say so.'

'And cause of death?' Shona said.

'Blow to the skull, no question. Subdural haemorrhage.' Sue leaned back against the desk as her assistant stapled closed the Y-shape incision on Emma Johnstone's chest. She leafed through the photographs taken at the scene. 'You're asking me, did she fall or was she pushed?'

'Any ideas?'

Professor Kitchen picked up the dead woman's hand and examined the fingers. 'We've taken nail pairings, but her nails weren't broken and I can't see any other defensive wounds. There's some bruising to the lower spine area, but that's peri–mortem. Given the state of those steps, which were green with algae, I'd say she fell backwards and hit her head. I can't tell you if anyone else was present or if she was pushed. Could her bag and phone have floated away?'

'It's possible,' Shona said. 'Why d'you ask?'

'Because I'm seeing more and more of these.' Sue leaned back and mimicked holding a phone high above her. 'Selfie deaths.'

Shona remembered the first time she'd seen Emma. She was doing just that in the steep garden at High Pines. She felt a guilty rush of relief. 'It was dark, but I suppose it's a possible explanation,' she said.

They changed and Professor Kitchen insisted Shona had a quick coffee before she went upstairs to see Jamie Carlin. Ravi texted an update. So far, no CCTV had been found of Fergus Carlin leaving his flat by bike on the night of Tony's murder.

'Can I pick your brain?' Shona said, as they sat in the bright cafeteria that looked out over grass lawns and young trees.

'I hope you're not going to show me a rash. That's usually what happens when someone wants to pick my brain. Especially at dinner parties.'

Shona smiled. 'No, it's not that. It's about the Tony Carlin case.'

'What's the problem?'

'I have a suspect, but if I can't place him at the scene, then I'm beginning to think we'll never get a result.'

'How can I help?'

'I don't know. It's a bit of a punt. Can Tony Carlin's body tell us anything else?'

Professor Kitchen drained her mug and shook her head. 'I doubt it. Tony Carlin's body was exceptionally contaminated. There was nothing under his fingernails. What about your other forensic items?'

'We tested a bait box, a jacket and an empty wallet. None of them told us anything. The soldiers who cleared the grenades just piled everything in one spot. The tides bring in all sorts, hence the local name, Deadman's Point. Tony Carlin thought the MoD were greenwashing by bigging up their role in protecting rare plants, but I suppose even they can't be held responsible for the litter that washes up on the island.'

Sue pressed a finger to her lips in thought. 'You need to place a suspect at the scene?'

Shona nodded.

'Have you thought of consulting a forensic botanist?'

'How will that help?' Shona said doubtfully. There was always the whiff of dark magic around Slasher Sue, she was a gatekeeper of any number of obscure tests and fields of expertise. It was one of the reasons Shona valued her so highly.

'I'll give you the number of a colleague of mine at the university.' Professor Kitchen took out her phone and scrolled through. 'She's also a palynologist, that's a pollen analyst to you and me. She also does those forecasts you get on the news in the summer. We used to row together, though she doesn't fence,' she said, as if this indicated a major character flaw. 'It sounds like your location might have a specific pattern of vegetation. I know she's done work tracing where drug shipments came from and even discovered where a batch of fake condoms were manufactured.'

Shona's phone pinged as the contact details arrived.

'You see,' Sue said and grinned. 'You never fail to bring me something interesting.'

# Chapter 30

In the brightly painted family room, Laura Carlin looked frailer than ever. Shona stepped forward to hug her. A frost of awkwardness had descended on their friendship. She wanted to tell Laura she didn't judge her for the choices she'd made, and she could be honest with her over the affair with Fergus. But they'd moved to a place where Laura's response would need recording and probably the presence of a solicitor. Kate updated Shona that the doctor was on her way.

Laura's friend Karen came in carrying two plastic cups of coffee and gave Shona a curt nod. She was followed by a short woman with a wide smile, who wore a hijab and a doctor's white coat and introduced herself as Habiba Mansour, a consultant in Respiratory Medicine at Glasgow's Queen Elizabeth Hospital and a researcher in the effects of chemical warfare.

She shook Shona's outstretch hand. 'Call me Biba.' She smiled.

'Is he awake?' Laura said.

Biba's smile widened. 'Yes, he's awake.'

'Oh, thank God!' Laura exclaimed and for a moment, the five women's faces all reflected the joy of that simple fact. 'Can I see him?'

'Yes, we will take you through shortly,' Biba said.

Shona drew the doctor aside. 'I'll need to interview him as soon as possible.'

'I understand this is in relation to a crime,' Biba said, her face serious. 'He's very weak and may be confused, but you can have a few minutes with him.'

'What are Jamie's chances, long term?' Shona said, keeping her voice low, conscious of Laura's glances towards her.

'We're still learning about the chronic effects of nerve agents,' the doctor replied, matching her quiet tones. 'In addition, he may exhibit signs of PTSD, which will magnify the effects. Research shows significant structural brain changes occur in veterans exposed to nerve gas and in the survivors of the Tokyo subway attack. Long-term effects occur even after low exposure. Loss of dexterity, decline of memory.'

'Jamie's just a child,' she said. 'Will it be different for him?'

Biba pursed her lips and looked grave. 'We know from survivors, like the Kurdish children of the 1980s, that effects are always higher in younger victims. He may have problems with his vision, dermatological issues and chronic respiratory diseases. My team will be following Jamie's case in the future and hope to minimise the symp-toms.'

'I see,' Shona said. 'I'd like to go in with Jamie's mother in case he says anything, and then have a few minutes with him alone.'

'Of course. Mummy may become distressed, but we can support her and allow you to do your job,' Biba said firmly.

Shona and Laura donned gowns, masks and gloves. In his weakened state, the risk to Jamie from infection was high.

At the door of his room, Laura grasped Shona's hand.

'I'm glad it's you that's coming in with me,' she said.

Shona squeezed her friend's hand. 'Laura, I think it's best if you don't mention Tony to him.' She wanted a first account, if she could get it, unbiased by any other input.

'I think that's wise,' Biba agreed. 'When he's stronger he may ask, and we can decide together how to break the news to him.'

Jamie was propped up, an oxygen mask over his mouth, eyes closed. His hands were swathed in dressings and wires ran to monitors. The swelling had gone from his face, replaced by blisters and the crusted scabs of his burns.

Laura stopped and gripped the door frame. 'He's not in pain, is he?'

Biba put her arm around Laura's waist. 'He's being treated with a topical anaesthetic, as well as IV pain relief, so he's quite comfortable, but a little sleepy.'

'Can I touch him? I cannae hold his hand,' she said, on the verge of tears.

'Why not touch his shoulder?' Biba said.

Laura went forward, Shona and the doctor on either side of her, and placed her gloved hand on Jamie's narrow chest.

'Jamie, darling, it's your mum.'

Jamie's eyes flickered open and Laura sobbed. His lips moved behind the plastic oxygen mask and formed a word. Mum.

'You're in the hospital, darlin'. D'you know what happened?'

Shona was about to intervene, but Jamie just blinked at his mother and didn't answer.

'His voice is not strong due to the ventilator,' Biba said in Shona's ear.

After two minutes, two nurses in gowns and masks came in and Biba tapped Laura's arm. She'd assured him his brother Jack was at home waiting to play their favourite computer game. When he got back, they'd get a puppy. As agreed, she'd made no mention of his father. Laura looked about to protest that Shona was getting time alone with her son that should be hers, but in the end, she allowed the nurses to lead her out. Shona could hear her crying in the corridor.

'Jamie, it's me, Shona.' She smiled and thought there was a flicker of recognition. 'I came to get you on the beach. Can you remember what happened? Just nod your head if you do.'

Jamie looked at her through half-closed eyes and swallowed. His mouth formed a shape. Mum.

'No, it's Shona,' she said.

He winced, swallowed again and moved his head from side to side in a shake.

'You don't remember?'

A pause and another shake.

'Okay Jamie, thank you. I'll let you rest and get better. I'll be back to see you again.'

'How is he?' Kate asked when Shona met her in the corridor.

'Unrecognisable,' Shona replied. 'He'll have long-term problems according to the doctor.' Shona sighed. 'He says he doesn't remember what happened. If he did stab Tony, why is his DNA missing from the knife?'

'Could he have cleaned it before he discarded it?'

'Maybe,' Shona replied. 'But that suggests a level of organisation and I don't think Jamie had that. I want you to stay here in case he does say something, but as of now, I'm not looking at Jamie Carlin as a suspect, although he may still have more to tell us. And if he does remember, he may feel he needs to protect someone else.'

'His Uncle Fergus?'

'My thought exactly,' said Shona. 'If he turns up here to see his nephew, he doesn't get access, understand? If even sets foot in the hospital, call me.'

# Chapter 31

Outside the hospital, Shona found a bench and took out her phone. The forensic botanist, Professor Angela Macrae, answered Shona's call and listened while she explained her problem.

'I can help you with that,' she said straight away. 'Hang on while I look it up.'

Shona thanked her lucky stars for straight-talking Glasgow women. There was no *email me and I'll look at it* nonsense.

'Okay, part of Kilcatrin Ranges is a triple-SI, a Site of Special Scientific Interest. There's MoD Integrated Land Management Plan in place, which co-ordinates the needs of training with the overall ecology of the area,' she read.

'Is that good?' Shona said.

'It's very good,' Professor Macrae replied. 'It means many species survive that would otherwise be lost if it were to be developed commercially. Each area has its unique pollen print. I'll need to visit and take samples. I'll create a map and then we can compare those against your suspect's clothing.'

'It's been over a week. Will that make a difference?' Shona asked.

'It's a relatively indestructible fingerprint. Even if you put clothes through a washing machine, the pollen profile will remain. I can be there tomorrow, if you can arrange the access.'

Shona thanked the professor, ended the call and dialled another number.

'Simon, are you still at Kilcatrin?'

'Yes. It's pretty quiet here, just the hard-core protestors who haven't got jobs to go back to.'

She'd heard the clean-up operation was packing up. The flow of armaments onto the beaches had trickled to almost nothing. Until next time, Shona thought.

'Jamie Carlin just woke up, but he claims to remember nothing about what happened on the beach.'

'It's good news he's awake,' Wallace said. 'His recall might improve.'

'That's what the doctor said.' Shona remembered what Robocop had told her that morning about the MDP requesting Shona's team stay on the case. 'Thanks for the vote of confidence, by the way.'

'I couldn't possibly comment,' he said.

Shona laughed. 'Can I come and see you tomorrow?'

'I'd be delighted.'

'I'm bringing a forensic botanist.'

'I can live with that,' he said. 'I'll arrange access. Text me the details.'

As Shona drove back to the office, she thought through her plan for the forensic botanist. Fergus claimed he'd never visited the area. Should they test anyone else? They already knew Jamie was there, although Shona was convinced he couldn't have wielded the knife. Then she remembered the old Kilcatrin map with its hidden tracks and overgrown gates. Fergus grew up in that house and still visited it regularly. He would have seen the map. Who else might have seen it? Potentially anyone who visited Old Jimmy.

She'd get one shot at this and she had to be thorough. For the technique and to stand up in court, the jury had to believe it worked. The only other person who had seen the map regularly was Laura. For elimination, they'd test her too. If both of them were telling the truth, that they'd never visited Kilcatrin, then she was right back where she started and probably a few thousand pounds lighter. She could hear Robocop's derision, *you spent a couple of grand on a forensic florist?*

When she got back, Murdo came into her office. He'd shed his jacket and his shirt had become untucked on one side. 'We've picked Emma up on CCTV at the harbour.'

Shona followed Murdo to where Vinny sat behind his curtain-wall of monitors. On the screen, a grainy Emma Johnstone was getting out of her car. A figure walked up and joined her. She swung long braids over her shoulder.

'I recognise that lassie,' Murdo said.

'You should,' Shona said, her heart thumping. 'You saw her yesterday when she got off the boat. Her name's Willow Moon.'

Shona checked the CCTV time clock on the screen. Two hours before this meeting, Willow had stood on Kirkness seafront and told Shona she was taking Becca tree planting. A few seconds later, Shona's worst fears were confirmed, when Becca, her long dark hair tied up in a scarf, walked into the frame and shook Emma's hand.

'I know where they are,' Shona said, taking out her phone and calling Becca's number. Straight to voicemail. Youngsters never turned their phone off. She either had it on silent or was chatting to her mates about the piercings.

'They're both at a tattoo and piercing parlour in town,' Shona said, forwarding the picture Becca had sent her earlier. 'Do me a favour, Murdo, go and pick them up. Take Rhys Marshall with you. I don't want to send a uniform patrol and give them a scare.'

While she waited for the girls, Ravi came into the main office and hung his funnel neck parka up carefully on the coat stand. He tapped her door and entered, carrying two takeaway coffees.

He put one down on her desk. 'I heard about the CCTV. Reckoned you might need the caffeine.'

Shona sighed. 'Thanks, Rav. Any joy with Fergus?'

'Says he sold the bike cash-in-hand to a guy in a pub.'

'You've got to be kidding me,' Shona said. 'He's smart enough to be forensically aware, isn't he? Think he's covering his tracks?'

Ravi took a sip of his coffee. 'Aye. I do. He had money problems he blamed on his brother, and he was shagging his wife. Got to be in the frame.'

'Then let's nail him. Give Vinny a hand, pal, would you? See if you can spot Fergus nipping out on his bike.'

Shona's phone rang. It was Simon Wallace.

'Just confirming permission for your professor. And thanks for the info from your contact in Cumbria. Useful,' he said. Shona had emailed him a brief roundup of what Harry Jackson had told her abound the historic arms dumping. 'We should have a chat about it tomorrow, discuss future safety protocols or active clean-up plans. Or we could brainstorm it over a drink sometime.'

'Yes, okay,' she said. Really, what was there to say? *MoD, sort your shit*, was the gist of it. Was he flirting with her? In person she might have been able to tell, though given Simon Wallace's demeanour, possibly not.

She had to admit, Simon Wallace had grown on her. Perhaps that very blandness that made him unmemorable also meant the absence of those personality snags which seem amusing at first, but quickly become grating. Also, he was a useful source of information and she knew he was as invested as she was in resolving the case.

'I've my hands full at the minute with the Carlins and an unexplained death in Kirkcudbright.' A thought occurred to her. 'The victim is Emma Johnstone, a blogger and journalist. She was digging around on Tony's death but my one of my team thinks she also had a pen name, The Insider. It's a column on Viva Caledonia covering environmental politics, and things like Faslane. Mean anything to you?'

'Yes, I know who she is. She's been here talking to the gate protestors. So she's your victim? Interesting. I'm not sure we knew she was behind The Insider. Thanks for that.'

'It's my DC Ravi Sarwar you need to thank.'

'I owe him a pint then.'

'Running up quite a bar tab with us, aren't you?' Shona laughed.

'Don't worry, I intend to pay my debts,' he said. 'See you tomorrow.'

Flirting. Definitely flirting, Shona thought.

Ravi put his head round the door. 'Willow Moon,' he said. 'Probably a good idea for you to see this if you've got her in for interview.' He held out a printed sheet.

'A change of name registration,' Shona said. 'I did wonder if that was her birth name. Michaela Campbell? Is that what she changed it from?'

'Aye,' said Ravi. 'But look who her father is.'

'Michael Campbell,' Shona said. 'The Michael Campbell who owns all the scallop boats, of Campbell Shellfish fame?'

'The very same. And she's his only child. The business is valued at around £20 million.'

So, not the poor abandoned child Shona thought she was, but a rich heiress. Material wealth could hide other forms of poverty, though.

'No wonder she was so well informed about the scallop business,' Shona said. 'Michael Campbell is a piece of work by all accounts. Perhaps she's got more than an ethical reason for hating the practice.'

## Chapter 32

Willow sat in an interview room with PC Christine Jamieson. Along with her partner PC Kirsten O'Carroll, they formed the formidable 'Two Kirsties', beat cops who Murdo termed 'handy lassies' and rated highly. Jamieson had taken off her stab vest and was chatting to Willow about the Gaia Collective and their aims. Becca was next door, giving Murdo a statement.

Shona put her laptop on the table and told Willow she wasn't being cautioned.

'You've not been arrested...' Shona let the *yet* hang in the air. 'I'm interviewing you as a potential witness and you can leave at any time. I'm sure you understand your rights, but feel free to ask me if you have questions.' With Willow's protesting past and arrest record, her knowledge probably matched Shona's own. Willow nodded and Shona continued. 'Was Emma a friend? If she was, then I'm sure you'd like to help us find out why she died.'

Willow folded her arms in her habitual attitude of defiance, but then she said, 'I didn't know she was dead till your guys picked us up. What happened?'

'She was found near the steps down to the water at Kirkcudbright harbour. She had a head injury.'

Christine Jamieson leaned forward and poured Willow a cup of water.

Shona opened the laptop and turned it to face her. 'Willow, I'd just like you to confirm this is you.'

The young woman leaned forward and looked at the screen. 'Yeah, that's us.'

'We know Emma arrived at the car park at three p.m. from the time on her ticket. Was your meeting pre-arranged?'

'Not really, she just texted me.'

'So you were friends?'

Willow shrugged. 'She writes about environmental issues. I knew her from campaigns. We catch up now and then.'

'We know she working on a story about Tony Carlin. Did Emma think you could help her with that?'

'Like I said yesterday, I didn't know the guy.'

'Was it something to do with scallop dredging? With your father, perhaps, and his business?' Shona saw immediately she'd scored an emotional bullseye, if nothing else.

Willow glared at her. 'I've had nothing to do with that man for years. I don't consider him my father,' she said stiffly.

'I'm sorry, it must be hard coming from Campbell Shellfish, knowing what the business involves.'

'That's not me, or my mother, and it never was,' she spat. 'Yes, Emma was working on the Beaufort's Dyke story and I wanted to help her. Maybe one of your MoD friends killed her, did you think of that?'

Shona had already dismissed that fleeting option. The location where Emma was found was the primary crime scene. There was blood on the top step. If someone wanted to do the job properly, they'd have slipped her body into the harbour and let the tide wash away all the evidence.

'Did Emma have a lot of enemies?' Shona said. The woman clearly had a talent for trouble. Another investigating officer would put Shona squarely in that camp.

'It's what happens when you tell the truth,' Willow said.

'And what was the *truth* about Beaufort's Dyke and Tony Carlin's death that she wanted to talk about?' Shona said.

'It's not the only environmental scandal out there,' Willow snapped. 'If you really want to know, she wanted to talk about the illegal cockle trade. That's an environmental crime you should be investigating.' Willow stabbed a finger at Shona. 'Now I've had enough of this. I'd like to go.' She gathered her jacket from her lap and stood up. Jamieson moved to the door.

'One last question, Willow,' Shona said. 'Did you meet anyone else with Emma?'

Willow shook her head and swung her jeans jacket over her shoulders. 'I think she was seeing someone later.'

'D'you know who?'

'That's two questions. And no, I don't.'

–

Becca was waiting downstairs when her mother finished. It was Shona's first chance to examine the nose piercing, a thickish metal ring in Becca's right nostril.

'That looks painful,' Shona said. 'Is it?'

'No,' Becca lied.

Shona had googled *nose piercing and aftercare*. It would be at least four months before Becca could swap it for something smaller. They'd all have to get used to it.

'I've read the statement you gave Murdo,' Shona said as they pulled out of the car park and edged their way through the traffic towards the bypass.

'Are you allowed to do that?' Becca said.

'Yes, although not because I'm your mother,' Shona snapped. 'Did you know you were going to meet Emma?'

'Didn't see any harm in it. She stayed at High Pines, didn't she?'

'And did she ask you about Tony Carlin's death or the family?'

Becca screwed up her face. 'Yeah, but what could I tell her? Murdo showed me the CCTV of us talking. It's horrible to think she died not long after that.'

'Did you and Willow leave together?'

'No, I caught the bus. Willow said she was gonna hang out there for a while.' Becca sounded a little peeved, as if the older women had excluded her.

'Willow told me you were going tree planting.'

'Tree planting? In May?' Becca snorted and looked appalled at the suggestion. 'That's an autumn and winter thing. We went shopping. Second hand stuff.'

Shona had goaded Willow over her father, using it as leverage to get an honest reaction. It had worked. She'd rather the girl had just parked her attitude and co-operated. Now, she realised Willow had played her. She'd taken Becca to meet Emma who, having failed to use Rob as a conduit, was now targeting her daughter. Emma really did have a talent for making enemies. It looked to Shona she'd made one too many, and this time it had gotten her killed.

Shona dropped Becca off at High Pines. Rob met them at the back door and Shona told him it was a flying visit. She had to get back to the office.

'Could you not have stopped her?' he said to Shona, pointing at Becca's nose ring.

'She's over the legal age,' Shona said. 'Only just, mind.'

He frowned. 'I'm not happy,' he said to his daughter. 'I think it makes you look like you should be in a pen at the Royal Highland Show.'

'Daaad! That's so offensive. You callin' me a cow?'

'I'm saying you are beautiful enough without iron-mongery in your face.'

Becca stomped through the kitchen and slammed the door. A second door slammed upstairs when she reached her room.

'Make her something to eat and a hot drink, will you?' Shona said. 'She'll need to take some painkillers or she won't sleep tonight. Remember, she's just given a state-ment about meeting Emma Johnstone before her death. Murdo took it, but he'll have been thorough. Think it shocked her a bit.'

Rob stood in the utility room, hand on hips and shook his head. 'What was she doing there?'

'It seems like Emma got Willow to bring her.' Shona stepped back through the open back door. 'She was asking about Beaufort's Dyke and Tony Carlin's murder. Perhaps Emma thought, since she couldn't get to you, she'd try Becca.' She checked the time on her phone. Better make tracks.

'And I suppose that's my fault,' Rob said, his eyes wide with indignation as he stared at her.

Shona took a deep breath, but it wasn't enough. Inside, she felt something snap.

Shona came into the utility room with such force that Rob took a step back.

'You've no idea, have you?' she hissed at him. 'If this turns out to be murder, Robocop will bring in another officer and that'll be it.' She pointed a finger in his face and had the satisfaction of seeing a crease of worry spring up across his forehead.

'It's all round the village about how you were carrying on with that lassie. She left High Pines in a hurry. It wouldn't take long to put two and two together and make five.' The rage she'd been holding at bay ever since she saw Rob and Emma on the terrace surged upwards.

'We were both here at High Pines. We're each other's alibi. I know neither you nor I had anything to do with her death, but that won't be enough.' Her voice rose and she couldn't stop it. 'It'll look like I covered up my husband's affair with a dead woman. Robocop will have me out and there'll be nothing I can do about it. Not even Mars Bar Munroe will be able to help me.'

She took a step towards the back door then turned back to face a grim-faced Rob.

'Even if neither of us are charged with murder or attempting to defeat the ends of justice, what about all that Milton McConnell shit you're in? How will that look? My case against Delfont. What he did to me. His corruption. Who's gonnae believe that now?'

—

It took the entire drive back to Dumfries for Shona to calm down. When a car pulled out of a side road, forcing her to brake sharply, she leaned on the horn. Foot off the gas, she told herself, or *Local DI in Road Rage Incident* would be the headline.

When she swept into her office, her face was so grim that people stepped aside.

Shona's desk phone rang. 'Yes?'

'Everything okay?' Dan Ridley said. He must have caught the edge in her voice.

'Yeah, sorry Dan, Just full on here at the minute.'

'Okay, I won't keep you,' he said. 'I left you a message.'

Shona took out her phone and realised she'd switched it to silent for the interview with Willow. There was a string of missed calls from Dan and also a message from the forensics team at Gartcosh.

'I just wanted to give you an update,' Dan said. 'The cockle rustling you mentioned?'

Suddenly, he had her full attention. Her own enquiries via the lifeboat had come to nothing. 'Go on.'

'I had a chat with some of the local community support officers in the port towns and also Harry Jackson had his ear to the ground.'

Dan seemed to have risen in his father's friend's estimation. Or perhaps the old man had developed an eco-conscience in the light of the Beaufort's Dyke incident.

'What's the news?' Shona said impatiently.

'I think you may be on to something,' Dan said, and she could hear the note of excitement in his voice. He didn't see eye-to-eye with his DI at Cumbria CID, which meant he was low on the pecking border for jobs. Anything beyond the mundane caught his imagination.

'There's rumour of net bags of cockles being loaded onto lorries,' he said. 'They're bound for the Dutch and Spanish markets. I spoke with the local inshore fisheries protection people. They've been on the lookout for gangs with rakes and buckets or tractors. But some beds out in the Solway can't be reached on foot from the shore but can be trawled like scallops. Their patrol boat hasn't caught anyone, but they're still looking.'

Shona updated Dan on the possibility that Emma Johnstone was pursuing the same story and that it was connected to her death.

'Okay boss, I'll follow this up,' he said.

# Chapter 33

Shona pulled up by the gate security post at Kilcatrin Ranges. A small knot of protestors waved placards, but otherwise ignored her arrival. A bright red camper van sat in the car park. The front seats had thick sheepskin covers and Shona thought since a forensic botanist must spend a lot of time in the field, quite literally, Professor Macrae liked to travel in comfort.

A text came from Simon Wallace, *ETA 5 min*.

A short time later, a Land Rover pulled up at the inner gate on to the ranges. Special Rhys Marshall got out, followed by a woman with a leather bush hat and a small backpack. She had on a long-sleeved pink shirt over khaki activity trousers well served by pockets. Her mousy hair was tied back from her round face. Walking boots of a sturdy nature brought her across the tarmac towards Shona.

'I'm sorry I couldn't be here to meet you this morning,' Shona said, offering her hand. She'd been delayed by a budget and strategy meeting and then tailbacks from an RTA that had forced her to drive the long way round. Fortunately, she'd sent Marshall ahead. He could put time spent at the gym to good use carrying bags and boxes around for Professor Macrae. The apology was also directed at Simon Wallace. She didn't want to give the impression she was avoiding him.

'It's fine,' Professor Macrae said with a cheery smile. 'Inspector Wallace here has been entertaining me. I'm Angela, by the way.' A warm hand grasped Shona's in return.

Shona looked at Simon standing impassively by and wondered how entertaining he could be. Probably not jokes or card tricks, she concluded. Definitely not karaoke.

'I've completed my sampling,' Professor Macrae said. 'I'll have a vegetation species map for you in a few days.'

'Forgive me,' Shona said, 'but how does this actually work?'

'C'mon, I'll show you,' Angela replied.

They crossed to the camper van. The professor opened the tailgate and retrieved a laptop from a locked cabinet, flipping open the screen.

'It's popular to say we live a surveillance society,' she said, 'but we're tracked by more than CCTV. You'll know from your work that each time we visit a place, it's possible we leave a trace, like DNA or fingerprints, but we also carry something away.'

Angela turned the screen to face Shona. 'Here, have a look. These are pollen grains from different plants.'

Shona peered at a multitude of shapes, from hairy lemons to elongated doughnuts and old-fashioned light bulbs.

'That'll give you an idea of the variety we're talking about. Dumfries and Galloway are home to approximately two and a half thousand flowering plant species, and pollen is all around you. Wherever you walk, the abundance of each plant is different. Kilcatrin has an unusual mixture. That gives a very specific profile.'

Professor Macrae pulled up a new series of images showing tiny shapes and pointed to a triangular object on the screen. 'This is hawthorn pollen magnified about a thousand times, and here's some other common plants.'

Shona saw the dandelion grains were jagged and spikey. Tulip pollen was rounded with a granular surface, and the wild garlic boat-shaped and smooth. All looked distinctively different.

'And the proportions of those on someone's clothing will show us where they walked?' Shona said.

'Precisely,' Angela replied. 'I'll be looking at the seams at the bottom of jeans. Zips and pockets. Anywhere that traps. I've taken a broad range of samples through the woods and down to the shore.'

'How specific will your map be?' Rhys Marshall said, then shot a fearful glance at Shona. She smiled her encouragement at him. She liked her team to expand their horizons.

'Very,' Professor Macrae replied. 'It'll show not just pollens, but seeds and plant fibres like dry bracken. Kilcatrin also has species like *Paris Quadrifolia* and *Erinus Alpinus*, commonly called Herb Paris and the Hairy Foxglove, that were introduced at some point only to the ranges so they're extremely rare in the region.'

Shona pictured the ancient trees, a wash of bluebells around their feet and the scent of wild garlic heavy in the air. The cliffs and shore were different again. She didn't know the names of the flowers but she could tell Kilcatrin Island, with its special status as a bird sanctuary, looked nothing like Ross Island, where they'd taken Becca and her friend, just a few miles away along the coast.

'Inspector Wallace mentioned there was a possible access route,' Angela said. 'Past the farm to a gate in the hedge.'

'We think our victim drove in that way, so it's possible his attacker did too.'

'In that case, specific pollen will be present in the air filters of his vehicle if you can identify it.'

'What about a bike?' Shona said.

'The principle's the same. Where the spokes meet the wheel rim or caught in the chain oil are good traps.'

Shona nodded, considering. Anything that tied the threads of a case more tightly together was a welcome possibility. And juries liked forensics. They'd seen it on TV and come to expect it. 'Thanks,' she said. 'I'll keep that in mind.'

'I'd better be off,' Angela said. 'I hope you locked that Landy. I wouldn't want my morning's work stolen,' she teased Wallace.

'Car theft isn't a big issue in this neighbourhood, Professor Macrae,' he replied.

Angela turned to Rhys, who was still peering at the images on the screen.

'If you help me with those bags, I'll tell you the story of how I traced a container load of fake condoms. Now that's a skill a young man like yourself might appreciate.'

The Special blushed as he set off with the professor to retrieve the remaining samples from the MoD Land Rover.

'I've already heard this story,' Shona said as Wallace looked at the retreating backs of the professor and her new assistant. 'Slasher Sue told me she tracked the consignment back to a factory in northern India, thus performing a service to mankind. And womankind.'

'It's a pity you missed our field trip,' he said. 'There's a whole forensic world of fungal spores we only scratched the surface of.'

'Sounds fascinating.' Shona grinned. 'I'd still prefer it to discussing budgets or sitting in traffic.' She gazed over the flush of green spreading from hedgerows to treetops. 'It's beautiful here. When someone isn't lobbing high explosive at it.'

'I think the era of lobbing may be coming to an end,' Simon replied. 'There'll still be a testing requirement but mostly the threat isn't from someone pointing a bigger gun at you. It's cyber. Or biological.'

'I'm sure we're a match for them.' Shona closed her eyes, feeling the sun on her face.

'For all our sakes I hope so.'

She opened her eyes again and found he was looking at her.

'There's "we", is there?' he said.

'I think we're on the same side,' Shona replied. 'But don't go taking that for granted.'

'Wouldn't dream of it.' A hint of a smile touched the corner of his mouth.

'Rhys,' Shona called to the Special loitering by the camper van. 'Now you've had a lovely day out, I want you to go back to the office and help Murdo with the forensic pick up of clothing from Fergus and Laura Carlin.'

'Yes, ma'am,' he said.

When they'd said goodbye to Professor Macrae, Wallace turned to her.

'What about you?' he said to Shona. 'You heading back?'

'In a bit,' she said. 'I've got half an hour. I believe you wanted to discuss systems for monitoring and safety of Beaufort's Dyke.'

'Do you require the discussion to be minuted?' he said.

'All I require is coffee.' Shona smiled.

'I think we can run to that.'

–

Back at Dumfries CID, the mountain of CCTV evidence from roads, private business and traffic cameras was diminishing, but it was painfully slow. Kate retrieved clothes from Laura's, Shona reminding her about the jeans and fleece the woman had been wearing when they first turned up to break the news of Tony's death. Fergus's garments were more of a guess, but his wardrobe wasn't an extensive one. The clothes would go to Professor Macrae's team so the forensics burden at Gartcosh labs wouldn't be added to. Ravi was still looking for the bike and had told her earlier that morning that he'd called the forensics lab and promised to send them all the chocolate they could eat if they'd prioritise Fergus Carlin's DNA.

When Shona saw she had a missed call from Gartcosh, it seemed like his tactic might have worked. She checked the clock. The forensics team was probably at lunch. She hit redial on the off chance. It rang out. She was just about to end the call when a breathless voice answered.

'Hello? You just caught me. I'm only in the door.'

'It's DI Shona Oliver down in Dumfries returning your call.'

'Ah yes,' the woman said. 'Been having quite a time of it, haven't you? Anyway, the full email report will drop later but I thought you'd like a heads-up on the fishing boat.'

'This is the fire damage report on the *Arcturus*?' It had slipped her mind.

'That's the fella.'

Shona could hear tapping on a keyboard.

'No phosphorous contamination, you'll be glad to hear. The fire was due to an accelerant spillage.'

'An accelerant?' Shona said. 'Which one?'

'Petrol.'

Shona thanked the woman. She stood up from her desk, crossed to the door and called Murdo in.

'Did we ever get a confirmed source of those cash payments to Tony and Fergus Carlin?' she said.

'Nope,' Murdo replied. 'Want me to refer him to the Revenue?'

'Not just yet. I may have just found his golden goose. Tell everyone to stop what they're doing. I want all out resources focused on a single line of enquiry.'

'Okay, boss,' Murdo nodded. 'Is Fergus Carlin the lucky individual?'

'He is. And you better send out for chips later. By the end of the day, I want all outstanding action connected to him completed. If he's so much as blown his nose in the last two weeks, I'll want to know about it. But we get our ducks in a row before we tackle him.'

They worked on, the slow deliberate sieving of evidence that was the mainstay of any enquiry. 'Not all car chases and shoot outs, is?' said Murdo as he refilled her coffee cup.

She was just wondering if she should text Rob and ask him to make her a midnight sandwich to leave in the fridge for later, when Dan called from Cumbria. 'I'm about to prove why I am your favourite detective constable,' he said, the excitement in his voice barely contained. 'And you should give me a job immediately.'

'Go on. Impress me,' Shona said.

'Your cockle rustlers. I've got them.'

Shona got up and tapped the glass of her office partition. A number of faces looked up, including Murdo's. She gave him a thumbs up. He came in, his face anxious. More heads turned throughout the office as staff sensed a breakthrough.

'What exactly have you got?' Shona said to Dan, putting him on speakerphone.

'The works. I've CCTV of the Carlin brothers in Silloth unloading stolen cockles, and I've got a witness,' he finished with a flourish.

'You wee star!' Shona said. 'You are my favourite constable and I don't care who knows it. Ping the video over to me.'

'Aye, the boy done good,' Murdo beamed when Shona hung up.

She went to the door of her office and leaned out. 'Ravi, take Bram the search dog's picture off the board. We have a new champion.' She updated the team on Dan's news. There was a round of applause. Ravi insisted he would get a frame and keep Bram on his desk as a virtual pet until he had a dog of his own.

Shona went back to her office. The video from Dan had dropped into her email. There was no doubt about the ID. It was dark and the camera's infrared sensor had kicked in, washing the images of colour, but there was the stocky swagger of Tony and his tall, slim brother hauling net sacks of cockles from the quayside into the back of a van.

A minute later, Ravi was in front of her desk, bouncing on the balls of his feet. 'We have a tie for constable of the week,' he said. 'My offer of chocolate to forensics seems to have done the trick. We've got Fergus Carlin's DNA back.'

'And...' Shona said.

'It's a match for the glove,' Ravi said.

'Well done. Ravi,' Shona said. 'Draw up an arrest strategy and I'll get started on an interview plan. Tomorrow morning, I want Fergus Carlin picked up and a full search of his flat.'

'D'you think he's a flight risk?' Murdo said. 'We went for his clothes today and he's got thon boat. Should we talk to the coastguard?'

Shona took out her phone. 'No need. I've been keeping an eye on the *Arcturus*.' She opened the Marine Tracking app that Harry Jackson had shown her. 'I learnt a lesson in new technology from an old seafarer.' She turned the screen to Murdo, the chart of the Galloway coast with Kirkcudbright at its centre. 'I've an alert on the *Arcturus*. The second she starts moving, I'll know about it.'

# Chapter 34

Every few hours, Shona woke and checked the app on her phone. *Arcturus* stayed at her berth. The arrest team, led by Ravi, would go in at five a.m. and search Fergus's flat. Dan was due over from Cumbria as the illegal catch of cockles had been landed there. It would be a cross-border operation. Shona wanted every bit of evidence gathered and no loopholes for Fergus Carlin to slip through.

By six a.m., Shona was at her desk. Ravi texted her. Everything had gone to plan. Fergus would arrive shortly at the custody suite and the search was ongoing. She took a vitamin pill and two painkillers, washing them down from the refillable water bottle Becca had got her at Christmas.

Fergus Carlin sat impassively in the interview room when Shona came in with Dan. His habitual black jeans and hoodie had gone to forensics, and he wore the standard custody costume of grey top and sweatpants. Shona recognised the man next to him in the dark suit as one of the duty solicitors. They confirmed their names for the record. Ravi and the others would be crowded around the relayed video monitors in the CID room.

'Fergus,' Shona began, 'DC Ridley from Cumbria would like to show you something.'

Dan had taken off his jacket and rolled up the sleeves of his blue shirt. He turned the laptop round and played the video of Fergus and Tony unloading the stolen cockles.

'Is this you and your brother in the video?' Dan said.

Fergus glanced at the screen, then looked away.

When he didn't answer, Shona took out two printed sheets from her file.

'I've yours and Tony's bank statements.' She ran her pen down the series of cash deposits. 'This is where the money came from, isn't it, Fergus? Not your cleaning jobs.'

The solicitor leaned forward. 'My client reserves his right not to answer your questions.'

'Thank you. I gathered that,' Shona said. 'But Fergus, it's really in your interest to talk to us, give us your side of the story, because right now, you're in a lot of trouble.

'It was a good ploy, making us think as fishermen you were too proud to tell us how you really earned your living. Well, are you proud of this?' She indicated the frozen black-and-white image of himself and his brother. 'Robbing cockle beds closed so numbers could recover. Robbing future fishermen like your nephews of any prospect of a living.' Shona paused and stared at Fergus Carlin until he looked up and met her eyes. 'But that's not all you robbed them of, is it?'

Fergus shifted in his chair, then leaned back and folded his arms.

'Tell me about the fire on your boat? It wasn't an electrical fault, was it?' She laid the forensic report on the table. 'Now, Inspector Wallace from the MoD thinks you were recovering armaments from Beaufort's Dyke for terrorist purposes.'

The solicitor sat up and a swift look of puzzled panic crossed Fergus Carlin's face.

'He may well want to talk to you, but I think this fire was about something else. The other night, a man was severely burned, Billy Kennedy of the *Harvester*, out of

Maryport. D'you know him? What have you and your friends been up to, Fergus? Are you trying to start a border war?'

Fergus's eyes were wide now and his leg jumped beneath the table, but his mouth was a firm line.

'But frankly, DC Ridley, illegal fishing and even the MoD are the least of your worries,' she said quietly. 'Tell me what happened at Kilcatrin the night Tony died?'

Fergus's leg stopped jumping. 'I've never been to Kilca-trin.'

'We know about your affair with Laura. There's video of you in a pub car park, all over your brother's wife,' Shona said, her voice rising. 'We were even called to a domestic at the house. Two months back. Were you the cause of that? Did Tony find out about you and Laura? What happened out at Kilcatrin, Fergus?'

'I dinnae know what you're on about,' Fergus shouted. 'I don't care about some old farm. I've never set foot in the place.'

His solicitor put out a hand to calm his client and opened his mouth to object, but Shona got in first. She pulled a photograph from her folder and slammed it down on the table.

'So, how do you explain this? A glove, recovered from the scene, with your DNA on it.'

Fergus stared at the photograph, then picked it up.

'You owe Laura and Tony's children an explanation, Fergus,' Shona said. 'What happened at Kilcatrin?'

Fergus sighed and then he said quietly, 'It was all Tony's fault.'

Beside her, Shona felt Dan edge forward in his seat.

'The money from the cockles was all that kept us afloat,' Fergus began, his eyes on the glove. 'Tony wanted to end it. He'd developed an environmental conscience and was going to expose the business.' Fergus stopped and licked his lips. 'You're right, we'd been threatened by other fishermen. They chucked petrol on the *Arcturus* and set it alight. It was a warning.' He shook his head 'What was Tony doing? He'd a family and Laura and he was just willing to throw that all away for this white knight fantasy that he was gonna save the world.'

Fergus met Shona's eyes, as if trying to convince himself as much as her. 'He wasnae gonnae save anything. If we hadnae taken the cockles, someone else would. A Scottish boat or an English one. And if Tony had talked to youse lot or the coastguard, he'd have got us both killed.'

'What happened at Kilcatrin?'

'I went out to reason with him, but he wouldnae listen. I didnae know Jamie was with him. It just happened.'

'How did you get out there? You've no vehicle.'

'Bike,' Fergus said. 'That's why youse were asking about it, wasn't it?'

'Thank you, Fergus,' Shona said. 'You're doing the right thing for Laura and the boys.'

'I know I am,' he said quietly.

'Okay, we'll take a break for a minute, then DS Ridley and Ravi will help you with your statement.'

Two hours later, Shona scanned through the charging document Murdo and the team had put together and forwarded it on to the Procurator Fiscal's office. The plastic glove and DNA had been a gamble. The defence might claim contamination at the family home or that the item was used by Fergus on a previous occasion and reused by Tony on the night of his death, but it had been enough to provoke his confession. She waited five minutes, then gave the fiscal a call. She had no real doubt about the outcome. Neither, it seemed, did the fiscal. The verdict was immediate. Charge him. An immense wave of relief flowed over Shona. It had taken ten days, but finally, they'd got their man. Tony Carlin would have justice. The wider damage to the family would take a great deal longer to heal, but finally, that process could begin. Today, she could celebrate a result for her team, and there'd be a few drinks that evening. Laura would need her support and now, for as long as it took, Shona was at last free to give it.

# Chapter 35

Shona phoned Wallace to relay the news.

'Are you coming over for a drink? I'm buying the first round. Dan Ridley's here from Cumbria CID. You should meet him. He's a useful officer, under-appreciated. And of course you owe Ravi a beer for the Insider tip,' she teased.

'Thanks, I'll be there,' he said. 'It'll be a farewell drink too. I'm back to Glasgow tomorrow.'

'Okay,' Shona said lightly. 'We'll see you off Dumfries style. I should give you the heads-up. Murdo's ex-rugby and can hold his booze, but he does tend to quote Rabbie Burns's poetry when he's had a few.'

'I'll consider that a warning.'

Shona ended the call and pulled together the papers on her desk. There was always a slight feeling of anti-climax after the initial euphoria of an arrest passed. Was that all it was? Several months of report writing and cross-checking lay ahead until the Procurator Fiscal was happy that Fergus's case could go to trial. Fatigue replaced adrenaline. She knew that, but below it all a sense of restlessness lurked. A weekend at home with Becca and Rob, and lifeboat training on Sunday morning would be a chance to reset.

There were a few other people she should break the news to. Laura she would see in person. Kate was up at the hospital with Laura waiting for Shona to arrive. She needed to discuss with Kate her FLO exit strategy and how she would transition Laura to the Procurator Fiscal's Victim Liaison officer, but that could be done next week. She'd speak to Robocop and he could talk to the press office.

She dialled DCI Robinson's number and received perfunctory congratulations.

'Thank you, sir,' she said. 'There's just a few outstanding points to clear up, but I'm sure they'll be tied up soon.'

'Wind it up by Friday, Shona,' he said. 'You've got a confession. His DNA's on the glove found at the scene, if not the murder weapon. That's unfortunate.'

He made it sound like her fault.

'But the jury will be made to understand. Killers are more forensically aware these days. There's an obvious motive, and opportunity. Just get your documentation in order and the fiscal will make it stick.'

He was right. They'd got what they needed.

'What about that other fisherman?'

'There was nothing to indicate Ben MacNeill's death wasn't suicide.' There was no note and they would probably never know what tipped him over the edge. It was another tragedy that could be chalked up to the fishing industry's decline, alcohol and despair.

'And the journalist lassie? That needs sorting, the press are saying she died in the line of duty. You know what it's like, some bampot will start a crusade. Anything to show it's suspicious?'

'We can't place anyone at the scene. Bag and phone are missing but given the location, they may have washed away.' Shona cleared her throat. 'Professor Kitchen ventured the theory she may have slipped and fallen taking a selfie, but that's difficult to prove. We're trying to get access to her cloud storage.'

'Well Slasher Sue knows her onions,' he said in a tone that convinced Shona he both agreed with the verdict and disapproved of Professor Kitchen in general. She probably scared the pants off him. 'Keep me updated. Get it done. Remember, Shona, clear-ups count.'

–

Shona walked between the young trees in the hospital garden, sipped her takeaway coffee and took a minute to prepare herself for the meeting with Laura. There was no sign of the environmental protestors, but someone had tied a bunch of flowers to the post in the car park with the homemade sign saying, *Close Kilcatrin Ranges Now!* propped up beside it. A sentiment she supported. Maybe Simon Wallace was right, and the day was coming. If the Russians were willing to send biological warfare onto the streets of Salisbury it was time to reassess exactly where the balance of threat lay. The protestors would claim their victory but in the end it would be the shifting sands of geo-politics that sealed the deal.

Shona made her way upstairs to the intensive care unit. Jamie Carlin's nurse told her he was doing well. Shona went to the inner door of Jamie's room and looked in. He was on his side, curled like a much younger child, his burns raw and yellow with the topical anaesthetic. She tried to console herself with the fact that if the lifeboat hadn't found him when they did, she'd be investigating two fatalities.

Laura was in the family room, reading a magazine and ignoring Kate. When Shona told Laura that Fergus had been charged, she looked blank and disbelieving.

'Where is he now?' she said.

'Don't worry, Laura, he's been remanded,' Shona said. 'It's over. You can concentrate on Jamie getting well.' She paused. 'We'll probably need to talk to you when we put the case files together, but don't worry about that now.' She didn't want to raise the spectre of Laura and Fergus's affair. It was bound to come out in court. 'There's just one thing I want to ask you. Was Tony ever violent at home?'

There were reports of Tony's drunken temper and Shona wanted to be prepared if Fergus's legal team offered self-defence as a factor.

'Not really,' Laura said, turning the pages of her magazine and not looking at Shona. 'It was nothing.'

'It isn't speaking ill of the dead, Laura. You can tell me, and there's trained counsellors to talk to.'

Laura shrugged, wound a strand of her fair hair around her finger, and shook her head. It was clear she wasn't ready to talk about it.

'Jamie's asking about his father,' Laura said. 'I had to tell him.'

'Okay,' Shona said, exchanging a look with Kate. 'I'll just pop in to see Jamie, then I'll leave you to it. We'll talk again soon. I'll call you.' She crossed and gave her unresisting friend a hug. 'Don't worry. You're not on your own. Everything will be fine.'

Shona put on her gown and mask with the help of Jamie's nurse. The boy was awake when she came in, drinking from a lidded tumbler through a straw. He held the beaker in his bandaged hands like he was wearing oven gloves. It constituted progress and earned a round of applause from the nurse.

'Good lad, Jamie,' the nurse said. 'Look, your Auntie Shona's here.'

'Hi Jamie,' Shona said and pulled a chair up to his bedside.

'Is it true ma dad's dead?' Jamie mumbled. His lips were thick and swollen, as much from the ventilator as his injuries.

'Yes,' said Shona. 'I'm afraid it is.'

'I tried to save him,' he said.

'I know. I came to the beach in the lifeboat to get you, d'you remember?'

Jamie nodded. 'Dad always said, in an emergency, press the red button.'

'That's right. You did the right thing.' Shona edged forward and put her gloved hand on his shoulder. 'How did you get to Kilcatrin, Jamie?'

'It was dark. I heard ma dad come back for his haaf-net, so I climbed out my bedroom window. He promised to teach me. I made him take me.'

'Do you remember anything else?'

Jamie thought for a moment, then shook his head. His lower lip began to tremble.

'It's okay,' Shona said.

'Can Jack and Uncle Fergus come to see me?' he said.

No one under sixteen was allowed in the intensive care unit, but hopefully Jamie would be moved soon. 'In a few days,' she said. 'Jack played Kate, the officer who's helping your mum, at Mario Kart. I think he won.'

Jamie nodded and sniffed. He didn't ask again about his uncle and Shona wondered if painful memories had begun to surface. They'd need a statement soon and Shona hoped the hospital would recommend a suitably trained counsellor to support him in the interview.

'D'you want me to send your mum back in?' Shona said passing a tissue to his bandaged hands.

He wiped his nose and handed the tissue back. He shook his head, then turned away from her, curled up and closed his eyes.

–

Shona had a drink with the team, restricting herself to one gin and tonic as she was driving. Wallace proved an easy-going and amenable addition to the celebration and seemed to hit it off with Dan and Ravi. Plans were made to go on for a meal, but Shona knew there were times when the boss needed to step back so the team could really let their hair down. There was also the long shadow of Harry Delfont's attack on her. A works drink, followed by a blank space, then the sickly realisation of what had happened. She was two years and hundreds of miles from that night, but Delfont, and others like him, still stalked the streets.

As she'd left the pub, Wallace had come up to her to say goodbye. He'd be leaving tomorrow. There was a moment of awkwardness as they shook hands. Then she'd said, *don't be a stranger*. Shona smiled to herself when she thought of his reply. *No danger of that.*

Shona reached home before it was completely dark, the lengthening May days stretching towards the summer solstice in a month's time. The estuary lay like blue velvet beneath a matching sky. She sat for a moment in the car on the tarmac at the side of the house.

Robocop had been right. When she'd got back to the office from the hospital, she found Murdo had taken a stream of calls from Emma Johnstone's editor at Viva Caledonia. He was convinced she'd been murdered as a result of her investigative journalism. However, he couldn't offer any firm suspects and accused the police of exploiting Emma's death by asking for her notebooks and live investigations so they could pursue her sources. Shona had phoned him back and offered assurances of a thorough investigation and asking for his co-operation. She stopped short of revealing the selfie death as a conclusion. Emma's phone records and cloud access might come tomorrow, and Shona was aware Viva Caledonia would have a field day with her if a suspect emerged after she'd suggested Emma's death might be in any way self-inflicted.

Shona found the kitchen quiet, but the light was on in the eye-level oven and a covered plate inside. A message alert sounded, but it wasn't Shona's. Becca's phone sat on the counter, a text visible on the screen. *Faslane is on.* *#Peacecamp!* A thumbs up and smiley face followed. Shona didn't have to look at the name to know who it was from.

She grabbed the phone and pounded up the stairs. Becca came out onto the landing, a towel around her hair.

'What's this?' Shona demanded.

Becca made a grab for the phone, which flew from Shona's hand and landed on the wood floor, a crack zigzagging across the screen.

'What are you doing, Mum?' Becca screamed, snatching up the phone. 'That's private!'

There were footsteps in the lounge above and Rob's head appeared over the banister.

'Shhh. What's going on? There are guests with a bairn downstairs,' he said.

'Did you know about this?' Shona hissed.

'Know about what?' He hurried down the polished stairs in his thick socks. He slipped the final few and came to rest with an undignified scramble on the landing.

273

'It's none of your business,' Becca shouted. 'You shouldn't be looking at other people's phones. You're not at work now.'

'Don't take that tone, Becca,' Rob said indignantly.

'She's hacking my messages.' Becca pointed at her mother.

'She's going off to Faslane Peace Camp with Willow,' Shona said to Rob.

'No, she's not,' Rob said. 'And can we just keep the noise down.'

'I can go if I want,' Becca replied, not moderating her volume.

'What about your exams?' Shona said.

'What about them? They're pointless anyway.'

'What?' said Rob. 'You mean I've just spent all this time home schooling you while trying to run a business and you're telling me it's pointless? Well, I'm glad I made the effort.'

'What about your other friends, Ellie and the lads?' Shona said. 'You had such a great time with them out at Ross Island. Are you just going to turn your back on them? Ellie's hardly ever over here now.'

'Willow said you can educate yourself if you keep asking questions.'

'Willow's dad is a multi-millionaire,' Shona said. 'Did she tell you that?'

'Willow isn't in contact with her dad,' Becca said, faltering.

'Maybe not,' Shona said lowering her voice and making a conscious effort to reduce the tension. 'I'm sure she really believes the things she says, and I agree, the way we treat the environment needs to change. But gluing yourself to the road is not the only way and it'll get you

274

a criminal record. You had a near miss with the drugs at school.'

'That was years ago. Why did you bring that up?'

'I know some of the campaigners think a criminal conviction is a rite of passage, a badge of belonging, but it's not something you can undo. It will follow you for your whole life.'

'Like mother like daughter then?' Becca shot back. 'I know it's not just about that court case, this is about police corruption. I heard you and Dad talking, and he's no better.'

From downstairs there came the long wail of a baby.

'Ah, shit,' Rob said. 'Look, let's all cool off. Your mum's just back from work. She's had a busy day. We've all got to be up early. Let her get her dinner and we'll talk about this tomorrow.'

Shona took a step towards Becca, her voice low. 'Corruption? Don't you ever say that about me. Not ever. You've no idea what you're talking about,' she said with such vehemence that Becca stared at her mother with wide eyes. 'Go to bed, now,' Shona snapped.

Shona and Rob were left standing in the hall as Becca ran up the stairs clutching her phone.

'Willow doesn't get in this house. Understand?' Shona said to Rob.

'Aye, fine,' he said. 'Your dinner's in the oven. Becca's not daft, she's got it too cushy here. You two need to stop knocking lumps out of each other. I'm going back upstairs and hope I've a business left in the morning.'

# Chapter 36

Becca's bedroom door was closed and the light off the next morning when Shona came downstairs. Rob fussed in the kitchen, taking extra care with the guests' breakfasts. There was a homemade fruit salad to go with his own recipe muesli. Danish pastries rose in the oven and a bowl and whisk stood by for scrambled eggs with smoked salmon if they wished.

'It's an apology for their disturbed evening,' Rob said, archly, when Shona helped herself to toast and coffee.

'Tell them it's a free life lesson. With a bairn they've got all this to come.' Shona took a bite of her toast. It was sulky and ungenerous and she hated herself for saying it. She should have gone with the team last night, had a curry, and staggered out of an Uber at four a.m., and the fight with Becca would never have happened. Other things might have happened, a small voice in her head said. Go away, Shona thought and finished her coffee.

'Should I wake her?' Shona asked Rob.

He took the tea towel tucked into his apron and lifted the pastries out of the oven.

'I'd leave it,' he said. 'I heard her on the phone half the night. I'll talk to her when she gets up.'

There were a few empty chairs in the CID office but Murdo was already sat at his desk. He looked slightly bleary-eyed, otherwise robust as he tucked into a bacon roll. His resilience had been honed by his years playing rugby for his hometown of Langholm. He gave her a wave and mimed raising a cup to his lips, but she shook her head.

Shona looked at calls list and dialled Mars Bar Munroe's number.

'Great result, Shona,' he said, and she could hear the genuine warmth in his words. 'You'll have seen the papers and know what this Beaufort's Dyke stramash has cost us, so a result like this is what we needed.'

He meant a result that didn't put the blame for a fisherman's death squarely on a government department, Shona thought. Murders were messy affairs, but this one was messier than most. Some papers might argue institutional bias by Police Scotland, but a trial and a conviction would silence them.

'What else do you have outstanding?' Munroe said.

'Emma Johnstone the journalist's sudden death,' she said. She outlined the lack of a second person at the scene, any witnesses, and the theory put forward by Slasher Sue that Emma's was a selfie death.

'That needs careful handling,' Munroe said gravely.

'I'm aware, sir,' Shona said. 'I'd like a few more days to be sure.'

'Well, I'm happy for you to go over this with a fine-tooth comb. As you always do,' he said. 'One other thing. Have you had a rethink about taking up a DCI post?'

Was that a hint that Robocop shouldn't get too comfortable in his temporary promotion? Shona felt a stab of satisfaction, but then quickly remembered why she'd turned Munroe down previously.

'I'm happy where I am, sir.' She meant it. She'd built a good team.

'That's fine,' he said, undeterred. 'I'll be off soon, but let me know if you change your mind.' He ended the call with the reassurance she could call him anytime if she needed advice on the journalist case, or any other matter.

The office filled up and tales were recounted of the night before, which had luckily resulted in no arrests. Simon Wallace, she was surprised to hear, had distinguished himself not on the karaoke, but on the dancefloor. He'd stuck to mineral water, but otherwise retained the respect of her team, with Murdo declaring him a top bloke.

She hadn't heard from Rob or Becca all day, despite her texts. At four o'clock, Murdo came in and said, if it was all right with her, he'd send everyone home. She raised an eyebrow. Quite a few had staggered in late after the night out, but she knew they'd put in the hours when it mattered so she told Murdo to let them go.

'You should get off yourself, boss,' he said. 'Everything okay with Becca?'

'Yes. Why?' she said, suddenly suspicious that her wayward daughter had been a topic of conversation around the pub table.

'She recovered from her birthday and that...' he pointed to his face; 'that nose-thingy?'

'It's a work in progress,' Shona said. Perhaps Murdo was right. There wasn't anything left on her to-do list that couldn't be done at home. She sent her laptop to sleep.

'That friend, Willow, is a bit of a character,' Murdo said, leaning on the office door frame.

'Did you know she's Michael Campbell, the scallop king's daughter?'

'Aye, so I heard,' Murdo replied. 'Jeezo, I pulled him out of a few barneys in his youth.' Murdo's beginnings as a beat cop had earned him respect and an encyclopaedic knowledge of local faces that Shona found invaluable.

'I'd say young Willow takes after her father,' he said.

'I'm afraid you might be right,' Shona said, picking up her bag and jacket. 'I'll leave you to turn the lights off. Thanks, Murdo.'

When she arrived home, Rob's car wasn't parked it in its usual spot by the detached garage. The house was silent. From the hallway, Shona saw light flooding the landing above and knew Becca's bedroom door must be open.

'Becca?' she called. No answer. They were both out.

She made herself coffee, revelling in the peaceful house, and took it out onto the kitchen terrace to drink. She texted Rob. *I'm back. Where's Becca?*

A few minutes later, she heard his car pull onto the tarmac behind the house. Shona walked round, cup in hand. Two new guests, a retired couple, got out. Shona nodded and smiled as they exchanged notes on the weather, their journey, the recent trouble with the beaches, until Rob led them to the guest suites on the ground floor.

'Did you talk to Becca?' Shona said when he came back into the kitchen.

'I had to go out. There was a B&B owners meeting. I'm mending fences over the whole Beaufort's Dyke fiasco. Then I had these guys to pick up. Is she not in her room?'

'No,' Shona said. 'So you haven't seen her all day?'

'No,' Rob said, with careful pronunciation. 'I've been busy all day.'

Shona ran upstairs and pulled open the wardrobes and the drawers in Becca's desk. Rob followed her and lingered at the door.

'Her bag's gone and her phone charger and some clothes,' Shona said.

'You sure?'

'Well, I could call a team and do a forensic search, but yeah, I'm pretty sure.' Shona lifted her phone to her ear and dialled Becca's number, which rang out, then went to voicemail. She glared at Rob. 'I thought you two were close. Didn't you have any idea?'

'Oh, I see,' Rob shot back. 'When things are going well, she's your daughter and when she's trouble, she's mine?'

'You know where she'll be, don't you?' Shona consulted her call list and found Willow Moon's number. She dialled, but it was switched off. 'You better stay here in case she comes back.'

At Bankend, the high wire mesh gates of the Gaia Collective were closed. Beyond, Shona could see some of the parked vehicles were up on blocks. The site was tidy, no rubbish. Around some of the wagons, the residents had created gardens from groups of repurposed containers: olive oil and coffee tins, old sinks. Old tyres stacked like a dry-stone wall. Shona thought the plants growing in the gaps might be herbs. In an allotment area, two children played on a rope swing, beside stacked pallets fashioned into tables and benches.

On the gate, an open padlock swung on a chain. A dog barked as she unlatched it and pushed through. A shirtless man in his twenties with dreadlocked red hair put his head out of an open caravan door. He came quickly down the steps, followed by two other lads.

'Private property,' he said, marching towards her.

She'd heard all private property was theft, but perhaps this wasn't the time to bring it up.

'Get yourself off, lady,' he called. His accent was northern England, Liverpool maybe.

'I'm looking for Becca,' Shona said, aware that dressed in her business suit, she presented the kind of state authority that wasn't always welcome.

'Behind the gate, lady.' The man ushered her back.

Shona stepped back and raised her hands in reassurance. 'I'm just looking for my daughter.'

'Well, she's not here,' he replied. 'Get yourself off, before I call the bizzies.'

Shona saw Willow step from a red, single-decker bus. She came forward and stood with her arms crossed.

'If I can just have a word with Willow,' she said.

'Like he said.' Willow eyed her. 'She's not here.'

Shona stared at the windows of the bus, convinced her daughter was watching. She itched to flash her warrant card. A single call to the control room would get a couple of cars over here, and she'd insist on a search. Drugs were an easy justification, but then she'd have a riot on her hands and Willow, and most of the other residents, would be sure to make an official complaint of police harassment and the true nature of Shona's visit would come out and God knows what else with it.

'I only want to talk to her, Willow. She's just sixteen.'

'I knew my own mind at sixteen, and so does Becca,' Willow said, a smirk of triumph on her face.

And look where that's got you, Shona wanted to say. But the truth was, Willow was right. Shona was powerless. There was very little she could do to stop Becca going off with Willow if she wanted to.

'Just get her to phone me, so I know she's all right,' Shona said, and searched the vehicle windows for a last glimpse of her daughter. That she needed Willow's co-operation stuck in her throat.

Willow shrugged and went back up the steps of the van and closed the door.

Shona returned to the Audi parked opposite the gates. The children on the rope swing were called indoors. No one was visible within the Gaia Collective, but Shona had the sense she was being watched.

She called Rob. 'I know she's in there,' she said.

'It'll be all right,' he replied. 'One night with a composting toilet and a freezing bed and she'll be back.'

'What d'you think this is, Rob? Some sort of hardcore sleepover?' Shona shouted down the phone.

'It's not like she's run away,' he said, exasperation creeping into his voice. 'We know where she is. Maybe it's just exam stress or good old teenage rebellion. She's with her friend.'

'Willow is seven years older than Becca and is not her friend,' Shona said flatly. 'She's got our daughter following her around like she's on a lead. Don't you appreciate how serious this is?'

'I do,' Rob said. 'I love her to bits, but ever since she was a kid, it's been one thing after the other wi' that lassie. Admit it, Shona. She's sixteen. It's time she realised her actions have consequences. We cannae be running after her all the time.'

You've never learned, so why should she, Shona thought. Instead she said, 'So you're happy to let her go? Get herself a string of public order convictions that'll mark her for the rest of her life. Employers don't see committed activist, they see criminal convictions. Thank you and goodbye.'

'I'm not happy and I'm not letting her go,' Rob said firmly. 'I'm just giving her space, like I do with you, when you go off on one. Tomorrow, I'll get a call, *Dad, can you pick me up?* It'll be fine, you'll see.'

'No, Rob, it's not fine and I don't see,' Shona said. 'This is my mother all over again. She went off and didn't come back.'

'It's not the same,' Rob said.

'But the point is, Rob. It could be. My mother didn't start out as some chaotic junkie. She began by taking one step away from the people who loved her. My mum thought she was making a choice, but she wasn't. She was in the grip of an idea that her life would be better if she just cut loose from all the things that were dragging her down. Work, family, me. And all I can think about is my beautiful daughter is going the same way, and there's no way I'm letting that happen.'

She ended the call and tapped her phone on the steering wheel. The panic she felt at losing Becca fluttered in her chest like a trapped bird. Was Rob right? Was she over-reacting, resurrecting a past abandonment until it swelled and engulfed all reason? Perhaps, as a mother. But as a police officer she also had first-hand experience of what could happen to sixteen-year-old girls who ran away. Her daughter was, and always would be, her number one priority and she'd get her home.

Smoke rose from the wood-burning stoves of the vans. Perhaps if she sat there all night, Becca would see the car and come out? But as soon as she thought it, she knew that wouldn't work. Becca wouldn't do the walk of shame to her mum's car, not in front of her new friends. She would have to find another way to win her back. Shona put the Audi into gear and pulled away up the lane.

## Chapter 37

At the lifeboat station, Tommy McCall stood on the apron in front of the boat hall as he welcomed home an old friend. The *Margaret Wilson* lay on her trailer and looked every inch herself. Shona couldn't help but smile at Tommy's satisfaction. When he saw Shona's face, his own smile moderated.

'Get the kettle on,' he said. 'I'll be up in a minute.'

Shona sat down heavily in the mezzanine crew room as Tommy backed the tractor into the boat hall below. A couple of shore crew shouted their goodbyes, and the station fell into silence. A moment later, she heard the coxswain's tread as he came up the stairs.

'What's happened?' he said. 'Not another injury from Beaufort's Dyke?'

'No, it's not that.'

Tommy shook his head as he lifted down the mugs. 'Fergus Carlin. I wouldnae have believed it. We'll sort out a collection for Tony and the family. Maybe do something here for the boys. I'll talk to head office.'

'It's Becca,' Shona said. 'She's run off.'

Tommy stopped, the teabag suspended in mid-air. 'Run off? Where?'

'She's at the Gaia Collective.'

He dropped the teabag back in the tin. 'Well, let's go and get her.'

'I've already been there, she won't come out.'

'She willnae say no to me,' Tommy said severely.

For a second, Shona considered it. Ravi was her other choice to flush out her daughter, but there was a chance it would backfire. At least Shona knew where Becca was. If she left, they'd have trouble keeping track of her. Becca might consider herself an adult, but in other ways she was in that strange twilight zone. She could get married without Shona or Rob's permission and vote in a Scottish independence referendum. But she was required to be in formal education or training until she was eighteen and she'd find it hard to claim benefits.

'No, Tommy,' Shona said. 'I'm worried she'll bolt. Her passport is gone. I've checked. Communities like Gaia have networks all over the country. Becca could end up anywhere.' Willow's mother in Spain was a potential destination.

Tommy leaned against the worktop and sighed. 'Aye, maybe you're right. Did you have any inkling she was gonnae do this? She seemed happy enough on Sunday.'

'She was,' Shona said. 'But the girl Willow has been a destabilising influence.'

'Oh aye, that's one word for her.' Tommy resumed teamaking and brought Shona a cup. 'Well, let me know if you want me to go and have a chat. I know one of the lads over there. He's into traditional boat building.'

'Thanks Tommy. That's good to know.' Shona sipped her tea and felt a little more hopeful. 'How's everything with the *Margaret Wilson*?'

'Grand,' Tommy smiled. 'I worried they might scrap her, but she's come through okay. What's the latest on ordnance washing ashore? Coastguard says the beach clean is being wound down.'

Shona nodded. 'The army is gone. The Ministry of Defence police too.' She thought of Simon Wallace and where his enquiries might take him next. She drained her cup. 'I'm keeping you back.'

Shona helped Tommy close up the station, then they stood overlooking the estuary. It was low tide, the water reduced to a snaking flow between the mud banks. Here and there, a faint puckering showed on the surface of the water.

'See that,' Tommy said. 'That's salmon coming up the estuary to spawn.'

Shona felt a chink of hope. Life returning.

She left Tommy and walked out towards the headland. As the sun dipped, one half of the bay basked in golden light. Here, in the shadow, cold crept up the back of Shona's neck, chill fingers in the roots of her hair.

Shona found herself alone on the beach, the tide far gone, perhaps a mile out beyond the solid-looking sands. Across the bay, she saw the remains of the stakes once used for salmon netting. Oak posts perhaps fifty years old, black like the stumps of broken, rotting teeth sticking out of the mud and slowly worn down by the tide. Is that how she would feel in ten years' time? Her life measured by what she'd endured? The dream of a fresh start on this sheltered shore hadn't turned out quite as she expected. It should have been a beginning for them all, but now she saw there were some things you never leave behind no matter how far you travel.

She climbed the hill back up into the sun, which sat like a copper disc on the far horizon. High Pines was bathed in its golden glow, the warmth on the outside in sharp contrast to the chill within.

Shona's phone buzzed and Becca's name lit up the screen. She felt her heart soar and a hard lump come into her throat.

'Becca?'

'I'm fine, Mum,' Becca said. 'Just leave me alone.' She ended the call.

–

Shona slept fitfully. She was exhausted by the demands of the previous ten days but each time her eyes closed, her mind dragged out some horrific fate for her daughter that she was now powerless to stop. Only when the sky lightened behind the blinds of the bedroom windows did she slip under and finally sleep.

When she woke, she was surprised to see Rob up and dressed in a dark suit. He stood in front of the mirror and knotted his tie.

'I'm off to the solicitors,' he said when he saw she was awake and staring at him. 'In Glasgow,' he added, when she still looked blank.

'What for?' Shona rolled over and blinked at the sun coming through the wide bay of their bedroom window.

'Dunno,' Rob shrugged. 'I told you last night. They called me yesterday, something about my statement. I'll be back early this afternoon.' He turned to face her. 'If Becca surfaces, she'll just have to wait.'

'I'll go and get her.' Shona sat up and swept back her dark curls.

'Sure you'll be able to?' There was a hint of doubt in his tone.

'Yes. I've got meetings but I can reschedule.' She looked up at Rob, suddenly tearful. 'I just want her home.'

'Hey, shoosh now.' He knelt on the bed and put his arms around her. 'It'll be fine. This is the lassie that thinks roughing it is having no ensuite. I tell ye, she'll be back tonight. Tomorrow at the latest.' He bent his face to look at her. 'Dinnae cry on my good suit. The prices lawyers charge, I might need to sell it.'

'Don't joke,' she said and wiped her eyes. 'Remember, full disclosure, or they'll trip you up on something. Call me afterwards.' She threw back the covers and stood up to hug him again. 'Oh, what about the guests' breakfasts?'

'I've laid it out. They just want continental,' he said and kissed her. 'Which is good, cos that's what they're getting.' With a last check in the mirror, he headed downstairs.

Shona flopped back on the bed. Recently, she'd been thinking about her own trips to Glasgow. Perhaps she should wind up her therapy. After Delfont's trial, the date of which still hadn't been set, she might feel differently. Since she'd admitted what had happened to her, the numbness of secrecy and denial had given way to a cool, watchful rage.

Shona got up and walked across the soft carpet to the curved windows. Below, the water was half fluid, half light. She felt as if part of her was perpetually waiting, ready, with spear poised, arm elevated, knife drawn for the opportunity not just for revenge but to wipe Delfont from the face of the earth. To eradicate him as if he'd never existed. But even as she felt that, she knew it was impossible. There was still the sense of payback owed. A court case would never be enough, but unless Shona wanted to end up in jail herself, justice was all that was on offer and she'd need to be satisfied with that. For all their sakes, she would be a survivor, and wouldn't live her life as another one of Delfont's victims.

She showered and went downstairs to check on the guests, then headed into Dumfries. Dan called her on the way. The marine patrol boat had nabbed some cockle rustlers.

'That's a feather in your cap,' Shona said, genuinely pleased for him.

'Couldn't have done it without you,' he replied.

'I just wound you up and watched you go.' She hoped it would boost his confidence. 'What's you guv'nor saying?'

'You know, he'll be happy to claim it. I don't mind. I'm glad I could help with Tony Carlin's case.'

'Yes, you did well there.' Shona slowed and turned into Cornwall Mount car park.

After a pause he said, 'I'd still be interested in working for you.'

'I haven't forgotten. If a post becomes available, you'll be the first to know,' she said, smiling. 'By the way, does this have anything to do with Kate?'

There was a moment's silence. 'No, of course not. We're just mates.'

Shona reckoned she could hear him blushing from across the Solway and was a little surprised at how much his reply pleased her.

She got out of her car and stretched. Either Ravi or Kate might opt to follow specialist training that would take them to a bigger posting. They were both capable of it, as was Dan. She had little doubt they'd all go far.

For the rest of the morning, Shona worked at her desk, one eye always on her phone, for Becca's call. She went through the checklist on Emma Johnstone's death. They were still waiting on phone records.

'Chivvy them, Murdo,' she said. 'And get Ravi to work his magic on forensics for anything outstanding.'

As the day waned and late afternoon came, and she'd heard from neither Becca nor Rob, she felt a creeping sense of unease. Just after four p.m., Rob's name lit up the screen and there was a leap of relief. Becca must have been in touch. Even now, she was on her way home.

'Hi,' she said brightly. The main thing was Becca was at High Pines and they'd work through it together.

'I've been arrested,' Rob said.

Shona blinked. Surely he hadn't been daft enough to grab a few drinks with his Glasgow mates and flout Scotland's strict driving laws. She wasn't sure they could run the B&B if he got banned.

'When I got to the solicitors, there were two City of London cops waiting. They've charged me with the concealment and removal of criminal property.'

'Where are you now?' Shona's heart thumped. She had visions of him being loaded into a car for the journey to London and a cell in Bishopsgate.

'Stewart Street police office. I've been bailed.'

Shona let out a long breath. At least he could come home.

'Are you okay to drive?' she said.

'Aye, I'll be back in a couple of hours.'

'Okay, drive safe. I'll be home when you get there,' she said. 'Any news from Becca?'

'Not a peep.'

Shona ended the call and sat stunned, staring at the far wall of her office. She needed to leave. What tasks were outstanding? Murdo had everyone under his eye and could cope without her. She scanned her laptop and found a budget return that needed to go.

'Ma'am?' The Two Kirsties stood at her office door in their fluorescent stab vests. Kirsten O'Carroll was taller than her partner, a more authoritarian figure. When Shona had seen them work together, Kirsten more often played bad cop to Christine Jamieson's conciliatory good cop. They were a powerful combination.

'I don't know if this of interest, it's about the Carlins.'

'Yes, what is it?' Shona said impatiently, her fingers flying over her keyboard, jabbing out the letters. She frowned at her screen. A zero seemed to have added itself to her costs this month. She had to get this done and be home when Rob arrived back from Glasgow.

'It's just, the relationship wasn't exactly cordial between the husband and wife.'

'I'm aware of that.'

The Kirsties exchanged an uneasy glance. 'Are you aware we were called to the house back in February? A domestic.'

'Yes,' Shona said without looking up. 'There's a record we attended. We know Tony Carlin had a temper and we're aware he could be violent.' Shona stopped short of revealing the source of that confidence was Laura herself.

'It wasn't him, ma'am, it was her.'

Shona's fingers froze over the keys.

'The whole thing was dropped,' Christine Jamieson said. 'He refused to pursue it. I don't think it was the first time either. It was her that was battering him.'

Shona turned to look at the officers. She studied them over her glasses. 'You're sure about this?'

'Aye, I think drink had been taken on both sides. It seems the father next door called it in.'

'James Carlin senior has dementia,' Shona said.

'Yes, ma'am. That was part of the difficulty.'

Shona remembered Laura's response to her question, had Tony ever been violent to her? *It was nothing.* Perhaps

Jimmy was mistaken, and she didn't want to draw attention to his action. Calling the police on a regular basis might alert Social Services to his, and the family's, inability to cope. She would never put Old Jimmy in a home.

It was a salutary reminder that her own problems were nothing compared to Laura's.

'Okay, thanks,' Shona said. 'Thanks for letting me know.'

Before she left, she phoned Mars Bar Munroe. He greeted her with cheerful anticipation, assuming his speculative enquiry about the DCI post the day before had worked on Shona's ambition. When she told him that Rob had been arrested and bailed, he fell silent.

'I'm sorry for your trouble, Shona,' he said. 'At present I'll not ask you to step back given the nature of the offences and your personal history. You've been honest with me and it does you credit. However, I'll have to refer this higher and what the outcome of that will be, I can't say.'

# Chapter 38

There was little Shona could say to console Rob. He ranted about the unfairness of the charges and the deviousness of Milton McConnell's attempt to shift the blame and spin a narrative of a few bad apples. He wasn't going down without a fight.

'What about Becca?' Shona said.

'What about her? Don't look at me like that,' Rob snapped when he saw Shona's expression. 'I'm as worried about her as you are. I'm just exhausted. I've had a round trip to Glasgow and four hours in the company of police officers.'

Welcome to my day, Shona thought.

'I'm sorry, Shona, I'm just done in. Becca's fine where she is. Let's deal with this tomorrow.'

Rob felt quickly asleep. Shona stared at her phone screen. Becca had taken her charger, but could she plug it in? There were some small wind turbines and solar panels at the Gaia Collective. She wasn't replying to Shona's texts. Had she even seen them? What if her phone was really broken after it fell on the hall floor when they argued? Stop it, she told herself. You're looking for things to worry about. Willow has a phone. She must charge it somehow.

The next morning, Shona checked the guests out, then she ran back upstairs.

'Quick, Rob, get up,' she ordered.

'What is it?'

She threw him his clothes. 'I've just had a message from Tommy. He's over at the Gaia Collective. Some of them are packing up. Becca's with them. They're going, Rob. Hurry.'

Shona swung the Audi into the lane and skidded to a halt, as a spray of gravel dinged off her paintwork. Tommy stood with the red-haired lad from Liverpool who'd asked Shona to leave on her last visit. He seemed less hostile, but not exactly welcoming.

'Where is she?' Shona said to Tommy.

Tommy nodded to the red single-decker bus, and Shona pushed open the gate, Rob at her shoulder.

As she reached the vehicle, Willow stepped out in front of her. 'Private property, you're trespassing.'

'Your Liverpudlian friend invited me in,' Shona said, and jerked a thumb to the lad stood with Tommy at the gate.

'So?' Willow said.

Shona took a deep breath and smiled. 'I'm not here to stop you leaving, if that's what you intend to do. I'm just here to speak to Becca.'

'She doesn't want to talk to you,' Willow replied.

Two vans waited on the roadside. A small group of young men and women loaded bags into the back. Bed rolls were stacked alongside boxes of food and bundled up banners. Shona could guess their destination. Inspector Simon Wallace's chums at Faslane were about to have a new round of faces to deal with.

'Look, Willow,' Rob said. 'This'll just take five minutes.' He deployed his charming smile at maximum volume, but to no effect.

Willow glared at him. 'You need to go.'

'Step aside, please, Willow,' Shona said in her officer's voice. They stood eye-to-eye and Shona braced herself in case the young woman took a swing at her. Go on, do it, she thought.

'It's all right, Willow,' Becca said, stepping down from the bus. Her bag was hoisted over her shoulder. She looked tired and somehow younger than when Shona had last seen her. Her hair was tied up in a scarf and the puncture wound of her nose ring looked red and angry.

Shona turned and walked across to where the rope swing hung over the pallets. Becca followed and Rob had the sense to hang back, giving mother and daughter some space.

'Are you off to Faslane?' Shona said.

'Yes,' Becca said cautiously.

'What do you think those protests at Kilcatrin achieved, beyond making a lot of local people angry about traffic?'

'It's good that people get angry about protests, it means they can't ignore the issues any longer.'

There was an echo of Willow's words to Shona at the fish van, but she let it pass.

'As long as no one gets hurt, you can't argue with that, Mum,' she said. 'And massive public pressure on politicians is the only way things will change.' Becca shook her head. 'But it's not about making people angry. It's about hope. That's why I want to be an activist, to show there's hope for change.'

'Come home, Becca,' Shona said. 'Your father needs you. I need you. What you want to do is important and we want to be a part of it, too. You're not Willow, you don't have to cut yourself off from your family to achieve what you want. My mother thought that, and she paid the price for it.'

Shona looked around the garden. 'I understand that you've made friends here and I'm not asking you to give them up. I just want you to consider there are other ways to make a difference. Being inside the system is also a powerful way to change it.'

She put out her arm and Becca moved into the space. 'Come home,' Shona said as she hugged her daughter. 'For as long as you want. Can you do that?'

Shona felt her daughter hug her back and then Becca's hair brushed her cheek as she nodded.

'Sorry about your phone,' Shona said. 'I'll get you a new one.'

'It's fine,' Becca replied. 'It's just the screen protector.'

'Come on, let's get home.' Shona linked her arm through Becca's. 'How's your nose feeling?'

'Horrendous,' Becca said. 'But Willow says the first week is the worst.'

Shona joined Rob as Becca broke the news to Willow. The girl shrugged but shot Shona a look of pure hatred as Becca hugged her.

Shona gave Rob the keys to the Audi. He walked back towards it with his arm around his daughter. Tommy walked beside them.

'I'm sorry about Emma Johnstone,' Shona said to Willow. 'I'll do my best to find out what happened to her. We're not really on opposite sides. I think we both want a safer world.'

–

Shona called Murdo, Ravi and Kate into her office. Emma Johnstone's phone log had arrived. If Rob's arrest meant a spell of gardening leave for her, then she wanted the investigation into the woman's death tied up and sent to the fiscal's office. It would be their job to come to a conclusion. She'd googled selfie deaths and found they were a growing phenomenon. A dizzying array of final pre-mortem shots showing heights, waterfalls and speeding trains filled her screen. There was nothing like this in Emma Johnstone's photo history but it didn't mean they could rule out the possibility.

Shona ran her finger down the phone numbers the journalist had called in the two weeks leading up to her death. It read like a who's who of the Tony Carlin case. Emma had tried Laura's number multiple times. Fergus's mobile was there, along with Shona's own. There was a stack of calls to Rob, but she attempted not to read anything into that, and hoped no one else would either.

'Where are we with the forensics backlog?' she said to Ravi.

'Almost there. There's nothing outstanding in connection to Emma Johnstone. The blood on the steps was confirmed as hers alone and there were no traces under her fingernails. And the second DNA on the glove came back. It's Laura Carlin's.'

'So likely domestic contamination?' Shona said, making a note on her pad.

'Aye,' Ravi said. 'It's what I was thinking. Does that raise the possibility that Fergus handled the glove at home too?'

'Possibly,' said Shona. 'But the forensic evidence isn't central to our case. We have the confession. He'll plead guilty. I think we can tell the lab to suspend testing on any other items. Just pack them for archive in case we need to come back to them later.'

They drew up a final actions list and Shona prayed it wouldn't also be her final action. She and Kate would diary a time next week to discuss her exit strategy as FLO to Laura Carlin. A representative from the fiscal's office would take over the role of conduit for the next step of the legal journey. Sometimes, the family came to rely on the FLO and found the transition traumatic. Shona didn't think this would happen in Laura and Kate's case, but she wanted to make the process as smooth as possible. If she was honest, she also saw it as a chance to build bridges with her friend. She'd missed Laura.

A few hours later, her desk was clear. She would break the news of Rob's arrest next week. She didn't want to leave them speculating over the weekend about her position and the possibility of a new DI. They'd earned a couple of days of peace, at least before whatever fallout was ahead.

'Boss,' Murdo tapped her door. 'A witness has just come forward, a painter who owns the gallery next door to the harbour steps. She didn't know about Emma Johnstone's death because she left early next morning in her camper van for the Galloway Hills. She found the door-to-door card through her letterbox this morning when she got back. A neighbour told her what happened.'

'Anything interesting?'

'Ravi's been out to talk to her. She saw Emma because it was late and there were raised voices. She went out to complain.'

'Voices?' Shona said.

'Aye, she thought it was a couple having a domestic.'

'Did she give a description?' Shona inked a line in her notepad.

'Didn't have to. She recognised the man. She says it was Fergus Carlin.'

Shona let the news sink in. Then she said to Murdo, 'Call Dumfries jail. Set up a meeting with Fergus Carlin for tomorrow morning. Let's see what he has to say for himself.'

—

Shona got home to High Pines to find Rob shouting down his phone at someone. Becca was upstairs and Shona hoped she was catching up on her studies. The exams began next week. She'd make time to take her daughter over to the private school in Cumbria where she'd sit them. They might even catch up with Dan. If Mars Bar Munroe couldn't plead her case, she'd have a lot more time for catching up. She was surprised to find it didn't alarm her as much as she thought it would.

'Can you bloody believe it?' he said, throwing his phone down onto the sofa and holding his head, his hands going through his hair.

She was about to ask him what had happened but suddenly the words just wouldn't come.

'Rob, I don't think I can't do this anymore,' she said quietly. 'It's turning me into someone I don't want to be.'

'What d'you mean?' His eyes narrowed.

'You haven't once asked how your arrest affects me,' she said quietly. 'But I don't want to fight about it. We're going to need each other's support, for Becca and the business. We were a good team once and maybe we can be that again. I don't know if our marriage will survive but if we do part, let's part as friends.'

'You want to leave me because of this court case? To save your job?'

She smiled. 'It wouldn't make any difference to my job if I left you. The damage is done. I just hope Munroe can convince Police Scotland to keep me on. What we need to do now is salvage what we can.'

# Chapter 39

On Monday morning, Shona arrived at the red sandstone turrets of Dumfries jail with Ravi at the wheel. Fergus had agreed to see them and asked after his nephew. Shona thought that was his prime motivation, and he must have understood that the next time he saw the boy would be by video link across a courtroom.

Shona gave up her bag and phone into the lockbox at the desk and was patted down, opening the jacket of her navy blue suit to show the female prison officer that she had nothing concealed in an inside pocket.

Fergus was already sitting in the interview room when Shona and Ravi came in. He smiled a hello and confirmed he didn't want a solicitor present. The guard left them, telling Shona to let them know when they were finished. Outside, Shona could hear the faint calls of children in the playground of the school next door and wondered how that affected long-term prisoners with families of their own.

Fergus leaned his elbows on the table. He looked calm and told Shona the food was better than on the boats and he was used to being cooped up in small cabins. At least these ones didn't throw you around. She had the sense he was putting a brave face on things. The shock of remand was perhaps lessened by his life at sea, but the realisation that four walls and not a distant horizon would rule his life was still to hit home.

'Fergus, I want to ask you about Emma Johnstone,' she said. 'We know she contacted you. Can you tell us about that?'

Fergus pressed his lips together and nodded. 'I thought that's what you'd come about. Did someone see us?' He looked at Shona with steady blue eyes.

'Just tell us what happened, Fergus,' Ravi said.

'I killed her,' he said with a shrug of his shoulders. 'But it was an accident.'

Shona held up her hand. 'Fergus, I'll have to caution you.' She recited the lines. 'Shall we stop while your solicitor gets here?'

'No, it's fine, carry on,' he said, leaning his elbow on the table and scrubbing through his cropped fair hair.

'Okay, Ravi is going to take notes and record this on his phone, but we may need to do this again formally.'

'I'm not going anywhere,' Fergus said with a small smile. 'It was an accident, though. She was on to us over the cockle fishing. Came to see me and said she'd keep us out of it if I helped her bust the whole operation. Who were the buyers? Which other boats were involved? That wasnae gonnae happen. We'd have been dead men.'

'Did she meet with Tony?' Shona asked.

'I don't think so. It's like I said before, Tony wanted to stop. I think he might have tipped her off anonymously and that's why she came down here in the first place. She's written other eco stuff. She wasnae to know all that Beaufort's Dyke stuff would kick off too. It must have been like journo Christmas.'

'So what happened that night?' Shona said as she glanced down at Ravi's notes. His writing was fast and neat with a flourish of strong loops. 'We have a witness who heard raised voices and recognised you.'

'The artist woman?' Fergus said, nodding in recognition. 'I thought it might have been her. She's always complaining about the noise the scallop boats make at night unloading. We try and keep it down, but it's a working port, not a touristy backdrop for her paintings.'

'What happened with Emma Johnstone?' Shona prompted.

'She showed me a video of Tony and me unloading the cockle bags in Silloth. She must have gotten it off somebody local.'

It was likely the same source as Dan's copy, but with Emma Johnstone it was more likely money had changed hands.

'I tried to grab her phone,' Fergus continued. 'Thought I could wipe it. She wouldnae let go. We struggled, she fell on the steps,' Fergus said. 'Simple as that.'

'Where's her phone now?' Shona said.

'Chucked it in the harbour. Her bag too.'

Now the story was told, the energy had drained out of him. Fergus slumped back in his chair.

'You can charge me with both murders, it's okay, I willnae withdraw my confession,' he said quietly. 'Like you said to me. It's Laura, the boys and my father I need to think about.' He shook his head. 'We did this to her, me and Tony, but he paid with his life. The doctor gave her tablets for the stress but we kept on piling things on her, my father, the business, the kids. She deserves a new start. The affair was never gonnae go anywhere, but she thought it was. That's my fault. You've got your killer, what more do you want.'

'Are you sure there's nothing else you want to tell me, Fergus?' Shona said.

'Yeah,' Fergus said, his eyes rimmed red. 'The Carlin men are cursed. Bad luck follows us, Laura's better off without us both.'

–

Ravi drove Shona back to the office. Fergus Carlin would be formally charged, probably with culpable homicide, to go with Tony's murder.

Shona's phone rang. 'Kate. Where are you?'

'I'm at the hospital. Jamie's asking for you. He's been moved out of IC and into a private room. I'm on my way over to see Laura. The hospital say Jack can come in for a visit.'

'That's good,' Shona replied. 'You may have to prepare him for Jamie's injuries.'

'That's what I thought.'

'Okay. I'll come over and meet you once I've seen Jamie.' Shona relayed the message to Ravi, perhaps the opportunity to take a statement from Jamie wasn't far off. It would tidy up their timeline and complete a significant section of their case for the fiscal.

'Those wee boys, Jamie and Jack,' Ravi said. 'Pure rips yer knittin', so it does.'

'Aye, it does,' Shona agreed.

–

The mood was sombre in the office. The result was welcomed but the speed of Fergus's confession had taken them by surprise.

'Murdo,' Shona said. 'Can we get Fergus Carlin brought down to Loreburn Street and formally charged, ASAP? And update his solicitor. He may want to cancel any holiday plans. He's going to be busy.'

'Will do, boss,' Murdo said.

'Do you want to sit in on my chat with Kate later? It's about her exit strategy for Laura Carlin. I get the feeling both can't wait to see the back of each other.'

'It's been a tricky case,' Murdo said with usual under-statement. 'I don't think you can lay all the blame at Kate's door. She's put in the graft.'

'I don't, Murdo,' Shona said rubbing her eyes. 'You can't hit it off with everyone. I'm just not looking forward to Kate beating herself up about it.'

'It's this case, it's hit everyone hard,' Murdo counselled. 'You especially. Kids are always difficult.'

'That's true,' Shona conceded. There was plenty of time to get Kate through an appraisal matrix and help her put some perspective on the job. Shona's phone rang and she saw it was the forensic botanist from Glasgow University, Professor Macrae. Shona felt a little guilty that her work would not now be needed but it had been a useful exercise and Shona would tuck the palynologist and potential expert witness away for another occasion.

'Shona,' Professor Macrae said, 'I've just emailed you over the results of my report. Would you like me to talk you through them?'

'Okay,' Shona said without much enthusiasm. Slasher Sue was sure to follow up on this and Shona didn't want to be questioned by her like a particularly lax undergraduate. But why should she suffer alone. 'Murdo,' she called.

Shona put the phone on speaker and opened the email to find two spreadsheets attached. Her heart sank. She was used to doing budgeting forecasts and overtime payments but found it was rarely an enjoyable experience. She double clicked the first spreadsheet. A list of Latin plant names greeted her in the left-hand column. Murdo leaned on the back of her chair and looked no wiser than she was.

'What am I looking at?' Shona said.

'These are the distribution matrix of the clothing recovered from your two individuals,' Angela said. 'Both claimed not to have visited the locus, is that correct?'

'That's correct,' Shona said. She knew it. It had been a waste of time.

'And you're sure these are the clothes they were wearing?'

Shona's heart sank further. She wasn't sure these were the clothes; it was a best guess. 'So what did you find?'

'Well subject A, the male individual, showed a wide range of locally present pollen. Unfortunately he was not a match for the Kilcatrin distribution.'

'Ah, I see,' Shona said. 'Well, thank you for your work on this, Angela.'

'However,' Professor Macrae cut in. 'Your subject B shows a clear profile that matches the Kilcatrin distribution.'

Shona blinked. 'The female subject?'

'Yes. The woman's jeans and fleece? They've clearly been worn at the locus. I can point you to the key indicator species, if you open the second spreadsheet…'

'Thank you, professor. I'm sorry, I'll have to call you back.'

The tests run on the jeans and fleece Shona saw Laura wearing the morning she came to break the news about Tony had tested positive. Laura had claimed she'd never been to Kilcatrin.

Shona remembered cradling Jamie. *Mum, Mum.* What if he wasn't calling out for his mother? What if it was a warning?

Shona snatched up her phone and called Kate's number. The phone rang out and then went to voicemail.

'Murdo! Get a squad car over to Laura Carlin's. Ravi, with me.'

# Chapter 40

Kate's car was parked in the quiet lane. The Carlin house sat mute, blinds drawn. The next door cottage also looked deserted and a sudden fear gripped Shona that something had happened to Old Jimmy. Kate was bound to mention that Jamie had asked for his Auntie Shona. Laura had been at her son's bedside and seen the improvement. She must realise the truth was about to come out.

'Ravi,' Shona said. 'Check James Carlin senior is okay.'

Ravi looked uncertain. 'I think I better come in with you, boss.'

'No, I'm fine on my own,' Shona reassured him. 'I'll go round the back and look through the kitchen window. I'll call you if anything's amiss.' She tried Kate's mobile again. It went straight to voicemail. 'Uniform are on their way but keep them back.'

'Okay boss,' he said, uncertainly.

Shona walked to the end of the house and took the passageway that ran up between the cottage and the detached garage. There was no sign of life. She checked the time on her phone. Jack would be finishing school soon. Laura's car was in front of the garage, so she hadn't set off to collect him yet. She took a deep breath. Laura and Kate would be sitting in the kitchen drinking tea. Karen could pick up Jack and keep an eye on Old Jimmy. Then they'd take Laura to Cornwall Mount and calmly discuss the forensic's findings and how the botanical fingerprint of Kilcatrin, a place she claimed she'd never been, came to be on Laura's clothes.

Shona walked quietly up the path and turned across the rough lawn. A kids' football goal, its net repaired with twine, sat back towards the bushes and Shona was instantly reminded of that morning on Kilcatrin beach two weeks before. Tony Carlin, burned beyond recognition, his haaf-net abandoned on the shingle as he'd stumbled around, fatally wounded and blinded by burning phosphorous eating through him.

And Jamie, lying on the stones, alone and injured. *Mum, Mum.* He wasn't calling out because he thought she would save him. He was calling out to warn his father. To ask her why she had done this terrible thing and left him alone to die. He went to his father's aid, only to become covered in chemicals himself as he tried to save him.

Shona edged up to the kitchen window. She could hear women's voices, not loud but there was an urgency in their tone that caused the hairs on the back of Shona's neck to rise.

Kate was wedged into the corner by the sink, her back to the window. As Shona moved further, she saw Kate hold her hands out in front of her in a placating manner. Laura stood opposite, her hand also extended. The knuckles showed bone-white as she gripped a kitchen knife.

Shona ducked down under the window and ran to the back door. The handle was stiff. She eased the door open and crept quietly into the passageway. She could hear Laura's voice, high and fast. A stream of words flowed out of her. *Cope. Love. Hate.* Then Shona was at the kitchen door.

Laura glanced around. 'Don't come in, Shona, it doesnae concern you.' She jabbed the knife at Kate. 'She did this. She poisoned my son. She made him say the things he's saying.'

'Jamie hasn't said anything, Laura.' Shona angled her head at Kate to move slowly to the open kitchen door. 'Kate has to go, she's needed on another job, but I'll stay with you.' She kept her voice low, her words matter-of-fact but her heart was hammering and her mind spun forward to all the potential outcomes.

'Jack will be home soon,' Shona added. 'You'll need to get the tea on, but we've time for a chat. Just you and me. It'll all be fine, Laura, you can put the knife down. Off you go, Kate.'

Laura looked at the knife in her hand as if she was only just noticing it. Kate stepped uncertainly towards the back door and Shona hurried her with a jerk of her chin. *Go*, she mouthed.

Laura blinked at the knife, then at Shona. 'Don't come near me.' She held the knife against her wrist. 'Don't come near me, I mean it.'

'It's okay, I promise,' Shona said. In the corner of her eye she saw a mop propped up behind the kitchen door.

'No. No, it's not. Is it?' Laura said. 'I can't do it anymore. I can't go on.'

'Laura, we can get you help, all the help you need.'

'You can't help me,' Laura replied, scorn blooming on her face. 'You can't help yourself. Rob, running around making a fool of you. Karen told me all about it,' she said with a look of triumph. 'That lassie, the journalist. She was gonnae pay me for my story. That money would have changed our lives, but now she's dead too.

'I knew where Tony had gone that night. Skiving off. He used to take me to the farm years ago, when we were courting. It's no' hard to get into the ranges if you how. But I swear I didnae know Jamie was there. Tony kept saying he'd teach Jamie about haaf-netting, that it was his hereditary right, but he never did. He was too drunk and selfish. Ditched his mobile so I couldnae call him, said he was rejecting the trappings of the modern world and we should return to a simpler way of life. Ma life was simple. Work. Work. Work. At home, next door with Old Jimmy, at my job, with ma kids. My life never stopped being simple.'

Laura sobbed. The storm was blowing itself out. Shona took a step forward, but Laura brought the knife up to her wrist again. Shona stopped. Beads of blood appeared on the pale, blue-veined skin of Laura's left arm.

'Laura, I'm sorry. Why didn't you tell me? I could have helped. I still can. The lifeboat family will support you too. Just please, put down the knife.'

'I couldnae let anyone see how bad it was because then they'd know. You in your big house with your fancy job. Karen with her school sweetheart and me with everything a failure. The business, my marriage, even my kids failing at school. I couldnae let people see that.' She pointed the knife at Shona. 'Maybe Fergus and I could have been happy but we'll never put it behind us. Tony deserved what he got, but not Jamie. I did that to my son and I can never forgive myself.'

The slice was swift. A spurt of red arced across the cream kitchen cabinets. Shona lunged forward but Laura stayed on her feet. A sting of pain lit up Shona's hand, and she staggered back. Laura fumbled the knife into her left hand and brought it across her other wrist, but the handle was now slick with blood, her grip less sure.

'No, Laura stop!' Shona reached for the broom, flicking it upside like an oversized baton, and knocked it sharply on Laura's left forearm. The knife fell from her grasp. Laura reached for it but Shona kicked it away as they both slipped on the bloody tiles. Shona's knee cracked on the stone floor as they tumbled together. Laura lashed out at her but Shona grabbed her upper arms and pinned her to the floor.

'No, no,' Laura screamed in Shona's ear. 'Let me die.' But Shona could feel her friend's energy leaching away with the blood that was now smeared all around. Pinning Laura's chest with her elbow, Shona reached up and grabbed a tea towel, wrapping it round the gaping wound on Laura's left forearm, part bandage, part tourniquet as she clawed at Shona's face with her other hand.

'Stop it!' Shona yelled as she wrestled Laura back down. 'You've no right. Jack needs you; Jamie needs you. You took their father, you've no right to take their mother too.' She panted as she yanked Laura's injured arm higher to reduce the blood flow.

Finally, Shona felt the fight go out of Laura as she fell back sobbing. Phone? Where was her phone? The towel around Laura's wrist was already sopping with blood. She grabbed a second one and wrapped it over the top. Shona felt for her phone but it had fallen from her pocket in the struggle. 'Get up,' she ordered Laura, through gritted teeth, and pulled her to her knees.

Still holding Laura's arm above her head, she hoisted the much taller woman's right arm around her shoulder and pulled her towards the front room. Outside, she could see the travelling beam of blue light crossing the front windows. Back-up had arrived.

'Walk, Laura. Just walk.'

They reached the front door and Shona fumbled with the lock. Laura was a dead weight. Her legs had gone from under her, the skin of her arm cold and clammy against Shona's cheek.

Shona hauled the door open. 'Paramedic!' she yelled.

Laura sagged forward and Shona went down with her and felt the tarmac of the road come up to meet her. Boots and hi-vis vests ran towards them.

'Show us your hands,' came the shout and, still holding Laura's towel-wrapped wrist, Shona lifted hers up and saw blood running from a deep wound on her own arm.

'Safe,' she yelled. 'DI Shona Oliver. Get a paramedic, now.'

Someone was lifting Laura away from her. 'It's okay. You can let go,' a firm voice told her.

It was only when she sat up that everything began to hurt. One of the armed response team wrapped her hand and arm tightly in field dressing. She wiped the blood from her eyes, not sure if it was her own or Laura's, and looked around for her officers.

An armed response vehicle had arrived. But it wasn't the presence of armed officers that caught Shona's attention. It was Ravi stood by the verge, his arm around Kate. Wonders would never cease.

# Chapter 41

One week later, the clouds cleared, the wind dropped, and the sunshine poured down on the serene face of the Solway. Far out in the Atlantic, squalls were waiting, but for now Mother Nature sent her most benign breezes, a glimpse of a summer yet to come.

Shona idled the engine of the *Margaret Wilson*. Four crew members, including village postman Callum Stewart and the plumber Dave Thomson, knelt in the lifeboat wearing their full immersion suit kit. Ahead, the starboard side of the *Arcturus* turned her blue flank to the silent crowd lining Kirkness quayside set off with Tony Carlin aboard, making his final voyage to Kilcatrin. At the helm, Tommy McCall in his dress uniform and peaked cap. Beside him Jack Carlin, a lifejacket over a dark suit that was a shade too big for him. At his shoulder stood his two older cousins from Aberdeen, sons of fishmen themselves.

Shona brought the lifeboat's nose round and opened the throttle. They fell into position behind *Arcturus*. The stitches in her right arm protested. They felt tight and itched, but the cut was healing. The blood tests had come back clear of ill effects from the rescue at Kilcatrin Island, although a follow-up in six months was advised. A trip to the specialist optometrist at the DRI had showed her eyes were fine and it was age-related issues with her vision that caused the headaches. Get more sleep, the specialist told her. Cut down on your stress and screen time. When she'd relayed the news to Tommy he had grinned. Like that's going to happen, he'd said. You'll be forty soon, it's all downhill from there.

As they left the shelter of the estuary, a line of fishing boats of all sizes waited. They fanned out behind the *Arcturus* like a flock of birds. Silloth's Atlantic class and Workington's all-weather lifeboats brought up the rear.

The procession headed west. The green flanks of Kilcatrin Airds rose from a calm sea and Shona followed the *Arcturus* in. They landed at the slip near the causeway to the island where she'd come ashore that first morning. A welcoming party waited on this occasion, too. Gone were the tankers and paramedics, instead it was a sombre suited group of haaf-netters. One of them had received permission to bring his long-wheelbase Land Rover on to the ranges. They loaded Tony's sealed coffin onto the back of it and took it to the top of the hill. They carried him on their shoulders into St Catrin's kirkyard to a plot next to his parents' grave. At a signal from the clifftop, the ships below sounded their horns. And so, the tragedy on Kilcatrin Island obeyed tradition and Tony Carlin was buried close to where death claimed him. Only for this fisherman it was also a homecoming.

Murdo was there in his suit, shaking hands with the haaf-netters and the family. A regular churchgoer, he managed to strike just the right tone with faces both familiar and new, compassion written in his every move. As the party dispersed, Shona was surprised to see Simon Wallace standing at the edge of kirkyard.

'I see you opted for conventional funeral dress,' she said, indicating his well-cut black ensemble and tie over a white shirt.

'I see you didn't,' he replied.

Above his breast pocket was a medal ribbon bar and suddenly Shona wondered if his desire to stop a terrorist chemical weapons attack was rooted in what he'd already seen. Iraq? Afghanistan? He might well have served there. She thought of Dr Biba and the Kurdish children. Shona was having therapy for an attack she couldn't even remember. The damage needn't be physical. Witnessing the horrors others suffered never really left you. One day she'd ask him about it, and he might tell her. But not yet.

They stood on the clifftop in silence as the mourners picked their way back down the hill. Two minibuses waited for those who weren't returning home by boat.

'What will happen to the boys?' Wallace said.

She followed his gaze to where Jack stood, looking down at the *Arcturus* in the bay below, his tall, fair-haired cousins watching over him. Even if he never returned, this would be a view, a moment, fixed in his memory forever. Perhaps, like his grandfather, Jimmy, Jack Carlin would live to be an old man and travel far, yet still see Kilcatrin in his dreams. One of the cousins tapped Jack on the shoulder and they set off back down the hill.

'The boys will go to relatives. Jamie is being transferred to Aberdeen Royal Infirmary. They've a good burns unit, what with the North Sea industries close by. Victim Support and Social Services are looking at residential care for their grandfather there too, if it can be arranged.'

'And the boat?'

'It'll be sold probably, along with the house. The business has debts, but there might be something left for the boys. I doubt they'll follow their father into fishing, but you never know. Some traditions are hard to break.' Shona hoped the next generation of Carlin brothers had better luck than previous ones.

Simon Wallace nodded.

'That tip off about the Carlins recovering arms from Beaufort's Dyke,' Shona said. 'Did it come from another fisherman, by chance? In Cumbria? The Isle of Man?'

Nothing in his expression gave away the answer, but then he said, 'I'd like to say that it was a piece of malicious mischief-making. I really would. But I'm afraid it's still an ongoing investigation, and we've a new lead.'

Shona let the implications of that sink in. A dirty bomb in some city, maybe even back in her old neighbourhood in London. She was glad she'd proved that Tony and Fergus Carlin were innocent, of that crime at least. But the idea that her patch of this beautiful coast and rolling farmland was divorced from the threats of the wider world was false. It was a crossing place and that brought links with far-flung lands and peoples, whether you liked it or not.

'I understand you were a friend of the Carlins,' Wallace said.

Shona sighed. 'I thought I was. Maybe that's why I almost missed the truth. Fergus wanted to protect Laura and she'd have let him go to jail for something he didn't do. Do you know what gave her away in the end?'

Wallace searched her expression then shook his head. 'What?'

'Old Jimmy's mother and her chickens. She must have planted forage crops for them in her garden along with the tulips. Now, they grow wild on the ranges. It's what Angela Macrae found when she looked at Kilcatrin's botanical fingerprint.' She smiled. 'Old Jimmy told me he still sees his mother feeding her hens. Turns out Professor Macrae saw her too.'

'I wasn't sure I'd be welcome today,' Wallace said. 'But I wanted to pay my respects.'

'I'm glad you did,' she said.

'You know,' he began. 'There's a job coming up in Glasgow with the MDP. It would be a better outlet for your skills.'

'I'm not looking for another job,' she said evenly.

'Don't you miss Glasgow?' he said. 'It's a chance at a more senior role that's still operational. Pleasant as this is, it must seem...' he considered for a moment, 'restrictive after the City of London Police.'

'Oh, we seem to have plenty of excitement here,' she replied lightly.

'Don't you want more?'

Shona turned away and her hair, blown around her face by the westerly wind, hid her expression. When she didn't answer, he reached out and took a piece of dried grass that had caught in a strand of her dark curls. He looked at it before letting the wind carry it away, then he smiled.

'You should smile more often,' she said quietly.

'I might, if you'll promise to think about what I said.'

She returned his smile but shook her head. 'I wouldn't make a very good MDP officer. I like to do my own thing. And the MoD aren't riding high in my opinion at the minute, present company excepted.'

Her face became serious. 'I'll be knocking on doors and pushing for reparation for Jamie. Someone has to be responsible for all that poison in Beaufort's Dyke. It needs sorting. I don't want it on my beaches again. It might not make me too popular with your bosses.'

'Well, I'll be sure to draw my own conclusions.'

'Anyway,' she said quickly, 'my daughter starts her exams next week. My life is here.'

She wondered if he knew about the charges Rob faced and how she may be forced to resign. It wouldn't take much digging for him to have learned about Harry Delfont, the court case that lay ahead and the potential fallout from that too.

'Things change, Shona. We have no choice but to change with them.'

Shona looked at the benign curve of the bay. The lifeboat crews were making ready to return to service. The *Margaret Wilson* sat on the shingle beach of Kilcatrin Island, the two larger boats had already turned, their wakes white arcs across the blue water.

'Maybe,' she said, smiling. 'But some things are worth hanging on to.'

# Acknowledgements

A great many thanks, as ever, to my editor Louise Cullen and her assistant Siân Heap for keeping this book on track through challenging times. Thank you also to my agent, Anne Williams and everyone at KHLA, and to my copy editor Deborah Blake and proof reader Miranda Ward, all of whom saved my blushes and helped me knit in those inevitable loose threads. My appreciation also to all at Canelo Crime, particularly Francesca Riccardi and Elinor Fewster who work so hard on behalf of DI Shona Oliver.

This is a work of fiction but I'm obliged to a great many people for their factual insight. I'm enormously grateful to Steve Austin, Lifeboat Deputy Launch Authority at RNLI Cleethorpes for his technical advice and wisdom. Also, my brother Eric McEwan, Structural Engineering Group Manager at Subsea 7, for the hazards that lie beneath the waves.

A chance encounter on the Solway coast one night led me to the ancient tradition of haaf-netting and I owe my thanks to Kevin for his generosity and knowledge. If this ancient fishing practise has piqued your interest, I recommend www.annanhaafnets.org for further information.

Like many crime novelists, I'm indebted to the pioneering work of forensic scientists, particularly forensic ecologist, botanist and palynologist Professor Patricia

Wiltshire whose story inspired my own. Thank you to Charles Simpson for pointing me in the right direction.

This book began while I was still working on my master degree at the University of East Anglia Creative Writing programme, and I owe a continuing debt to my tutors Henry Sutton, Tom Benn, Nathan Ashman and Julia Crouch, and my fellow students Sharon Bale, Katherine Black, Libby Brookes, Hannah Brown, Mandy Byatt, Virginia Cole, Alan Jackson, Denise Kuehl, Simon Margrave, Pat Page and Sue Thomas, for all their talent, generosity and unfailing enthusiasm.

Finally, thank you to Thomas Poulter for the shed building and persistent good humour, and to my parents and Cath, Mickey, Leo, Sam and Chloe for all their love and support.

Do you love crime fiction and are always on the lookout for brilliant authors?

Canelo Crime is home to some of the most exciting novels around. Thousands of readers are already enjoying our compulsive stories. Are you ready to find your new favourite writer?

Find out more and sign up to our newsletter at canelocrime.com